MW00438186

Broken Lights Can't Shine

Erin Sievers

Chapter One

The wind paused, took a deep breath, and began conducting wildly. The orchestra of trees and branches and metal fences picked up in all the wrong measures, completely out of tune. The wind was angry, bouncing the baton more forcefully to get the instruments back in time, but it was no use. The piece was drawing to a close, and the wind sighed for another failed performance.

The tension in Lily's shoulders loosened before she shuddered again, her muscles squeezing in a fight to preserve as much warmth as possible. The orchestra was supposed to help her relax, but it achieved quite the opposite. The fence was the worst part, with its metallic banging and clanking right next to her head. It hurt her ears and rattled her brain.

Lily curled her legs up to her stomach and wrapped her barely-covered arms around them. Her jeans were freezing and her skin repelled the cold material with its army of goosebumps. Lily wanted to cry, but she knew better—tears would only chill her skin and rubbing her nose on her sleeve would make it sting to the touch. She sniffed, her sinuses somehow stuffy and clogged while dripping snot at the same time. She pressed her face into the frozen ground, hoping the cold would calm the heat that was rising behind her eyes. But all it did was give her a headache.

A single, colorless leaf fluttered to the ground. It was shriveled, its tattered edges curled in, as if the lightest touch of a fingertip would make it crumple into dust. As soon as it reached the ground, the wind blew it away, no doubt as a punishment for such an awful concert. Lily followed it with her eyes until it blew behind the fence and became indistinguishable from the rest of the world.

Lily squinted at the sky through the branches of the tree towering over her, but there were too many reaching out for something to hold on to. She stretched her arm up to help, but she was too short. Or they were too tall, growing away from her as she watched. The branches didn't want her help. They knew there was no hope in holding onto her for support; if they did, everything would collapse. She dropped her arm.

The wind picked up again, though not as intense as before. It slithered up the sleeve of her jacket and trickled up by her neck, making Lily jerk her shoulders up by her ears. She licked her lips out of instinct and with no hesitation, the cool breeze rushed in for a kiss. But the gesture wasn't loving or soothing or caring. Nothing ever was. The wind only did it to cause her pain, to draw attention to how rough and cracked her lips were. Lily swiped her tongue out again and tasted blood. She wiped her mouth with her sleeve so the air wouldn't dry it out even more.

Lily raised her head to flick the hood of her jacket up and a piece of mud fell from behind her ear. She went to brush it away, but all it did was swing in front of her face. It wasn't mud. It was her hair, stuck together with dirt and dried into a long clump. One of her jagged fingernails scratched her cheek as she tucked the strand back behind her ear, but she didn't wince. She was too numb.

Nothing on the other side of the fence was moving out of its own will. Leaves were jumping from the tree's branches as a sacrifice for the wind to stop blowing—so it would stop chastising them—but they didn't know it was a hopeless cause. They were killing themselves for nothing.

Lily's eyes crossed and she had to blink a couple times to refocus. By the time she did, there was a shadow bounding in the distance. It slowed to a stop and appeared before the line of trees.

Her breath hitched. This was the first deer she'd seen since the temperatures dropped below a comfortable level. She sat up, her hood slipping off, but she didn't care. The deer was gingerly stepping towards the fence. Lily inched towards it, but could only go so far before the rope around her neck forced her to stop. It was pulling a little too tightly for her preference, but still she stretched until she could wrap her fingers around the frigid metal wiring. The deer startled and stood in place, darting its eyes around to find the danger.

Lily held her breath. She waited for it to run away, to leave her like all the animals inevitably did, but its hunger won out. It bent its head to pick through the weeds at the base of the fence. Lily drew her hand back slowly, keeping her eyes on it, and ripped the remaining green grass from the ground. She stuck it through the chain-links, in front of the deer's face, and its velvety black nose twitched as it contemplated Lily's offering.

"Lily, what do you think you're doing?" Brian boomed. Lily jumped and dropped the loose grass. The deer galloped away.

The temperature hit Lily all at once again and she curled into a ball. Brian stomped over to her, red anger crawling up his neck and planting itself on his face, nearly steaming off his glistening head.

"What the hell are you doing? Now it's gonna think it can come around here whenever it wants. Idiot," Brian grumbled. "Are you listening to me?" he shouted.

Lily squeezed her eyes shut. Brian's foot connected with her side, her back, her head. She couldn't help but whimper at every blow, even though her teeth were digging into her bottom lip to avoid any sound escaping.

"You shut up," Brian hissed, "Don't talk back to me. You shouldn't be talking at all, you know that."

Brian paused and Lily thought he'd lumbered away. But when she tried to sit up, she was met with an explosion of pain on the top of her head. A muted ache dripped down her skull and collected in her ears. Somehow she was on her back, and her vision was wavering; the stars above her blurred in and out of focus and the dark sky rippled and waved like a puddle of water. She rolled onto her side before the movement of the sky made her sick, and saw brown shards of glass scattered on the ground. Brian's fingers dug into the soft skin below her shoulder and he ripped her off the ground.

"You little shit," he snarled. "You made me waste the last of my beer."

He shook Lily, her eyes rolling in her head even more than they did before. He continued to shout obscenities at her, but all Lily could concentrate on was the rancid smell of his breath. She felt nauseous again.

"I can end your eight years of life right now. Would you like that? Huh? Do you want me to kill you?"

Lily felt the familiar burning twist of bile in her stomach and her cheeks puffed out as it rose in her chest. It rushed out of her mouth and added to the ever-growing collection of stains on Brian's shirt.

"Ugh!" he threw her to the ground. "That's disgusting. Ugh." Brian scrubbed at his face and Lily wiped her mouth.

"You're lucky we don't have neighbors who could hear you," Shannon slurred from the doorway.

"Shut up, you're not the one covered in puke." Brian stomped on Lily again. "You're the reason she's here; you're the reason this all happened." Brian gestured to his shirt and Lily.

"Yeah, I'm the one who hit her over the head with a bottle," Shannon said.

"That's not what I mean and you know it."

"You don't have to stay here."

Brian mumbled, mocking Shannon. He went back to the house. "You better clean this off, I need it for work tomorrow," he said. "Do it yourself."

"You really think I'm gonna touch this?"

Brian disappeared around the doorway and Lily deemed it safe enough to hide her face in the ground and mouth the words Brian and Shannon just said. Her mouth tasted bad.

"And you," Shannon croaked, "no food for you tomorrow." She snorted. The door banged and Lily couldn't help but flinch.

"Shut up, shut up, shut up. Kill you, waste my beer. Clean your mess, shut up, kill you," Lily whispered in between hiccups. The sounds her mouth made and the intense concentration on making the correct noises calmed Lily down and almost let her forget the life she was living. She was in a trance, repeating the words over and over again, until she rolled over and a piece of glass stuck in the side of her head.

Lily moaned as she pulled the glass out, and threw the shard down in frustration. She winced and her hand stopped in midair. The sharp edge had sliced her finger. The blood pooled up, but soon couldn't handle its own weight and trickled down her hand. Lily longed for the soft fabric of the dog bed she used to sleep on to wipe her hand off and stop the bleeding. Her jacket was already gross enough.

The dog bed was the only luxury she was allowed after Brian and Shannon kicked her out of the house. Before, when she lived with them and was actually cared for, Lily was treated like a normal member of the family. She was allowed inside the house—except for their bedroom—and she had free range to go to the fridge, sit on the couch, or even to play in the yard.

The couch in the living room pulled out into a bed, and that was where Lily slept every night. The sheets weren't changed or washed often, but she had her own blankets and pillows. She even had a well-loved stuffed bunny that she cuddled with when she was scared.

Lily was treated well for the first few years of her life. Shannon changed her diapers and sometimes made her meals, but she was told to stay out of Brian's way. They never interacted all that much, until one day a couple months after she turned five.

Brian and Shannon had been in their room, but the door was open. Lily had been sitting on the couch, jumping her bunny up and down like it was real. Her parents were fighting, and they didn't bother to keep their voices down.

"She's used up *all of our money*, Shan. What're we supposed to do? We're gonna starve," Brian shouted. Lily placed her bunny in a comfortable position on the couch, then stood up and went to the fridge. She scrounged around for something to eat, unaware that she was subconsciously distancing herself from their argument.

"Well, what do you want me to do about it?" Shannon fired back. "I can't just leave her on the street to die."

"Throw her out back. God, all you ever do is buy her new clothes and give her all of our food. And she doesn't even do anything besides get in our way," Brian said. Lily found an apple behind the milk and took a big bite. "Besides, I can see it. You don't want her here anymore."

Shannon paused. Her voice was completely neutral when she said, "We can't just *kill* her."

"That's why we keep her in the back. She's not around us all the time, she won't eat all our food—" Brian rounded the corner. "Dammit, this is exactly why we need to do something."

He stormed over to Lily, the apple halfway to her mouth, and grabbed her arm. Lily yelped and dropped the apple, fighting to get away.

"You don't need to hurt her," Shannon said. But she didn't do anything to stop it.

Brian yanked Lily towards him. "You don't know how long I've waited to do this," he sneered in her face. He dragged her with him as he stormed towards the back door.

"Mommy," Lily cried. She twisted her arm, trying to get out of Brian's grip, but he was too strong. "Stop!"

Lily turned and pleaded with her eyes for Shannon to help. But all Shannon did was follow behind like she wanted to watch the show.

Brian dropped her on the ground in front of their old doghouse. "This is where you're gonna live now. This is where you deserve to be." He crawled inside the doghouse and appeared again with a rope in his hand. "And this is so you don't get any ideas about running away."

Lily scrambled to her feet and ran to Shannon, pulling on her leg and begging her to do something. But Shannon just pushed her back into Brian's grasp. Lily looked at her, frozen, dumbfounded. Brian looped the rope over her head.

"No!" His meaty hand clamped over her mouth.

"Don't you dare scream," he said, his hot breath branding the skin near her ear. The loop was too small to fit over her head easily and the abrasive material was scratching her face. Lily scrabbled to get ahold of it before it was too late.

"Shannon, get her arms down."

Shannon stepped closer, but stopped before she got to them. She shook her head. "I won't hurt her. Not like that."

Brian huffed. The rope pressed over Lily's nose and slid down her chin, landing loosely around her neck. Brian let go and she waved her arms to keep her balance, leaning backwards at an uncomfortable and awkward angle to stay on her feet. Lily pulled at the rope, trying to get it back over her head.

"Don't touch it," Brian yelled, knocking her hands off. He shoved her shoulder and she fell back, landing hard on the ground. "You hear me? I don't wanna see you in the house or out on the street. You're gonna stay back here with that rope around your neck."

Lily shrunk away. Brian had never been this loud towards her before. Sure, he'd grumbled something or knocked into her a few times, but nothing this extreme. He only ever yelled like this at Shannon.

And she seemed relieved that his aggression wasn't directed at her. She glanced at him and stepped closer. She bent over so her face was level with Lily's. "You won't get any food if you take it off."

Lily whimpered and Brian sneered. "That's how you do it."

Lily cried. Loudly. Her parents were being so mean. She wanted to go back inside and she wanted everything to go back to normal. So she cried.

Her eyes were closed so she couldn't prepare herself for Brian lifting her shoulders and slamming them back down, pinning her to the ground. She wailed even louder, this time for the pain in her shoulders and neck and head and every other place that was hurting.

"No. Shut up," Brian shouted. Lily cried harder.

Then Brian's hand was around her neck. She choked, gasping for air.

"I don't want to hear you out here," he said, tightening his grip. "You don't speak and you don't cry. You sit out here silently. Got that?"

Lily nodded the best she could. He let her go.

She ducked her chin, trying to quiet her shuddering breaths, but not before seeing Brian and Shannon go inside.

Lily glanced at the doghouse. She didn't want to go in there. She didn't want to have to abide by Brian and Shannon's rules. But she'd already been given an example of what would happen if she disobeyed. So she dropped her head and went in the small shelter.

There was an old discarded dog bed on the floor. Lily crawled onto it but was stopped short by the rope around her neck. She turned around, silently crying, and inched backwards. She could lie down with only a little tug from the rope if she had her head near the opening.

At that time of year, it wasn't extremely cold out, but she was shivering all the same. She burrowed deep into the packed-down stuffing and pulled the sleeves of her jacket over her hands. The wood around her protected her from the wind and elements, and for that she had to be thankful. But she didn't know just how thankful until nearly two years later, when during one particularly bad storm, a branch from the tree above her fell on the doghouse—luckily missing her by inches—and tore away the whole back wall. It wasn't long until the rest of the rotting wood collapsed on her. Before the night was over, the exposed dog bed was sopping wet and cold, ripped of its cottony filling. Lily found the ground to be more welcoming than the bed, so she laid on the grass. Soon after, a gust of wind made the bed roll away from Lily while she was sleeping. From that moment on, Lily was forced to deal with whatever weather the day decided to bring. Thankfully, where she lived, the winter temperatures didn't drop all that low.

Shannon made frequent trips outside to give her the least amount of food possible, but Brian only ever came out to torment her. They replaced the rope a couple times when they determined it was too worn down or too loose or too long. Her rope now was half the length of the first one she had, and much tighter.

In the beginning, Shannon cared about giving her enough food to sustain her. She had stopped giving her new clothes and forgot water every now and then. But as time wore on, and the chore of keeping Lily alive had become too much, Shannon forgot her vow of not harming her. She never physically beat her, but the damage her words did—before Lily learned how to block them—had hurt Lily more than anything.

Lily thought she was bleeding. Or maybe it was raining. She opened one eye to see why her head felt so wet.

"Good morning, rat." Shannon smirked. Lily brought her hand up to her head to wipe away the wetness, but Shannon screwed up her mouth and spit on her again. She took a long drag on her cigarette before speaking.

"You didn't wake up when I kicked you," Shannon said, and shrugged, as if that justified anything. She flicked her stringy black hair over her shoulder. "Anyways, me and Brian are going to the casino. Don't go anywhere." She snickered. Shannon took one last drag, leaned down in Lily's face, and blew the grey smoke out of her lungs. She leered at Lily's recoil, and pressed the cigarette on Lily's skin, only twisting it harder when Lily's eyes rolled back in her head. By the time the pain had subsided enough that Lily could open her eyes, Shannon was gone.

Lily let out the breath she was holding. She sat up and shrugged her jacket off her shoulder so she could press the burn against the cold metal pole. She scrunched up her face as she waited for her arm to go numb, and eventually she felt relief.

With the pain mostly gone, Lily could turn her attention to the real problem at hand. She tried to squeeze her grimy fingers between the rough material of the rope and her skin, but it was wrapped too tightly. She yanked on the length of the rope that connected her to the pole, but nothing happened. She crawled to the pole itself and attempted to pull it out of the ground, but her small hands wouldn't fit around the width of it. She had to stop and shake out her hands because the metal was so cold, it burned her.

Her hands were seared and she was already panting from the exertion, so Lily laid down. Another day, another failure. It didn't matter how many times her parents left her alone—she never made any progress. The rope continued to rub away at the skin at the base of her neck.

"Ha, yeah, give up. You're never going to get out, so why bother even trying right?"

Lily rolled over. She squinted at the darkened form standing before her.

"Mailman."

Mailman was evil. He came from inside Lily's head even when she didn't want him to. She never wanted him to. Mailman brings Brian and Shannon the bad letters called bills. They always yell about money and they yell at Mailman to take the bills back because they're not gonna pay them. They yell at each other to stop spending so much. Then one of them storms outside to yell at

Lily, saying how much of a burden she is. They ask how they're supposed to be able to live while she's out her doing nothing but using up all of their cash? After days like those, Lily could predict the amount of time she would have to go without food by the number of bruises Brian left.

"You're weak. You're small and stupid and weak," Mailman said. "How do you think you're going to escape? Look at you. You can barely hold your head off of the ground."

Mailman sounded a lot like Brian and Shannon. He used their words, the same tone. The only difference was that Mailman always stayed in the shadows. Lily had never seen his face, and to be honest, she didn't really want to.

Lily glared at him. "Mailman," she hissed.

"Wow, you're so witty aren't you?" he mocked. "You'll never get out. You'll be tied here forever. Even if you did manage to leave, where would you go? No one's out there. No one will take you in. You're filthy. You're an animal."

With every word, a layer of Lily's resolve was peeled away until she was exposed. She knew he was right. Everything he said was true. She ducked her head so she wouldn't have to look at him anymore.

Days passed, and life went on as usual. Lily's nose ran from the cold so she rubbed it until it was red and raw. She ate the scraps left over from Brian and Shannon's meals, Brian hit her once or twice, but it wasn't anything she wasn't used to. And, every day, she would practice her words.

Words were the only thing keeping her sane. When Brian was beating her, and shouting horrible things, Lily focused on what he was saying. Trying to remember the words helped her ignore his painful blows. Or, when Shannon was attempting to drain Lily emotionally with her vile insults, Lily would put up a wall to deflect all meaning and only strain the letters through. When they would finally leave her alone, Lily would mumble everything that stuck. And, piece by piece, she was building her own mental dictionary.

Brian and Shannon were off gambling somewhere, so Lily could practice speaking as loud as she wished.

"Good morning, rat," Lily used Shannon's words as her own when Mailman appeared.

He rolled his eyes. "Congratulations, you can say words."

Lily put her hood up and pulled her arms inside her zipped jacket so she could condense her body heat as much as possible. Practicing usually distracted her from the cold, but sometimes not even the words could warm her.

Lily continued to drill herself with phrases to say forwards and backwards, and saying each word individually. When the sun finally settled right above her, the air was a little bit warmer, and the low temperatures weren't as harsh as before. She laid on her back, staring upwards, watching the clouds lazily roam the sky. She muttered to herself as she imagined the clouds descending from their peaks to come say hello to her.

But she never stopped talking. She mumbled words and sentences, forced to hold up both ends of a one-way conversation until Brian or Shannon got home or Mailman came and berated her.

"Do you really think you're smart enough to talk? You can't even make your own words, you have to steal from other people."

When Mailman would chide her into silence, Lily would retreat into her other favorite pastime: her imagination.

Her fantasies could only reach from fence to fence. Her memory was limited; she'd been too young to remember much more than the smallest details from living inside the house. So she was stuck with the grimy back of the house, her rope, and the sky. The yard was her whole world. But however limited her sights, she worked wonders with what she had. Lily would go into a trance and imagine that the house and the fence were picked up by the wind and blown away. The rope would loosen from her throat and fall to the ground, and she would take a big, deep breath to fill her lungs. She would start running as soon as she could, in case the rope were to find her again, and as she sprinted, the grass would grow taller and taller until she couldn't see over it. In her daydreams, her legs would never get tired, and she would run for miles. She can run and skip through the ever-growing grass forever.

But it never lasts. The house always comes crashing back to Earth, and the rope ends up pulling tighter around her neck.

One day, the house crashed as the back door opened. Lily opened her eyes—surprised because somehow night had fallen while she was away in her imagination—and saw Shannon marching towards her.

"Why are you still here, you stupid brat?" Shannon slurred.

Lily knew better than to answer, so she filed the words into the back of her mind for later.

"We never wanted you, you know. You weren't planned. Your real father left me because you were born. You're why I'm with that miserable lump of fat in there. I'll never know why I didn't get rid of you earlier. I'm never gonna want you. No one will ever want you. "

Shannon bent down so her face was directly in front of Lily's and almost fell on top of her. Shannon opened her mouth to speak, but burped instead. Lily recoiled at the strong smell of beer on her breath.

Shannon lowered her voice. "Me and Brian almost won big tonight. Imagine that. You know, if we won, the first thing we would do is buy a big fancy house. We'd go far away from here, and you know where'd you be?"

She didn't wait for an answer. "Right. Here," she spit. Lily wanted to reach up and wipe the saliva off, but she chose to keep her pride.

"We would leave you here to rot, tied to this stupid, broken yard light." She perked up. "Wait. That's exactly what you are. A stupid, broken light."

She cackled and tapped Lily on the forehead. "You hear that? Yeah, that's right, there's nothing. Your lightbulb's gone out. Either that or you never had one in the first place."

When Shannon laughed, she threw her head back and opened her mouth wide, and Lily could see all the disgusting browns and yellows of Shannon's teeth. Lily imagined centipedes and spiders crawling on Shannon's tongue and out her nose.

Shannon decided she was bored of insulting Lily, and she weaved and staggered away. She stood at the door for a while like she didn't know how to use it. She finally pushed it open, leaning into it since she could barely stand up, and didn't even close it all the way behind her.

Already, Lily was in her safe haven of repetition. "No one wants you, stupid brat. Broken light, no one wants you. There's nothing, leave you here to rot. No one wants you."

Lily turned her head so she didn't have to see the house anymore. She was tired, hungry, lonely. She wanted the deer to come back. She wanted the rope off. Lily closed her eyes and pretended the clouds were sweeping her off to a better place.

The only sound besides the hum of the machinery was the bristles on the broom scraping along the cement floor. *Sweep. Swish. Sweep. Swish.* Ben cocked his head. When he pulled one way, the broom went *sweep*, but when he pushed it back the other way, it went *swish. Sweep. Swish.*

"Would you cut that out? I think the floor's clean enough," Brian said.

Ben kept his eyes trained on the speckled pattern of the floor, like he was searching for every particle of dust to sweep away. Brian was almost always hungover, and his snide comments were just another part of life that Ben had to endure. Besides, they were all a little grumpy today.

Despite the fact that there had only been two customers in the past four hours, three men were working at the gas station. And, since Ben was the "least experienced," he was stuck on cleaning duty. Just in the past hour, Ben had swept the floors, wiped down all the shelves, and scrubbed the bathroom until it shined. But did the other men offer to help? Not at all.

A burst of obnoxious laughter made Ben tighten his grip on the wooden handle. The other two men joked unintelligibly and roared again. Ben curled his hand into a fist to try and control himself, but when the laughter rang through the store a third time, he slammed his fist down onto a shelf. The initial bang was followed by a few thuds as some products fell onto the floor.

"Hey, be careful over there. Don't want to screw up any of the merchandise," Henry called. Henry was the other greasy man sporting a gut that stuck out farther than his lower jaw.

Ben closed his eyes and counted to ten before plastering a fake smile to his face and saying back, "Sorry, it's just that I really have my hands full here. It'd be nice to have some help."

He waited for a response, but the two men were already engaged in their conversation again. Ben rested the broom against the shelves and kneeled to scoop up the fallen items. He shoved them back into their places with little care; he was about to explode and needed to get out of there before he did something worse than knock a few cans on the floor. He stormed to the back room and threw the broom inside.

"I'm taking my break," he said as he passed Brian and Henry.

"Man, who pissed in your cereal this morning?"

Ben shoved the glass door open with both hands and the bells hanging from it jingled madly. He was hit with a blast of chilly air, so he pulled his jacket tighter around himself.

The place was deserted. Nobody was pumping gas or getting ice, no cars were driving by. Ben tried to take a deep breath in, to clear his head so he wouldn't be so irritable, but the smell made him gag. The disgusting combination of oil, smoke, and grease was typical for a rundown gas station like this, but Ben hated it nevertheless. He took a deep breath through his mouth rather than his nose and coughed. The icy air stung his throat and burned his lungs.

"Only a few more hours," he said to himself. "Then I get to go back to my stupid dingy house where I'll be all alone and have nothing to eat." He shoved his hands into his jacket's pockets. "Amy, you stupid bitch. It's all your fault."

He needed to stop thinking about her if he was going to make it through the day without killing someone. He wiped his dripping nose and found a stone to kick as he strolled around the gas station. After four laps he kicked the rock as far as he could, smoothed out his face so he seemed normal, and headed back inside. The tinkling of the bells was less aggressive this time.

Brian and Henry were staring at him, all conversation ceased, but Ben just offered a smile as he walked past. He went to the back room and picked up the broom to continue working.

The bells on the door rang.

"Hi," Henry said.

"Hello."

Ben went around to the front to see who was there. It was a woman with a small child holding her hand and sticking close to her leg. The woman was pretty, with long brown hair and delicate features. And her kid was a spitting image of her, wearing a cute pink dress with tights, and had hair that hung down to her waist.

The woman looked nervous and Ben didn't blame her. She was beautiful and had a child to look after. And here she was, in the middle of nowhere, surrounded by three men. She was probably scared out of her mind. A pang of sadness hit Ben's heart as the little girl lifted her arms for her mother to pick her up. As soon as she was rested on her mother's hip, she stuck her thumb in her mouth and rested her head on the woman's shoulder.

"Cute kid," Ben said, intending for it to be a compliment, but it came out gruffer than he expected. The woman flashed him a quick smile but dropped her head to look at the floor.

"Um, where's the bathroom?" she asked. Henry pointed it out to her and she scuttled away.

Ben watched her until the pair disappeared behind some shelves, but he looked back in time to see Henry and Brian exchange smiles.

Brian opened his mouth to say something, but Henry didn't let him speak. "Dude, you're married."

"You have a girlfriend," Brian countered.

"She has a kid, leave her alone." Ben's voice sounded tiny and weak compared to the older men, but he had to say something. They were like vultures circling prey.

Both men looked at him, offended, appalled. Henry scoffed, "Whatever," and sulked away. Brian held his stare with Ben as he picked up a rag and forcefully wiped the glass countertop.

The woman came out of the bathroom with her daughter and basically ran out the door.

Brian grumbled, "Why'd they got three of us working here today. That lady was like, the third person we've seen and she didn't even buy anything."

Henry called from somewhere in the store, "I don't know, man, but I don't care. It's keeping me away from my girlfriend; she ain't been leaving me alone lately."

Brian laughed and said back, "Yeah, Shannon's been bagging on me like, 'When're you gonna start making me some more money?' But then it's like, 'You never spend time with me anymore.' What'd you want me to do, get more hours or laze around all day with you?"

When Henry laughed his whole gut shook. Ben smiled so he wouldn't be shunned by the men, but inside, he was fuming.

They don't know how lucky they are, he thought. *To have a wife or girlfriend that actually wants to spend time with them.* Ben had to shove down the rising desire to snap at Brian and Henry, to tell them to spend time with the people that love them, because they have no idea how long it'll last. It doesn't matter if they're married or seem committed to each other—no. The relationship could be over in a blink of an eye.

After three more hours and two customers, it was finally time to close up. The three men walked out at the same time and got into their respective cars.

"See you tomorrow, boys," Henry said as a goodbye. Brian left the parking lot first, with Ben right after. Ben hated getting stuck behind Brian. Everything about his car was annoying, from the excessive exhaust spurting out to the huge dent above the back tire. And now he had to stare at it the entire way home.

They got to their neighborhood—a loose term to describe three connected streets—and Ben turned onto his own while Brian continued up to his. They were only one street apart, definitely not enough distance between them for Ben.

Brian's house sat alone on a long street. There were no houses surrounding his, just a big clump of trees separating his and Ben's yards. Ben's house had a few surrounding it, but to his knowledge, no one lived in any of them. Sometimes he would catch some homeless guy seeking shelter in one, or a drug addict, high out of his mind, shooting up on one of the porches. This was the worst side of town to live on, and everyone knew it.

Ben pulled into his cracked driveway and chided himself for not being able to afford to get it fixed. He avoided the web of weeds and grass growing out of the cement and went inside to fall on his creaky bed. The springs in the mattress pressed into his back.

This bedroom was the only separated room in his house. The kitchen and the living room were melded together, with the couch set as the dividing line between the two, and then there was the basement. Ben thought he was lucky to even be able to afford a house with a basement, but he had heard a rumor from the guy who sold him the house that the previous owners had used it as a drug lab. Now Ben was using the space to store all of the stuff from Ben and Amy's old house. All of the stuff she left behind.

Ben never used to live like this, but after Amy picked up and walked out of his life, he'd had to fight to make ends meet. He was barely making any money to begin with, and when he started drinking all the time, he'd had no chance. He didn't know how he had managed to survive this long.

Ben pressed the pillow over his face and moaned into it. His heart hurt. For his old friends, for Amy, for his daughter. He fell into a restless sleep, still in his work uniform and shoes, with the pillow soaking up his tears.

Chapter Two

Lily was daydreaming again, but the grass had barely reached her shoulders when Shannon shattered the image by running into her view. Shannon squealed in the way young girls do, and she hopped and skipped and did a little twirl.

"Guess what?" she asked ecstatically. "Brian won last night. He always told me making all those bets would pay off, but I never believed him. I've never been so happy to be proven wrong."

Lily hadn't even known they were gone. But she was hopeful now, turning her face up and widening her eyes, subconsciously trying to make herself loveable enough that Shannon might take pity on her. But she never so much as glanced Lily's way.

Shannon clasped her hands in front of her and sighed dramatically. "I feel like I fell in love all over again." Then Shannon huffed. "I mean, at least he actually got off his ass long enough to take care of me. He was barely making anything with that dead end gas station job he has. But hell, if he thinks he gets to quit now, he's got another thing coming."

She took a deep breath before continuing. "He's out buying us a new TV right now. I think he's gonna grab a computer too. Life is so good."

Lily had put her head down to the ground so she could start mouthing the words Shannon was saying.

Shannon scoffed, affronted. "Are you mocking me? Hey. Look at me."

Lily turned her face towards Shannon.

"This is why you're treated this way. You're disrespectful, ungrateful, and you don't care about me or Brian. So shut up and actually pay me some respect. I *am* your mother you know."

Shannon held Lily's blank stare, but when Lily didn't respond, she rolled her eyes and went away.

Lily cowered in her defensive position, which she had adapted after barely a month of Brian's torment. She laid on her side, legs curled up to her chest and arms wrapped around her knees, with her chin tucked down. It protected her from Brian's blows and deflected the worst of the damage.

Lily peeked out of the corner of her eye to watch the clouds leisurely pass overhead. The sky was starting to change colors like it does before it gets dark, but the peacefulness was interrupted by commotion in the house.

"Shannon, get over here and help me with this."

"You know I can't lift heavy things."

"It's not even heavy, Jesus. Just pick it up and carry it into the house."

"Brian, I don't know what to do with this."

"Just put it down anywhere. It's not that hard. Now come here and lift the other side of this box."

"Dammit Brian, I think I threw my back out."

"Would you stop complaining for just one second?"

Lily could hear the exchange punctuated by heavy thumps and curses, but the swirling colors blending into the gradual darkness calmed her. She tried to drift into her fantasy, but the shouts coming from inside kept making her lose the grasp she barely had on it.

"Just throw the boxes out back," Brian said.

A couple seconds later, the back door opened and out flew a few cardboard boxes.

"Here, play with these, brat," Shannon said.

"The guys at the gas station are never gonna believe this," Brian said, coming up behind Shannon and putting his hand on her shoulder. He twirled her around so she was facing him. "Imagine the look on their faces when I say I won fifteen grand. And sweetheart, I'm gonna take you out to dinner every single night. I'm gonna buy you beautiful dresses and shoes for you to wear with them. Here, take this, and go get yourself the best smokes money can buy." Brian led Shannon away and closed the door.

Brian never called Shannon any pet names. Crude insults, maybe, but nothing sweet, nothing romantic. Lily prayed that this new change in attitude would mean that they would forget about her. She didn't want any more abuse. She wanted them to leave her alone.

For a few days, Lily was happier than she'd ever been. She had a bunch of new words to practice, the boxes had blown over so she could sit on and sleep in them, and the weather was abnormally warm for the season. Her jacket was thrown haphazardly on the ground now, rather than wound around her shoulders. Lily hardly noticed, at first, that she hadn't been fed. She almost didn't care. Almost.

The meals Shannon brought every few days usually consisted of whatever scraps her and Brian had left behind: the crusts of bread, a bruised apple or orange, a little bit of cereal if they were feeling generous. Lily had to drink from their old dog's water dish, but she couldn't be picky.

Lily had gotten pretty skilled at rationing her food, but now, after four days of receiving nothing, she was all out.

Neither Brian nor Shannon had ventured into the backyard at all. Lily knew they were still living in the house, though, because the electronics shined a blue glow through the thin curtains and there were different voices and sounds coming from inside. And, every night as promised, Brian took Shannon out to dinner. Lily could hear the rev of the car's engine, and she would listen to it fade as her parents drove farther away, leaving her behind.

At first, Lily was fine with being alone all the time. She would practice her words louder if the rumbling of her stomach became too much to handle. She could claw at the rope around her neck and the pole without anyone screaming at her to stop.

But eventually, along with intense hunger pangs, loneliness made her crave human interaction. And seven days after the arrival of the TV, Lily didn't care whether it was Shannon yelling at her or even Brian smacking her around. She was getting weaker by the minute, and she desperately needed food. She was beginning to regret her wish of being left alone.

Lily could barely sit up anymore. Her stomach was trying to eat itself and her mouth was so dry, she couldn't move her tongue to practice speaking. She tried to yell, to be loud and annoying, in hopes that one of her parents would think of the daughter they had wasting away outside, but either they couldn't hear her or they didn't care.

"Help me with this. Look at me," Lily tried to shout, but the words only came out as a raspy whisper. "Life is good."

Mailman appeared. He clapped his hands dramatically. "Very good. You became so worthless that they actually forgot about you. Ha! Life *is* good."

"Help me with this."

Mailman shook his head and clicked his tongue. "Sorry, can't. You've already descended too far into nothingness. What did I tell you? Brian and Shannon don't love you. Your life is only going downhill from here." He whistled as he mimed a person jumping off a cliff, then smacked his hands together and made a *splat* noise with his mouth.

Ignoring his cruel words, Lily bent her head to suck the dew off of what little grass blades were left.

Mailman scoffed. "No wonder they hate you. You're no better than a wild animal."

Lily laid down, her soul crushed and her physical state declining by the second. She had her jacket on again, although she was pretty much numb already, and she didn't have the energy or spirit to practice her words. Like her body, her mind was deteriorating. Soon all that'd be left was a pile of mushy gunk where her brain used to be. She could no longer imagine the house flying away and the grass growing taller. All she could do was lay on her side, willing the back door to open and for one of her parents to come out.

By this point, the fumes of the gas station had taken residence in all of Ben's uniforms and seeped into his skin. His ears constantly rang from the whir of the slushie machine and the clangs of the heating unit, even when they were broken and silent. Row after row of candy and chips and cans that begged to be straightened and rearranged haunted his dreams. The *ding* of the cash register made him twitch every time the drawer scraped along the glass countertop. But this is what he had to do. Amy had brought in the big bucks, so Ben had to work long hours to get any scrap of food in his mouth.

Most days at this wretched place were boring. Dragged out. People milled around, messing up the shelves even though Ben had just fixed them, and Ben had to trail them, to clean up their path of destruction. But sometimes something interesting would happen. A drunk guy might stumble in, or some kid would rip open a pack of candy, and the parents would shout at them because they would have to pay for that. Ben was disgusted at people who screamed at their kids. He wanted to scream right back in the adults' faces that they're the only kids you have so you better love them. Let them do what they want before they grow up and become just like you.

But he never did. He just smiled politely and rung up their purchase.

Today, though, was the most interesting of all. Henry wasn't there; it was just Brian and Ben in the store.

A string of people pulled up to fill their tanks and drove away without ever coming inside, but some stopped in to buy a water or a snack. But there was a lull and, unoccupied by Henry, Brian turned his attention to Ben.

"So, kid," Brian started.

Ben, facing away from him, closed his eyes and tilted his head back. *Stop talking right now.*

Brian couldn't hear his silent plea, and continued on. "I was over at that casino on…on…oh, what's that street's name?" He snapped his fingers, trying to jog the memory. "I don't know, but it's about ten minutes from here?"

Ben nodded and turned to face Brian. He knew the place all right. That was where he had tried his luck and lost almost all of his savings. He never went back there again.

"Well get this." Brian motioned for Ben to come closer. He leaned his head in and looked around. "I won. Fifteen grand."

Ben's ears perked up, but he wasn't about to let Brian have the satisfaction of knowing he had piqued Ben's interest.

"Wow," Ben said, monotone. "Lucky you."

"I know. I've already bought me and Shannon a brand new TV and computer. Put the rest of it in a box under the sink—Shan doesn't trust banks and, I think, what's the point if I'm just gonna be spending it all the time anyways?"

Ben didn't answer at first—he would be so much better off if he could get ahold of some of that cash—but Brian was looking at him expectantly.

"Oh, yeah," Ben mumbled. "That's probably best."

"And the best part is I barely have to leave my house anymore. If the casino's too far away"—Brian waved his hand—"I can just pull up some site on the computer and—"

"Great," Ben said, his thoughts no longer on the conversation. How easy would it be to get into Brian's house and grab a couple bucks? Just enough to get some food in his mouth before he starved. He smiled to himself. "Hey, Brian?" Ben didn't realize he'd cut Brian off mid-sentence.

Brian raised his brows.

Ben grinned and licked his lips—a lion ready to attack its prey. "You think, since you got that TV set up, I could come over and watch the game on Saturday? I've been dying to watch on something that's more than twelve inches across."

Brian laughed and clapped Ben on the shoulder. "Of course, man. Be my guest."

Ben nodded, giddy. He hadn't been this happy in months.

Ben combed through his hair with his hands and smoothed out the front of his shirt. He glanced in the mirror to make sure he looked presentable, scrutinizing his image before stopping. What was he doing? It wasn't like he was about to go out. He was just going over to Brian's. He was just going over to Brian's and all he was going to do was steal his money. That's all.

Ben huffed at himself and closed his eyes, forcing his heart to slow down. He wiped his sweaty palms on the front of his jeans and headed out of his room. On his way outside, he glanced out the back door, seriously contemplating walking over so he wouldn't waste precious gas. But if he managed to succeed tonight, he wouldn't have to worry about gas anymore. He got into his car.

Brian's house was worse than his own. Ben parked in the street and treaded carefully on the driveway, though loose stones and clumps of dirt scattered with every step. Ben had to wade through grass and weeds that were halfway up his shin just to reach the front door since any walkway there might've been was completely overgrown.

Before he could even knock, the front door swung open. Thin strips of paint fluttered to the ground and a horrible smell wafted out like it had been trapped inside.

"Saw you pull up," Brian said with a grin. "Come on in. Welcome to my humble abode." He swept his arm, gesturing Ben inside.

Sure is humble alright, Ben thought. But he plastered on a smile, just like at work, and stepped inside.

Ben gagged, but covered it up with a cough. "Hey," he said, his fist up to his mouth. He cleared his throat. "How's it goin'?"

"Well come on in," Brian urged. "Oh, don't worry about your shoes."

Of course you wouldn't care if I tracked mud through this place.

Brian led Ben over to the TV. There was some sort of yellow-brown puddle pooled on the tile that was leaking into the carpet. It had a stench that made Ben's nose sting and his eyes water—he hoped it was beer and not anything else.

"This is it. And I sit here in my"—Brian relaxed into a chair with a sigh—"recliner. I've got a pack down here at the ready, too." He patted a mini fridge that was sitting beside his chair.

Ben grimaced. "Nice."

"Uh huh. And I set the whole thing up by myself. Shannon wanted me to pay some idiot to come and hook it up but I was like, 'Shan, I'm good.' She threw a fit but whatever. She's not complaining now."

"I wish I knew how to do that," Ben said, monotone. He had wandered over to the thin cream curtains. He slid one between his fingers and determined that he couldn't even consider them curtains. It was more like someone had hung toilet paper in front of the window.

"Oh, nothing's out there," Brian said suddenly, too loudly. Ben whirled around, surprised at the sudden outburst. "Me and Shannon haven't had time to go fixing that up yet; don't want you thinking we live like trash around here."

Ben scoffed silently. "Yeah, wouldn't want that."

A toilet flushed and a door to what Ben presumed to be a bedroom opened and Shannon hobbled out. Her permanently hunched shoulders and spindly fingers made her look like a witch, and her black hair didn't help anything.

"Who're you?" she grumbled in greeting as she went to the kitchen.

Ben rounded the couch and stuck his hand out. "Hi, I'm Ben. I work with Brian."

She scoffed. "Work? I wouldn't call it that. Now what *I* do— that's work."

Ben was taken aback. Brian always talked about her like she was awful, but he would've expected that from him. But this woman was truly nasty. He tried to be civil. "Oh, what do you do?" It came out snarkier than he wanted.

"I break my back every day slaving over a hot stove, tending to—" she faltered, her eyes skirting to the backyard. "Well, I have to *clean* the house so *Brian* likes it. I have to cook dinner so *Brian's* happy. I have to—"

"God, Shannon, would you be quiet? He doesn't wanna hear about all that crap," Brian said. He was elbow deep in the crack of his recliner, struggling to find the remote to turn the TV on.

Shannon rolled her eyes and dug around in a drawer. She found what she was looking for—a pack of cigarettes—and lit one, taking a deep drag and blowing out the cloud of smoke slowly and seemingly deliberately into Ben's face. He recoiled and pursed his lips together so he wouldn't breathe any in. It didn't work. He coughed and waved a hand in front of his face.

"You want one?" she asked, holding out the pack.

"No." Ben coughed again. "I don't smoke."

She sneered at him. "'Course you don't."

"Aha," Brian said. He held the remote like a trophy. "Shan, shut up. No one wants to listen to you anymore."

"Uh, maybe I should come back another time..." Ben said, backing up. The money wasn't worth this back and forth—not tonight at least.

"No, you stay"—Brian pointed the remote at Ben— "Shannon, goddammit would you quit smoking? When we're at all those fancy restaurants every night you're gonna ruin our image if you have to step out every two minutes to light one up."

Like you could ruin it any more than you already have, Ben thought. "You go out to dinner every night?"

Brian turned smug. "Sure do. Now that we're rich I get to eat good."

Shannon crossed her arms, tapping the cigarette mindlessly. "And because Brian here thought it would be a good idea to brag to everyone he talks to, I gotta worry about someone breaking in."

"Aw, come here," Brian cooed. He sat down and she fell into his arms, bending their heads close to each other. "No one's gonna break in."

Ben grimaced and looked away. "I wish I could afford eating a peanut butter sandwich every night," he said, staring into the darkened backyard through the glass.

Brian laughed and pushed Shannon away. "You'll get there one day." He opened the mini fridge. "Want one?" he asked, holding up a beer.

"Oh, no. I don't really drink anymore."

"What?" Shannon exclaimed. "You don't smoke, you don't drink. What do you do?"

"Work." He put air quotes around the word.

Shannon threw her head back and laughed. "I like you."

"Ben, come over here. Sit down. I didn't realize, the game's already started." Brian turned around. "What're you doing all the way over there?"

Ben looked around. He hadn't realized that he'd been edging towards the sink. He was so close that if he twitched his hand, his fingers would touch the cabinets beneath it.

"Come sit," Shannon said. She patted the cushion next to her.

Ben smiled with his mouth closed. "Yeah, coming." He sat on the very edge of the couch, purposefully avoiding the dark stain near the back. He couldn't even pretend to be interested in the game or the drab conversation he and Brian were having, and it wasn't because of the smell that was somehow becoming more intense or the fact that there were consistent noises coming from the backyard—Shannon was inching closer to him and kept knocking her knee against his own. He was about to jump up and make up some excuse about why he had to go when there was what sounded like a shriek from outside the window.

Shannon slammed her hand on the couch. "That *shithead* raccoon won't leave us the hell alone."

Another shriek.

Ben looked towards the curtains. "Um, that doesn't sound like a raccoon."

Brian rolled his eyes. "Go deal with her Shannon."

"Her?" Ben asked, slightly amused. "So you're well acquainted I presume?"

Brian laughed. "Too much so."

The shriek rang out again, but quieter this time.

"I think it's going away," Shannon said.

"Just go out there. You don't know what it's doing."

Ben couldn't help but notice that Brian didn't call it a "her" that time, and that he was sending his wife out in the dark to what seemed like a rabid raccoon. "I can help," he said.

"I got it," Shannon grumbled. She stalked out back.

Brian settled himself again, but after about five minutes, when Shannon didn't come back, Ben had to speak up. "You sure she's okay out there?"

"Ugh." Brian heaved himself out of his chair. "She can't do anything herself." He stormed outside, closing the door behind him with finality.

Awkwardly sitting on the couch, alone, Ben raised his eyebrows and pursed his lips. The night was turning out weirder than he expected.

He sat up straighter and his heart pounded. Here was a prime opportunity to make his move. He couldn't waste any time. He walked to the kitchen quickly, sparing a single glance at the small window on the door, praying they weren't looking in his direction, and crouched by the sink. He opened the cabinet, rummaging past a few sticky cleaning supplies and landing his hand on a metal box.

A bead of sweat dripped down his temple, but he brought the box close to his body, cradling it in his arms. He flipped it over and around, and his heart dropped. A small lock held the top and bottom together.

Ben dropped his head back. Now what?

He dropped the box back where he found it and closed the cabinet. There was a clatter by the door. Ben stood quickly and turned to the fridge, pretending to look for something in there.

"I told you to pick up those boxes," Brian said to Shannon. Then, to Ben, "You hungry, man?"

Brian's face was red now. Circles of sweat stained his underarms and he was rubbing the fingers on one hand with his other.

"Actually, no, I just remembered—is everything okay out there?" Ben asked. Shannon looked like she was about to explode.

"We're fine," she growled.

"Alright..." Ben said. "Well, I just remembered, I have to leave. I—there's something—so yeah, I have to go."

"No worries. I'll show you out," Brian said. He wasn't putting up much of a fight in trying to convince Ben to stay.

On the porch, Ben turned around once more, to explain himself or say thanks or something, but Brian was already closing the door. But he didn't close it fast enough, not before Ben saw something silver glint on his back. A key. Hanging backwards by a chain on Brian's neck.

The previous night, Lily's prayers had been answered. After straining to hear the new voice in the house and enduring one terrifying moment where a Mailman-like figure stood unmoving in front of the window, Brian and Shannon had finally come outside.

Lily had been whining and moaning, willing whoever was inside to come out and give her something—anything—to eat, to drink, to interact with.

First it was Shannon. She spit in Lily's face and hissed at her to be quiet. Then Brian stormed out. He grabbed her by the hair and brought her ear right up close to his mouth.

"Shut your mouth or I'll make you be quiet," he said. His breath was hot on her skin.

He threw her head to the side and she curled up, moving her mouth to his words. Brian and Shannon went back inside, and the new voice soon left.

"Told you," Mailman had sneered from the safety of the shadows.

At that point, when twinkling stars began to replace the clouds who had stubbornly refused to separate all day, Lily was done. The rope was pulling at her neck, rubbing painfully and cutting off her breath, but she didn't care anymore. The moon had dipped and was replaced by the sun, where it now shone in all its glory above her, but Lily's eyes were too heavy to hold open. It was her seventh night without food but she didn't feel hungry anymore. It was like her stomach had accepted that eating was an impossibility.

Luckily she knew how to ignore pain. She closed her eyes and swallowed, hoping the thick saliva would sustain her for the time being.

"Hey, Brian?" Ben asked, quieter than he normally would have. Henry was in the breakroom—he'd just arrived for his shift—but Brian was about to leave. Ben needed a way to get back into Brian's house, and he'd spent all night thinking of what to say. He was nervous that Brian would be suspicious about why Ben suddenly cared so much for him, because if he ever noticed any of the cash missing, he would without a doubt trace it back to him.

"Hmm?" Brian was leaning on the counter, flipping through a magazine. He didn't look up.

"So you said you and Shannon go out to dinner every night."

"Yeah, what about it?" Brian's voice was gruff.

Ben ran his hand along the back of his neck. "I'm worried for you."

Now he had his attention. Brian looked up at him and raised his eyebrows. "Why?"

"Well, because"—Ben glanced around and leaned in, for both Brian's benefit and his own—"my house got broken into a couple months back." It didn't. "They took my wallet and all the extra money I had laying around." They didn't. "I just don't want that to happen to you, too, especially because you brought in that new TV recently."

"I didn't know that happened. I never saw any police or anything over there."

"Didn't want them to get involved. Don't trust them, you know?" Ben laughed and pushed harder on his neck.

Brian huffed. "Well, what am I supposed to do about it? Shan won't let me put it in a bank."

"Oh, geez, I don't know, man," Ben said. After a pause, he said, "Wait, maybe I could watch your house for you. I could stay over while you're out and no one would try to break in 'cause my car would be out front and there'd be lights on."

Brian froze. "No, no, that's not—you don't need to do that."

"I was just thinking—"

"No, we're fine," Brian said. His words were rushed. "I'll lock up and maybe keep a lamp on or something."

Ben's heart sank. "But I—"

"We don't need anybody." Brian leaned over and the neck of his shirt fell down. The key dangled around his neck; Ben wanted to grab it and run.

He'd have to get the money the hard way, then. Hopefully he wouldn't get caught.

The last shred of hope left in Lily's heart was torn off by the car speeding away. She squeezed her eyes shut, hoping to form even one tear to relieve the headache throbbing in her temples, but any water her body might've stored had long since evaporated. Her anger at Brian and Shannon for putting her in this situation, and at Mailman for taunting instead of helping her, dissolved into irritation at herself for not being strong enough to do anything.

Not long after Brian and Shannon left, there was some scuffling around the fence that sounded like an animal searching for food. Lily wanted to tell it to go look somewhere else, because there was nothing there. The fence near the house creaked and a section of it opened up. Something came through.

Lily was unable to lift her head to see what was going on, and her eyelashes were blurring her vision. She strained her eyes in the darkness, and she could make out the figure of a man. *Mailman?* she thought.

But no, it couldn't be Mailman. He never came out of the shadows. Lily had come to believe that there were only three people in the world: Brian, Shannon, and herself. Yet here was a new man, standing in the moonlight.

He had a full head of blonde hair, mussy and floppy over his forehead. He towered over Lily and his arms and legs were stick-thin. She looked down at her own arms and determined them to be not much smaller than the man's. He went to the back door and wiggled the handle, but it must've been locked because he couldn't get inside. He had a backpack and he swung it around to his front so he could unzip it. Lily couldn't see what he extracted, but he went over to the window. He glanced around, and turned his attention back to the house.

Ben twisted his pocket knife into the lock on the door handle. He was surprised at how easy it was—under a minute of fiddling around, and he was inside.

He slapped his hand on the wall to find a light switch and flipped it on, taking care to close the door softly behind him, though he didn't know why—no one was around. Ben tiptoed to the cabinet below the sink. His brow started to sweat. He glanced over his shoulder and hurried to retrieve the box. He pushed aside half-empty bottles of cleaner and trash that didn't make it into the bin, and his hand hit the few pipes there were, but the box wasn't there.

"Dammit."

He stood, sliding his knife into his back pocket and taking a step forward. The single light above the table did little to illuminate the rest of the home, and the darkened living room looked foreboding.

Too afraid to turn on any more lights, Ben crept through the kitchen—being sure to feel around any nook and cranny he could find—and made his way to the living room. He lifted all the cushions and peered behind the couch. He even checked the mini fridge, but there was only two unopened bottles.

There was only one room left to check. Ben inched to Brian and Shannon's bedroom and pushed the door open slowly. For some reason, this room felt different. It felt like something was trying to keep him out.

"All the more reason," Ben said to himself.

He combed through the dresser's drawers, the attached bathroom's hidden crevices, and the closet that seemed to have more junk than anything of value. Ben was about to leave, discouraged, but on a whim, decided to check the bed. He lifted the mattress and the blankets, but nothing was there. But as a last resort, he pressed into each of the pillows and struck gold.

Ben tore the box from its hiding spot, pocket knife ready in his hand, and went to work on the lock. He had to be more careful with this one, because it was smaller and more fragile. Not to mention cheaper than the one on the door.

Only the tip of his knife fit in the keyhole, but after a few seconds of maneuvering, he managed to get it open.

Ben laughed out loud. "Yes," he murmured. He flipped open the lid and nearly shouted with joy. "Yes!"

Lily's vision began to waver. Her eyes crossed and came back into focus. She couldn't tell if it was the lack of food or the lack of sleep, but either way, she couldn't lose consciousness. There was a strange man in the house, and he might come back out to the yard. He might be dangerous.

Just as she thought, the man came back out the same door he went in, but now he was holding something close to his chest. He closed the door and when he turned around again, he pumped his fist in the air. Lily gasped at the sudden movement and the man whipped around.

"Who's that? Who's there?" He stuffed whatever he was holding into his bag, but a few loose papers fell to the ground. He bent quickly and grabbed them, and shoved those in the bag, too.

Lily held her breath, though she was sure he could hear her pounding heart.

"Hello?" The man squinted and scanned the backyard. His eyes landed on Lily. "Hello?"

He padded over to Lily, and as he got closer the moonlight elongated the features on his face, stretching them to monster-like proportions. He gagged at the smell surrounding her and covered his nose with his hand. Lily tried to shrink down so he wouldn't be able to see her anymore, but it didn't work. He crouched next to her.

"Are you okay?" he asked. "What're you doing back here?"

Lily didn't answer. She pressed her face into the crook of her elbow and rocked back and forth, willing the man to leave her alone. Fingers brushed her neck and Lily gasped and pushed herself back.

"Woah," the man exclaimed. "Sorry, I was just trying to see what's on your—" He ran his hand along the length of the rope. "What the hell? What's going on?"

Lily couldn't do anything but stare. She ran her hands up and down her arms, lightly scratching the bruises and scars snaking them. Her skin somehow simultaneously felt like it was loosely hanging off her bones and clinging to her like wet clothing. Her stomach rumbled as if to answer his question.

"Aren't you freezing? Do you need water? I have some. Here let me…" The man went to his bag, keeping his eyes on Lily the whole time like how she did with the deer. "Here, sweetie." he tried to move the bottle to her mouth, but Lily flinched and tried to scoot away.

"Woah, woah, it's okay," he said, holding out his hands as though he were calming a wild animal.

Lily was shaking horribly at this point, but her wide eyes stayed focused on the man.

"Oh here, I have an idea."

Ben pulled a thermos out of his bag. He unscrewed the lid and poured some water into it. He carefully slid the lid towards Lily, and brought his hand back quickly as if she was going to bite. She let her body relax enough to lean forward and peek at the contents in the lid. He leaned back on his heels, and Lily shot back.

"No, no. It's okay. You can drink."

Lily, desperate for water, bent her head to lap it up. Her tongue sopped up the liquid like a sponge, and she looked around for more.

"My name's Ben, by the way," the man said as he poured more water into the lid. "What's yours?"

Lily didn't answer.

"Do you need food? I have a granola bar."

As he was digging around in his bag, headlights reflected off of the metal fence, and in the moment they illuminated his face, Ben looked scared. He swung the bag over his shoulder and promised Lily, "I'll be back tomorrow."

He jumped up and over the fence behind her in one clean swoop, and just like that, he was gone. Lily didn't know what to make of him. She couldn't trust him. Could she? She had no way of knowing his intentions, but he gave her water. He filled her stomach slightly, and that was enough for Lily to want him to come back.

Brian's obnoxious voice and Shannon's snippy response pierced the quiet night and Lily was somewhat relieved. At least she knew what to expect from them.

"Don't get used to that. He's not going to treat you right, just like everybody else. Why would he help you?" Mailman asked.

Lily didn't even look at him. Some sort of emotion rose in her chest. She couldn't tell if it was from happiness or fear, but for the first time in a long time, Lily fell asleep hoping she would wake up the next morning.

All throughout the next day, Lily anxiously awaited Ben's arrival. She was terrified that he would come back but she was petrified that he wouldn't. She needed to stay alive, and he was her only hope. Lily willed the clouds to move across the sky faster and for the sun to begin its descent.

Finally, Brian and Shannon left for dinner. Her heart was about to beat out of her chest, but it was painfully and forcefully stopped by her ribcage. After what felt like forever, the fence creaked.

She heard, rather than saw, Ben walk over to her. The moon was covered today, so Lily couldn't see his face.

"Hey, sweetheart. I brought snacks," he said.

Ben unzipped something and crinkled some wrappers.

He spoke as he took everything out and showed it to Lily. "I made peanut butter and jelly for you. And I brought you more water."

Lily was still wary of Ben, so she kept her eyes on him, but the grumbling in her stomach overpowered any fear she had. She snatched the sandwich and held it against her chest as though Ben was going to take it away, and scarfed it down, paying little attention to the pain in her teeth and gums.

"Woah, slow down. I don't want you getting sick."

He poured water into the lid again and pushed it towards Lily, tilting his head. "You know, you're about the same size as her." He reached his hand out to push Lily's hair behind her ear. She nearly jumped out of her skin, startling Ben.

He laughed a bit and whispered, "You remind me so much of my daughter."

Lily, although she wouldn't have responded anyways, knew he was just talking to himself. She listened, not because she was curious about who he was talking about, but because maybe after he was done, he would give her something else to eat.

Ben sighed. "Okay, I have to leave now. But tomorrow I'll bring a blanket or something. And I'll bring more food, too."

He went back the way he came, creeping through the opening in the fence, and was gone.

Though Brian and Shannon still ignored her, Lily now had the comfort of Ben's expected visits. Without fail, after her parents would leave, he would come through the fence and give Lily food, warmth, and company. Very gradually, Lily became less weary of him. She was even able to start practicing her words again, and now she had Ben's vocabulary to add.

Lily knew it was all too good to be true. She knew something would end her good fortune; something always did. And sure enough, one night her parents started screaming at each other.

"Brian, you idiot. How could you lose *all* of our money? What the hell were you thinking?" Shannon screamed.

"I was on a roll! How was I supposed to know what was gonna happen?"

Lily closed her eyes. Her parents' argument didn't float through the air like their normal conversation. It flew right to Lily's head and stabbed and sliced her brain with its jagged words. She covered her ears and turned away from the house, squeezing her eyes shut, in attempt to drown out their voices and escape into her imagination. Nothing helped.

The shouts died down eventually, but Brian and Shannon didn't leave to go to dinner. Lily listened for the sputtering engine of the car, but it never started. The lights stayed on in the house and the TV blared all night long.

Lily waited for Ben to come, but he never did. Disappointed and abandoned, Lily decided to go to sleep. Nothing ever hurt her in her dreams.

"What did I tell you?" Mailman said. Lily huffed and rolled to her other side so she wouldn't have to look at him. "Even Ben got sick of you. He saw how ugly you are, how bad you smell. He realized you're stupid and worth absolutely nothing. That's why he didn't come tonight. He doesn't love you any more than Brian and Shannon do."

His words didn't cut like Brian's and Shannon's did. His cycled through her mind on an endless loop, before melting and mixing in with her own thoughts so she believed them too. Ben had given her hope, but plucked it out of her reach the moment he had the chance.

She was beginning to think she was all alone in the world.

Chapter Three

"Well apparently, it's all my fault we don't have any money, so I'm going out to make more."

For days now, Lily had to endure Brian and Shannon's constant yelling at each other. They'd been fighting more than ever, mostly about trivial things like who gets the remote and what they're going to eat for dinner.

"You can't just abandon me like this. Do I need to remind you what day it is?" Shannon shouted.

Lily could almost hear Brian rolling his eyes. "Oh my God, I know, but what're we gonna do? We barely have two pennies to rub together, let alone waste it on some stupid presents or dinner."

"Well, I'm sorry for wanting attention from my husband on the day I was born."

Lily didn't think Shannon sounded sorry at all.

"Shut up. You are so—I'm actually going to kill you if you don't stop talking."

Lily could picture what Brian looked like right now. His face was red and his hands were shaking. Shannon better back down soon or Brian was going to start hurting her like he does Lily.

"Brian, you are not leaving this—" Glass shattered and Shannon yelped.

Brian cussed. Shannon started to yell again.

"Did you just—you broke my skull! That's an actual glass bottle. You could've killed me, what the hell were you thinking?"

Brian shouted in frustration, but Lily couldn't make out his words.

"Excuse me, loving husband, I'm bleeding out over here. Take me to the hospital. Now."

"I swear to God I will hit you so hard you will *wish* you were dead. Let me think. Stop screaming at me for two seconds!" Brian's silhouette was pacing back and forth behind the curtain. "Fine. Fine! We'll go to the hospital," Brian said. His silhouette threw his hands up in the air. "But you're not gonna say a word about what happened. I'm not about to get arrested. We're going to tell them…we'll tell them you were getting out of the shower and you slipped and hit your head on the counter."

"Or maybe I'll tell them you attacked me. Jail time would do you some good."

"Do you want me to take you or not? And hurry up before you bleed all over the house."

The light flicked off and Lily was left in darkness. She didn't care that Ben wasn't going to return—or at least that's what she told herself—and she had been steeling herself against the inevitable hunger that would soon eat away at her until nothing was left. She shivered. She tucked her hands into the sleeves of her jacket and rubbed her arms to warm herself up.

With Brian and Shannon still at the hospital, Lily entertained herself by pulling the moon up with her eyes until it barely peeked out from above the tree. She sniffed and wiped the tears off her cheeks. That must've been more difficult than she thought; her eyes were watering now from the strain.

Movement from the front of the house caught Lily's attention. She thought maybe she missed the car pulling back into the driveway, that maybe Shannon was hurt so badly she couldn't talk anymore, but they weren't home yet. Ben came through the fence, looking so crazy that Lily actually backed away from him.

When he spoke, his words were rushed. "Hey, how've you been? I'm so sorry I haven't been able to come for the past couple days, but the lights were on in the house and I didn't want to get caught back here. But they were off tonight, so I figured I'd risk it."

Lily flinched, frightened by Ben's intensity.

Ben took a deep breath. "I want to get you out of here."

Lily didn't understand.

"Okay, we have to hurry though. I'm late today. I wasn't even going to come by, but at the last second I figured I should check just in case. You gotta work with me on this, okay?"

He reached into his bag and pulled out a knife. Lily shook her head and scrambled back even more. The last time someone came out here with a knife, she almost lost a couple fingers.

"No, I'm not going to hurt you. I just want to cut the rope. Okay? C'mon, I need to do this!" Ben raised his voice and Lily curled up.

"Do you want to get out of here or not?"

Lily furiously mouthed words into her knees to distract her from Ben's rage. She braced herself to be beaten, like Brian would've done, but no fists landed on her. She knew better than to look up, so she just rocked back and forth while she focused on moving her tongue and mouth in the right way.

The yard was quiet for a couple seconds, but Lily could still hear Ben breathing. There was some shuffling and then a noise Lily had never heard before. It almost sounded like when Brian came out to cut off some branches off of the tree, but crunchier. She stopped rocking and mouthing words so she could listen.

The pull on her neck loosened. She shot up to a sitting position and crawled away. But this time, there was nothing stopping her from going back forever. One end of the rope followed her like a snake as she moved backwards, and she opened her mouth to scream. Before she could make a sound, Ben's hand clamped down on her mouth, and she whipped her head from side to side and kicked her legs.

Ben was whispering fiercely into her ear, "I need you to stop. You need to be quiet. I'm trying to help you, please, stop."

But she couldn't. As horrible as her life was, she wasn't sure she wanted to leave. She had no idea what was beyond the fence, and she didn't think she was ready to find out.

Headlights illuminated Ben's face for a second and he looked just as distressed as Lily.

"Oh shit, shit, shit."

Car doors opened and slammed.

"I told you it wasn't anything serious," Brian said.

"Stitches are serious, dimwit. How do you think we're gonna pay for this, huh? And we still have Lily out back, what're we supposed to do with her?"

"Why're you so concerned about her all of a sudden? We'll just keep doing what we've been doing. Just leave her out there. She'll rot eventually," Brian said. "And if you had let me go out tonight, maybe I would've won more cash, you ever think of that?"

"Oh, believe me. This is *not* how I wanted to spend my birthday."

While Lily's attention was focused on her parents, Ben hoisted her off the ground. She involuntarily cried out, but he kept his hand over her mouth. It tasted like sweat and dirt. He flung his bag over his shoulder and bounded the few strides it took to get to the fence. He not-so-carefully deposited Lily onto the ground on the other side, and leapt over it himself. He held her in his arms and bolted for the woods.

Lily was dazed. Her surroundings were passing by at an alarming speed and the dull colors were flying by in a blur. She was dizzy. Her head was rolling back and forth, almost like her neck wouldn't support it. Her body was being jolted and bounced and each of her senses was being overwhelmed by something different. She saw a bunch of trees flying by, then everything went black and she could only hear Ben huffing and the crackle of leaves and twigs on the ground. Then she went deaf and her whole body was hyper-aware of all the places she was touching him.

After what seemed like ages, Ben stopped running. He set her down so he could bend over and put his hands on his knees.

Lily patted the ground around her. The grass was softer here, and greener too. She was overcome with fatigue, so she laid down and closed her eyes.

"Oh, no. Don't sleep yet, sweetie, we're almost home." Ben's voice was considerably softer than it was at the house. And, even though she was so far away from her pole, she still had a rope around her neck. Everything was just...wrong.

Ben grabbed Lily by the arm and helped her stand up fully for the first time in three years. Her legs were so thin and weak, she collapsed as soon as her feet were flat on the ground.

"Okay, here we go," Ben said, his voice strained as he picked her up. He carried her like a baby once more and walked towards a new house that Lily had never seen.

And there was her pole, but it wasn't in the backyard, it was in front of this house. She struggled in Ben's arms and tried to push herself away. In the background, from somewhere deep in the woods, Mailman cackled. "You'll never get away," he called.

"Woah, woah," Ben said. He squeezed her tighter to his body to control her. "It's okay, it's not the same one. Look, we're just going to walk past it..."

But not being able to get out of his grip made her strain against him even more. She wanted to be back at Brian and Shannon's. At least there they didn't force her to go places she didn't want to go to.

Help me with this. Please. I need you to stop, she thought, but couldn't make her mouth move.

Fear burst through her chest like someone had squeezed her heart until it popped like a water balloon. It slowly trickled into her legs and up her neck and down her arms, and it was turning her to stone.

Lily could do nothing to resist as she was carried through door after door and around corner after corner. Distant memories of Brian and Shannon's house flashed all around her, but it wasn't the same. They were in a maze that didn't have an end.

Lily was dropped onto a bed. The cement that had paralyzed her shattered with the soft impact and she scrambled to her knees. She thought that maybe this was Brian and Shannon's bed, and she panicked. She wasn't supposed to be in here.

Lily almost forgot that Ben was there, but he gently pushed her shoulders down so she was laying on her back. She grunted and panted and tried to jump off the bed, but Ben held her firmly in place until she stopped moving. She stared at him with wide eyes, trembling.

"It's okay, you're okay. You can trust me. This is all supposed to happen," Ben murmured soothingly. "Just go to bed, sweetheart."

With one hand still on her shoulder, he used his other to pull blankets on top of her. This was the first time all winter that she was truly warm, but something didn't feel right to her. Her heart had refilled its water balloon, but it wasn't slotted in the right place. It felt...off.

She flailed her arms under the blankets and tried to make herself melt so she could slide through Ben's fingers. She thought that if she could just get out the door she'd be able to go back and everything would be normal. Lily didn't like this new place. She wanted to go home. She grabbed her rope that was still attached to her neck and tugged until it felt familiar.

Help me with this, help me with this, help me with this. Lily repeated this mantra in her head, unable to say it out loud, and it hypnotized her. Her eyelids started to feel heavy and each blink was getting longer. First they were closed for a second, and they snapped back open. Ben was still there. They closed for a couple seconds more, and this time, she could only open her eyes halfway. They closed for the night, and she wouldn't have been able to force them open if she tried.

"What did I do?" Ben whispered. He was tugging on his hair and he was still baring a creepy smile despite the fact that she had passed out a while ago.

"No, oh no, oh no," he moaned. An ache set deep in his stomach like someone dropped a lead ball down his throat, and his stomach molded itself around it, twisting and turning in unnatural ways. In the heat of the moment, Ben was so pleased with himself. But now, watching her sleep in his daughter's old bed, clutching the rope like a treasured stuffed animal, he wanted to throw up.

"Someone's gonna find out. I'm gonna be arrested. I can't go to jail. I can't have another one taken from me."

She stirred, and Ben stiffened. He didn't even let himself breathe until she settled. He inched out of the room, his eyes never straying from her delicate face. The floor creaked under his heel and he froze again. Waking her up would make him face the full reality of what he'd done.

"What am I supposed to do?"

In the empty basement, his concern almost seemed to echo back at him, eerily swirling around and consuming his mind. Like a little kid afraid of the dark, Ben bounded up the stairs two by two, just in case his thoughts were chasing him down, ready to grab him.

He burst out of the basement and pressed his back against the door, protecting himself from the demons down there

The sliding glass door in his kitchen faced the back of the house. A minimal amount of light shone from the front yard to the back, leaving elongated shadows that made Ben shudder.

He stared into the near complete darkness, daring someone or something to jump out and scare him. He didn't turn his back to the door, but hurried into his room where it was safe. Ben pulled out his phone, and without thinking, scrolled down to Amy's name. She was the one he could always confide to, the one person he trusted with all of his secrets.

Ben wanted her to tell him that it would be okay. That he could keep Lily and no one would come after either of them. That she could come home so they could start over with a new daughter. No bad memories or regrets. Just a new family.

His hand shook as he stared at the number on the screen. His thumb was twitching madly back and forth as it slowly moved downwards to press the call button.

Ben heard her voice screaming at him in his head: "If you call here again, I swear, you'll never see Claire again."

"Arrggh!" Ben shouted and threw his phone across the room. "You can't do that. She's my daughter too."

Ben realized something. "I have Lily now. She's mine and you can't take her away."

The rest of the night was spent checking out the windows for red and blue flashing lights or the wide silhouette of Brian coming to steal his daughter back.

Ben didn't let himself close his eyes. He didn't even blink.

Chapter Four

Ben rolled over and groaned into the pillow damp with salty tears from a memory shining with the unreal glow of dreamland.

He and Amy had taken Claire to the playground so she could release some of her pent up energy after being locked inside for months. That winter had been brutal. Day after day they were trapped in the house, wrapped in blankets with mugs of hot chocolate in their hands, watching the snow that never seemed to stop falling. But there was one day, a week or so after the snow had melted, where they were able to go outside without getting frostbite.

Despite how beautiful the day had been—no clouds in the sky, chirping birds and dancing worms, bright green grass and colorful flowers poking through the dirt—no one else had been at the park. It was almost like they were afraid the cold weather would attack if they were out enjoying the sunshine.

"Do you want to go over by the lake?" Ben asked.

"Lake? That's too small to be a lake," Amy said. "That's a pond."

"Pond?" Ben repeated, shaking his head. "That's too big to be a pond. That's a lake."

Amy laughed. "Whatever you say." She patted his shoulder.

"Oh no, this isn't over yet," Ben said, wagging his finger in her face. "Claire, can you come here for a second?"

Claire ran back to them from where she had been skipping ahead and stopping every now and then to inspect something on the ground. She bounced to a stop in front of Ben. Before he could get to her, Amy picked her up and swung her around. Claire threw her head back and screamed, scrunching her face up in delight.

Amy balanced Claire on her hip and whispered something in her ear.

Claire giggled and nodded, covering her mouth with her hand. "It's a pond, Daddy."

Ben let his mouth fall open in shock and set the picnic basket down. "What did you say?"

Claire shrieked and wiggled out of her mother's safe embrace. Ben made his hands look like claws and stretched his arms over his head. "I'm gonna get you," he said in his best monster voice. She squealed again and ran away. He let her outrun him for a few steps before he swooped her off of the ground and tickled her.

She couldn't stop laughing.

Ben brought Claire back to the blanket where Amy had started unpacking their lunch.

"Tell Mommy who's the best," Ben instructed Claire.

Claire had looked between Amy and Ben with a small grin. "Daddy."

Amy had pursed her lips to stop herself from smiling and shook her head. Her eyes had found his. "He really is."

Claire had only been three years old. Long time ago.

Ben closed his eyes to recapture the comfort of that day, the whimsical feeling that yes, you *can* love someone that much. But now the memory was almost completely gone; it was like the wisps of the cloud in the sky that day: stretching so thin they were almost nonexistent.

Ben groaned as he pushed himself off the couch, stretching his back from the long night spent there. He didn't mean to fall asleep. He shouldn't have fallen asleep.

"Oh, shit."

Ben hurried to the window overlooking the front yard and stood to the side, only peeking around the edge to stay out of sight from anyone outside.

But no one was there to see him. No police, no Brian. He was in the clear. For now.

Ben swiped the curtain closed and crept to the sliding glass door in the back of his house. The sun was just starting to rise, but the world was barely awake. That is, except for the trees standing like a line of guards, daring somebody to test their will. Row after row of soldiers prepared to keep anyone from entering—or getting out.

At first, the trees seemed to be protecting him and Lily from danger, from someone who would want to take her away. But then Ben's vision shifted, and they were a wall of prison guards and he was stuck behind bars.

Ben shuddered and turned away.

"No work today," he said, letting out a low whistle. "Good timing on my part."

He massaged his face with his hands and ran his fingers through his hair. The TV was on from last night, but muted. When did he turn that on? He leaned over the couch for the remote to turn it off, but stopped and turned the volume up instead.

Ben half expected a picture of himself to flash across the screen and for the news anchor to be reporting about the little girl who was stolen from her home the night before. But she wasn't saying anything of relevance to Ben, so he pressed a button and it flicked to black.

Last night was just the first streak of paint on a white canvas. The start of something big, something unknown. Ben felt like he had woken up in a strange place, wanting to look around, to test the waters, but afraid of what he might find.

He was too alert now—too on-edge—to go back to sleep, but he didn't want to wake Lily up. She needed to rest.

The hours crawled by as if the clocks were having a competition to see who could tick the slowest. Ben wasn't going to leave the house and Lily alone, but the agonizing silence and overwhelming lack of activity was torturous.

The fridge never magically created any new food, no matter how often he checked. He counted his steps going from his bedroom to the front door, but the distance never changed. The blankets on his bed had never been neat before, but now the sheets were pulled taut and the edges crisp.

Ben tried to watch TV, but it was too loud in his head, too distracting from what he needed to think about. But when it was off, his thoughts rushed at him all at once and battered him to the point of frustrated tears. He swiped at his face and stabbed the mute button, anxiously bouncing his knee up and down while he waited for something to happen.

When Lily woke, she felt strange. The clouds were so thick above her head, she couldn't see any blue or grey or soft yellow. Not one sliver, not one dot of color. The whole sky was white. And it was so quiet. Brian and Shannon weren't shouting at each other, at her, at anything, and the wind wasn't arguing with its musicians. Lily could clearly hear her own breath, and if she strained her ears, there was a thumping noise coming from inside her chest.

"Good morning rat, don't go anywhere, life is good," Lily whispered. She curled up, but something got all tangled in her legs. She couldn't see her body; she screamed and kicked but couldn't get the thin piece of fabric off.

She pushed the blanket aside and sat straight up. Everything was different.

Lily sniffed, then blew out, trying to clear her blocked nose. She coughed. Her chest hurt. Everything was gone except her cold.

Flashes of memories—dreams?—danced and leaped and twirled through her mind: the woods rushing forward to meet her, her pole chasing her through a dark maze of looming figures and outstretched claws, herself floating a dizzying height above the ground.

The ground. She needed to get back on the ground. Lily slid off the bed and her feet jarred into the floor, jolting pain through the bones in her legs. She crumpled, catching herself on her hands, and winced when that hurt too. She rubbed her wrists and ankles but stopped when her hand brushed the stuff she had landed on. There was no hard grass here—it was soft. It was like dandelion fluff. Brian and Shannon's house had stuff like this, but theirs was grey and stiff and dirty. This stuff was squishy, like clouds.

Lily marveled. She must be in the sky. The clouds had finally answered her pleas and sandwiched her between them. They picked her up and were taking her with them on whatever adventures they always had.

She rubbed her face on the lower layer of clouds as a thank you for taking her away, but stopped short when the prickly end of the rope scraped her cheek. Her eyebrows furrowed and she held the rope in the palm of her hand. She touched her neck and it was still there, but the pole wasn't here. There was just the bed and a smooth brown box in the corner. The clouds must've taken the rope from the yard so Lily wouldn't be as lonely. They were so thoughtful.

Lily braced her hands on the ground, ignoring the twinge of pain in her wrists, and pushed herself to her knees. She wobbled for a second, wind-milling her arms, but regained her balance. Her core was already starting to ache from the exertion.

She clutched a handful of the blanket that was hanging off the side of the bed and heaved herself to a standing position. But her knees buckled and she was on the ground again, this time flat on her butt. She looked at her legs in bewilderment. Brian and Shannon walked all the time. What was wrong with her?

Lily huffed and squared her shoulders. She shifted onto all fours again and shuffled over to the box. She hoisted herself up until she was on her knees, leaning most of her weight against the wood.

Now that she was closer, she could see that there were smaller boxes inside the big one, and each had a handle on it that was made out of the same material as her pole.

Lily glanced around to make sure she was still alone and grabbed one of the handles. She pulled at it and it flew out, knocking her on her back from the force. When her heart started beating at a normal rate again, she righted herself and pulled on all the handles, albeit less aggressively.

She stared in awe at the inside of the boxes. Each was filled with clothes: t-shirts, pants, heavy long-sleeved shirts, underwear, socks, shorts. All different colors, all clean. As far as she could tell, none of them had holes or mud smeared on them.

Lily reached out so she could feel the fabric, to make sure she wasn't imagining it, but stopped herself and looked around again. The last thing she wanted was to get in trouble in this new haven. She didn't want the clouds to get mad at her and drop her somewhere strange, or worse, back in the yard. She pushed the boxes shut, trying to make as little noise as possible. She glanced up to see if the upper level of clouds had dissipated at all, but no sky was peeking through.

"Sun. Wood. Tree. Cloud."

Besides a light on the small table next to the bed that looked like the top part of her pole—the part that used to light up before it broke—there wasn't really anything else Lily could explore. So she sent her words out into the air, her breathy whispers searching for and residing in every nook and cranny she couldn't reach herself.

Unable to grip the box to hold herself up any longer, Lily sank to the ground. She ran her hand over the fluff underneath her and squished it between her fingers. Not even two seconds later, one of the doors opened. Lily's heart flipped and she scrambled away until her back hit the wall. In the doorway was the outline of a man.

Brian, her pounding heart said. *Mailman.*

"Hey, it's okay," the man said. He stepped into the light, so the shadows disappeared off his face. "It's just me."

Ben smiled a little, and took a couple steps closer.

Lily folded herself over her bent legs and shoved her hands behind her knees to stop herself from shaking, but it wasn't working. She rocked back and forth with her chin down, and there was a loud rattling noise, but she didn't know where it was coming from.

Why was Ben here? Shouldn't he be down on the ground?

Ben's smile faltered and he grimaced when he sniffed. He held his hands out a bit as he walked, as if he were calming an unfamiliar dog. He kept coming closer. He wouldn't stop. Lily whimpered and trembled more violently.

She clenched her jaw and the rattling stopped.

Ben brushed his hand over her shoulder and Lily jerked back. Ben yanked his hand away as if the metaphorical dog were about to bite him. He laughed uneasily, and rubbed his hand on the back of his neck.

"Lily," he said softly.

She jerked her head up at the sound of her name and it hurt her neck. Her teeth started to clatter again.

"Your parents said it back at the house. Your name's Lily."

Lily's breaths became more ragged as she desperately tried to fill her lungs. The air was so thick with everything they were leaving unsaid that it was hard to breathe.

"I didn't even realize last night, I didn't cut the rope off your neck. You probably want that off, don't you?"

Lily swallowed hard, trying to get the lump stuck in her throat to go down.

"We'll take care of that in a little bit, once we get out to the kitchen. I'll bring a knife down so I can cut it off," Ben said. He clapped his hands together. Lily wanted him to stop making so much noise. "Anyways, I, um, hope you like your room. I didn't have time to paint the walls, and the bedding is a couple years old, but it was all I had. I hope you like pink, 'cause that's what her favorite color was."

Ben trailed off and fixed his gaze on a spot on his wall, and Lily guessed she wouldn't be told who the "her" was. She glanced at the blankets and thought *pink*, correlating the color with the word.

"I tried to make it comfortable down here for you." Ben stood up and walked to the big wooden box. "This dresser used to be my mom's, so don't go scratching it up." He laughed softly, uneasily.

Dresser, Lily thought. *Basement.* So she wasn't in the sky. Her shoulders dropped.

He opened a drawer. "These clothes in here are all for you. I mean," he paused, tilting his head at her, "I'm pretty sure you'll fit. These are her clothes from a couple years ago, but you're smaller than her anyways."

Ben went to the second door in the room and swung it open. "And this is the closet."

Closet.

"If you have any clothes that won't fit in the drawers, you can hang them up in here." He flicked at a hanger. "They took most of her clothes with them, but they didn't take the ones that she grew out of. And I'm sorry about the lack of toys," Ben added. He raised his voice. "They pretty much took everything."

Lily winced. She waited for his next outburst to be directed at her, but he just pinched the bridge of his nose.

"Sorry. I'm sorry," he said, his eyes closed. He shook his head. "I'm still a little upset. But that's why I have you now. That's why you're here with me. We're all going to start over."

Start over? There wasn't anything to start over.

"Okay, enough about that. Do you wanna see the rest of it?" He held out his hand, but she didn't know what he wanted her to do. He grabbed her hands himself, and she tried to pull back out of habit, but Ben had a strong grip. He yanked her to her feet, and she stumbled trying to place her feet in the right spots.

"C'mon, you can do it. Here just…no, like this." Ben grabbed her ankle and put it down for her. She kicked him off.

Lily put one foot down flat, but when she tried to put the other one down, the first foot came up again. She grunted, frustrated. Ben let her use his hands for stability and waited patiently while she repeated this process a million times. He kept her from falling as she tried to walk on her own.

She took one step, another, and another, but her legs couldn't hold her up for very long and her knees knocked together. She collapsed into Ben's arms.

"I got you, don't worry. I'm here," he muttered.

She twisted a little and pulled away. She didn't want him to have her. But more importantly, why couldn't she do this? She taught herself how to eat and drink, ration food and water, and how to lean up against the pole when her back hurt. She learned how to pull the neck of her shirt up underneath the rope when the abrasive material became too rough, how to defend herself against Brian's attacks, how to put up a mental block against her parents' harsh words. If she could do all that, why couldn't she figure out how to walk?

Ben laughed. Lily wrinkled her forehead and craned her neck to look at him. Why is he laughing at her? She tugged her arms, but Ben wouldn't let go. If anything, he just held on tighter.

"It's okay, this will probably take a while to learn. We'll just have to practice every day to make your legs stronger," he assured her. "In the meantime, can I carry you? It'll make things a lot easier."

Lily didn't answer, so he decided it meant he was free to pick her up and balance her on his hip. He flicked the loose end of the rope over his shoulder, but she brought it back to the front so she could hold it. Lily leaned as far away from him as she could, so she was touching as little of him as possible. He walked out of the door he came in from and said, "So that, obviously, was your bedroom."

Lily stared in wonder as the room she was in expanded into a huge house that was so much bigger than her yard.

They went forward a couple steps and he showed her what he called the "living room".

"As you can see, there's not much to this. The couch is from upstairs, same with the rug, but I can't afford a TV down here. I could hardly afford the one that's upstairs."

They turned left and passed a huge stairwell.

"These are the stairs. You're not allowed to go up these. Okay? You have to stay down here."

He walked straight forward and pointed out the kitchen.

"This is where you'll eat," he said, patting the wooden table. "And I set up the microwave and fridge that were already here, and I'm going to stock these cupboards with plenty of food. You're never going to be hungry again."

They turned right and stopped in front of a bathroom.

"Now, judging by the smell of the backyard, you've never had a place to go to the bathroom. Well, this is where you do it. That's a toilet, and the sink is for when you wash your hands afterward. That tub is for taking showers and baths."

Besides the few things floating back to her from when she lived inside Brian and Shannon's house, Lily was overwhelmed with all of this new information, and she tried her best to store the words in her memory. It was hard to keep up with everything Ben was saying.

"And that's pretty much it," he said. He put her down into one of the chairs around the table and sat across from her. He folded his hands in front of himself.

"So, how do you like the place?"

Silence.

"You're not gonna talk to me anytime soon, are you?"

Lily swore she could hear a cricket chirp nearby. Her ears perked up; that was a familiar sound. But she didn't take her eyes off Ben's.

"You're going to have to speak to me at some point, you know."
He raised his eyebrows. "Yeah, we'll work on it. Just like," Ben
sighed, "All of the other things we need to work on. But it's okay.
It's okay. And you know why? Because we have plenty of
time."

Lily wasn't paying attention anymore; she was going over all
the new words she heard and connecting them to the pictures of
the objects in her mind.

"I'm going to bring you lots of toys and books and games. I'll
give you food and spend so much time with you. And again, I'm
so sorry I don't have more to give you. I'm kinda low on money
at the moment." Ben rubbed the back of his neck and slid his
fingers through his hair so he could have something to do with his
hands. That's what Brian needed a lot of the time. Except instead
of rubbing his own neck, he had his hands wrapped around Lily's.

Ben jumped up. "I'll go get a knife."

He bounded up the stairs and came back with a small blade.

"Ready?" He asked, waving it around.

Lily's mouth widened with her eyes and she scrambled
backwards, tipping the chair over and taking her with it. She
screamed and threw her arms over her head, her elbows
connecting hard with the ground.

"Lily!" Ben yelled. She heard the knife clatter to the floor. "Are
you okay?"

Lily was shaking, and cried out when Ben tried to help her up.
She shuffled away from him, but he wouldn't take his hand off.

"I'm not gonna hurt you. I'm just going to get the rope off."

The rope wasn't the problem, but Ben didn't seem to realize
that. He put his hand on her arm, and when she didn't jerk away,
he took it as a sign that he could continue.

Lily was too scared to move.

"That's it, there we go. See, we're okay now," Ben said. He
righted the chair and placed her in it, retrieving his knife and
bringing it towards her. "I'm gonna have to bring this near your

neck, okay? It's going to touch your skin, but don't freak out. I don't want you to cut yourself."

The cold metal slid in a line on her neck, and she lifted her head so the blade wouldn't touch her chin. She bit her bottom lip and pulled away ever so slightly.

Ben sawed at the rope. Lily dug her fingers into the underside of the chair, feeling her nails bend and scratch uncomfortably at the wood.

"Almost done, you're okay," Ben said. The crunching stopped and Ben backed away. He smiled at her and wiped his forehead with the back of his hand. "Phew! Got through that with minimal damage, didn't we?"

Lily could already feel the bruise forming on her elbow and the ghost of the cool knife hadn't yet left her skin. She gently touched her neck. The rope was lying limp in Ben's hands. He killed it. He killed her rope.

She reached for it, but Ben pulled it away. "Nuh uh, this is going right in the trash."

The rope wasn't around her neck, but she could still feel the weight of it. It was still choking her, still restricting her.

"Next order of business," Ben said, "is your clothes. Let's find you some new ones, shall we?"

In the bedroom, he pointed to the dresser, indicating which handle she should pull.

"You're going to bed soon, so let's pick out some pajamas for you to sleep in."

Lily pulled open one of the—she had to search for the word before it came to her—*drawers*. There were so many colors, she didn't even know where to begin. There was the color of apples, of her blankets, of the grass before it died, of the sky when a thin layer of clouds draped over it, of the sun when it shined without anything blocking it.

She shoved her hand into the pool of fabric and marveled at the wild contrast from her own stiff and dirty clothes. Lily stroked the materials. Some were smooth, others were fuzzy. She randomly grabbed one and rubbed it against her face.

Drawer, dresser, kitchen, clothes, bed, couch, she thought as she mouthed the words.

"Do you like that shirt?"

Lily could care less which shirt she wore, as long as it wasn't the one she currently had on.

Ben chuckled. He grabbed the top from her hands, and Lily whimpered.

"Don't worry, I'll give it back soon." He grabbed a pair of sweatpants and underwear, and mumbling the name of each as he picked it out.

"Time to take your very first bath." He looked back at her. "I mean, I'm assuming."

Ben picked her up again and Lily squirmed and leaned away, eyes squeezed shut, tongue moving in a series of silent words behind her closed lips.

Ben flipped on the light. He set her on the ground, but not before she caught a glimpse of another girl across the counter. A deep guttural noise escaped her throat and she crawled backwards until she was against the wall. She huddled in on herself and the coolness of the tiles soaked through her pants.

Ben didn't see how distressed she was. He was facing the tub, fiddling with the knob. To himself, he said, "If you take a bath, the water will get dirty really fast and we'll have to keep emptying and refilling it."

He turned on the shower and stepped back to wait for the water to heat up. He faced Lily and pasted on a big smile.

"I'm gonna help you out of those dirty clothes," he said.

Ben unzipped her jacket and shrugged it off of her shoulders. She shrugged it back on.

He gave her a pointed look. "No, you have to take your clothes off to take a bath."

As soon as her jacket was off, she wrapped her arms around her stomach, digging her fingers into the spot just below her ribs. She felt bare without the familiarity of the covering on her arms and torso. She felt exposed, like Ben could reach inside her skin and take out all the words she had written there.

"Lily, c'mon."

Lily knew that tone. That's how Brian sounded before he started yelling. She sucked in her trembling bottom lip and let Ben unravel her arms. She kept her eyes closed. She didn't want to see when he stole the only things keeping her alive.

But Ben didn't do anything.

Her words were still looping through her mouth and resting on her tongue. He didn't take them away.

"You know what, I'm not gonna push you. This is fine. I'll just wash you like this."

Ben grabbed her wrist and pulled her forward.

"You gotta open your eyes."

Lily peeked with one eye first, then both shot open. She stepped backwards, but Ben held her in place. He pointed the showerhead down, so she wouldn't be bombarded by the spray, and lifted her into the tub. She yelped, her eyes wide.

Lily didn't waste a second in trying to gain enough purchase to get out. But the slippery porcelain did little to help her stand or get on her knees like she needed.

"Hey, it's okay. Just sit down and relax," Ben said. "I'm going to spray the water on you now."

At first, Lily jumped at the touch of the water, but soon realized it was just like the rain, only warmer. She loved the rain. When the sky was crying and dark clouds brewed overhead, Brian and Shannon wouldn't come outside. They wouldn't do anything to her for the entirety of the storm. She closed her eyes and enjoyed the warmth of the water.

Ben's voice was soothing. "There you go, see, this isn't so bad."

Every now and then, Ben would say something like, "I'm going to touch your head now," or, "I'm going to lift up your shirt to wash your back."

Lily breathed in deeply through her nose. This water didn't smell like the rain.

Wait.

She sniffed. Now it did. She was going to the bathroom. She hadn't realized, but now that made sense. That was what her backyard smelled like, when the warm rain made the air humid and sticky and emphasized the odor.

Ben made a noise. He smiled, but his forehead and nose were all wrinkly.

"Yeah, we'll, uh, we'll work on that."

Lily turned away from him because there was magic happening below her. The dirt on her clothes and skin swirled around the bottom of the tub into pretty patterns. She was mesmerized. She almost forgot about Ben being there; she was lost in her own world.

The streaks of brown sliding off her body and down the drain reminded her of the mud at Brian and Shannon's house. Back in the yard, on those magical nights when water fell from the sky, Lily would watch in wonder as the dirt transformed into liquid that swirled when she touched it. The mud could form into any shape she wanted before being dissolved by the rain. She always made little sculptures of all the animals she'd seen.

But this mud ran away before she could sculpt it.

After she had been sitting there for a long time, Ben finally said she was clean enough for now, so he turned off the shower and plugged the drain. The water kept falling from another spout nearer to the bottom of the tub, and Lily expected Ben to pick her up. Instead, the water continued to rise from below. Her heart dropped to her feet and she crawled to the far side of the tub, but the water found her there, too. She looked at Ben for reassurance, and he smiled and nodded. He grabbed a bottle and squeezed, and it sputtered a few times before squirting something into the water.

"See? Bubbles," Ben said. He shook the bottle and squeezed it harder. "C'mon, I know there's more in here."

While Ben was struggling with getting the last few drops out, what he called "bubbles" started to appear.

Lily lifted her hand above the bubbles and brought it back down. The water splashed and some of the bubbles popped. She splashed some more and got Ben wet. He laughed and lightly splashed her back.

Lily still was completely expressionless.

Even so, she played with the bubbles. She learned she had to be gentle, otherwise they would pop. She picked them up carefully, and she discovered that when she took a deep breath and exhaled, they would go flying off her fingers like the leaves did off the trees. She imagined she was a giant who caused all the winds to blow. Sometimes she accidentally hit Ben with the bubbles, and he laughed, but each time she panicked and stared him down until she knew he wasn't going to hit her.

Ben let her play for a while, but he eventually had to get her out.

"I got the biggest, fluffiest towels that money can buy," he said. He held out the towel so it was the length of his arm span and wrapped Lily in it in a bear hug, rocking her back and forth, pretending he was wrestling with her. She didn't understand what was happening and she wriggled out of his embrace, but Ben caught her before she could get too far away and continued to dry her off, normally this time.

"We need to get you into pajamas, okay?" Ben said, rubbing her hair. He wasn't paying attention to where the towel was going, and it covered her eyes. She tossed her head around until she could see. "You don't want to go to bed in sopping wet clothes, do you?"

Lily wouldn't have minded. She'd done it before. But she was standing up now—before she'd always been laying down—and they were really heavy.

Ben raised his eyebrow at her and grabbed the bottom of her shirt. Lily turned her head but let him take off her old clothes and redress her in a big t-shirt and baggy sweatpants. She had to hold one side of the waistband so they wouldn't fall down.

"We're gonna tackle that hair in the morning. I don't have the energy right now." Ben yawned as if to prove his point. That made Lily yawn too, but she hid hers by tucking her chin into her shoulder.

Ben took Lily's hands in his and made her to stand up on her own.

"You're already becoming a master at this. You're doing great."

Lily didn't know how to react to praise. She only knew how to defend herself and put up mental blocks against abuse. The nice words couldn't get past her barriers.

With Ben's assistance, she took a few wobbly steps towards the counter. There was that girl she saw earlier. Lily touched her wet hair and gasped when the person on the other side of the sink copied her movements. Lily reached out at the same time as the other girl did, and recoiled as her fingers hit the cool glass.

"Don't be scared. It's just you," Ben said.

He had to tug on her shoulder to draw her eyes away from the mirror, and made her walk the few steps to the chair by the table. Her knees gave out a couple times, but he still congratulated her.

"You know," Ben said after Lily was seated, "you have a lot of stuff to learn. You have to know how to walk, dress yourself, shower, use the toilet. You up for the challenge?"

When Lily didn't respond, he laughed. "That's the spirit," he said. "Now we're going to get you something to eat, then it's off to bed again."

Ben left her alone for a second, and when he came back downstairs, he was holding a bag and a cup. He laid out her gourmet meal for the night in front of her: a crinkly bag of chips and a cup filled with water.

"Dig in."

The first chip she picked up broke because it was so thin, so she made sure to pinch the next one carefully. She set it on her tongue and her eyes widened at the flavor. She crunched down, wincing when the pressure sent a cold pain through her gums, but she managed to chew the food anyways.

"Those are potato chips. I haven't gone shopping yet, so I had to scrounge through my cabinet to find that," Ben said. "And I need you to drink the water too." He slid the cup closer to her. Lily stuck her tongue in to lap it up.

"Wait, no, that's not how you drink. Here, watch." Ben brought the drink to his lips and tilted the cup upwards. "See? No more drinking like a dog. Now you try."

Ben handed the cup back to Lily, and she gripped it with both hands. She put the edge of the cup in her mouth, imitating Ben, and leaned her head back with the cup. All of the water spilled onto her face and the cup clattered to the floor.

Ben was next to her in a flash, paper towel in hand, and was cleaning her off before she could even sputter.

"Oh, that's okay. You'll get it next time," Ben said. "But now you have to change again so you're not sleeping in wet pajamas."

Lily didn't want to have to change again, but she wondered why that was even a possibility. The supply of clothes here was endless. She clenched her fists by her side as Ben helped her into a new shirt and new pants. Why did Brian and Shannon make her wear those old ones all the time?

"There you go," Ben said as Lily's head popped out of the top of the shirt. "And I know you just woke up, but it's getting late." Lily could feel her eyelids drooping as he spoke. "You don't look like you're going to put up a fight. So let's go to sleep."

Ben gently laid Lily on the bed. She didn't speak or move her eyes from where they were locked onto his own. Her breaths were deep and rattling as if her lungs couldn't bring in the amount of air she needed and it made her chest shake as it rose and fell. Even the shirt she was wearing looked tired; it hung limply from her shoulders and she was so skinny, it could've just been lying flat on the bed.

Ben covered Lily up and tucked her in, and all he wanted to do was hold her tight. But he was afraid that if he did, she would crumble like dust between his fingers.

Her eyes flickered, fighting to stay open and make sure Ben wasn't a threat, but lost to the desperate pull of sleep. Ben tiptoed out of her room and closed the door quietly.

A sudden gaping hole in his heart took the place of his joy, and it took no time for him to figure out what was missing.

"Amy, you need to be here," he whispered. "We can start over with Lily. Please, come back."

Ben pressed his forehead against the door. "I don't know how, but I'll get us more money. I'll give you a great life. Lily, you're gonna love it here."

Chapter Five

Lily was shaken awake way too soon; she could've sworn she'd only been sleeping for a couple minutes.

"Lily, wake up, come on," Ben said. His hand was on her shoulder.

Her heart skipped a beat—two, three—and she inhaled sharply, her breath catching in her throat. The blankets had gotten tangled during the night and trapped Lily's legs so she couldn't protect herself. She moaned and kicked her feet, fighting with the blankets to free herself, and when she finally won, she curled up, mouthing words.

Bed, blanket, dresser, wake up, goodnight.

"Hey, you have to wake up. Breakfast is waiting."

Ben touched the sheets and crinkled his nose, and he pulled his hand back quickly.

"Okay, um, I'll take these upstairs to wash. It's okay, it happens to everyone."

Lily glanced up at him; she didn't know what was going on.

"You wet the bed," Ben said as explanation. He must've seen the confusion on her face. Lily made sure to relax her eyebrows and unclench her jaw so he wouldn't be able to see what she was thinking anymore. She moved to put her head back into her knees, but before she could, Ben grabbed her wrists and started pulling her off the bed.

"Come on, up and at 'em."

Lily shook her head, but Ben had already dragged her to the floor.

"Put your feet under you. Stand up."

He half carried, half walked her to the bathroom and sat her on the closed toilet seat while he fiddled with the knobs in the shower. Lily leaned against the tank behind her, and it reminded her of how she would lean against her pole back in the yard. It was cold like her pole, and it felt like the same material.

"You look like a mad woman with that hair sticking up all over the place. I don't know how I'm ever going to get it to calm down," Ben said, glancing over his shoulder. "Look over here now. Pay attention. You're gonna have to do this on your own at some point."

Lily felt every muscle in her stomach work to sit her up straight. She laid her hand over it like that would help make it feel better.

"So to turn on the water, you're gonna want to pull this out," he said as he demonstrated. Water gushed from the spout closest to the bottom of the tub. "Then you twist this to get the temperature you want, and you pull up on this little...thing."

It gurgled, and for a second nothing happened. Then water sprayed from the shower head and bounced off the wall and the bottom of the tub. Tiny drops misted her and some landed on her eyelashes. If she really concentrated, she could see the little beads of water. They only stayed in focus for a second before her eyes crossed and made them blur again.

"And this part," Ben continued as he grabbed the shower head, "this part is removable. And it stretches around too."

Lily blinked and wiped her eyes. She raised her eyebrows and looked at her hands like she had never seen them before. Her eyes didn't sting just then, when she touched them. Usually when she rubbed her eyes, dirt got in them and made them hurt. She flipped her hands over. There wasn't any dirt here.

"Are you gonna let me give you a real bath today or do you still want to wear your clothes?" Ben asked, his voice pointed. When she didn't respond, he reached for the bottom of her shirt, but she turned so he couldn't lift it up.

He sighed. "Okay, fine. Get in then." He nodded his head towards the tub.

Lily peered around him and took a small step forward.

"Alright, let's get you in there." Ben grunted and lifted her over the edge. "I'm going to take you through the motions, okay?" he asked when she was settled. "So you know how to do it later when I'm not here. Muscle memory and all."

Ben squeezed the shampoo into Lily's hand, but she flicked it off right away. It felt gross, like that one time she found a slug in the yard and accidentally held it too tightly.

"No, here," Ben said and squeezed more into her hand. Before she could shake the goop off, Ben pushed her hands together and made her rub them to make bubbles. She wanted to play with these bubbles too, even though they were so much smaller than the ones from the day before, but Ben guided her hands to her hair and moved them around. He had to keep stopping, though, to detangle her fingers from all the knots. He helped her rinse off, put conditioner in—or rather on, since her hair was so matted, nothing could get through it—and clean her body with a small rag.

Lily's nostrils flared. Something smelled sweet. Not the same kind of sweet as the apples Brian and Shannon used to put on her tray sometimes, but it was enough to make her twist around to see what it was.

"What?" Ben asked. He followed her line of sight down to the washcloth in his hand and chuckled. "That's not what smells good. Try this." He reached over her head to the notch on the wall that was holding a white rectangle.

Ben waved the soap in front of her. Lily grabbed at it and held it to her nose. She refused to give it back, so Ben had to be content with finishing cleaning her up himself. When the bath was over, he picked her up out of the tub and gave her the towel. He motioned what she should do with it, so she rubbed it on her stomach in small circles.

"No, Lily, you have to get your whole body."

He grabbed her hand with the towel and made her dry herself off.

"You need to try and dress yourself now. I'll help you a little, but this is something you really need to learn."

The getting-dressed process was long and difficult. Lily couldn't figure out which was the head hole and which was the arm hole. She was turning in circles trying to put her head through the small arm hole, with one of her arms sticking out where her head was supposed to be, and the other pinned against her body. Ben chuckled a couple times—two or three bursts of laughter that ended with a cough, like he was trying to cover them up.

"Oh, Lily. You're hilarious." He bit his lip to keep from laughing again, but couldn't hide his smile. "But no, you're doing really good, trust me."

He turned the shirt around the right way and her head popped through the correct hole, her hair even messier than it was before. Ben had her put on a pull-up before guiding her legs into jeans, which were soft and had no rips in them, unlike her old ones.

"Do you like that color?" Ben asked, pointing to her shirt. "I usually like darker purples, but the lighter one looks good too." Then he smacked his lips and said, "Now for the fun part."

Ben gingerly stepped over Lily from where she was sprawled on the floor, and went over to the toilet.

"Obviously you don't have much experience with these." He opened the lid. "When you have to go to the bathroom, you sit here. Well, I mean, first you pull your pants and underwear down, then you sit. You—you know—go, and then you take this"—he held up a roll of toilet paper—"and wipe your bottom."

Lily alternated her gaze from the toilet to Ben. Brian and Shannon had one of these. Lily had worn diapers for a long time, but as she grew, Shannon had gotten tired of changing them. There was one time when Lily had thrown out her own dirty diaper, but when she had gone to get a new one, the cabinet was empty. She figured she could go without it, so she laid down on the couch to take a nap. She woke to Shannon leaning over her and yelling, and Lily didn't even realize she was lying in a puddle of her own urine until Shannon grabbed her arm and dragged her into the bathroom. She tore Lily's pants down and thrust her onto the toilet.

"This is where you go! You don't go in your pants. Here. Not there!"

Shannon had walked away, mumbling to herself. That wasn't the first time she had yelled at her like that, but it was still scary. Lily felt herself peeing, but this time her pants were around her ankles. She hoped she was doing it right this time, if not for Shannon's sake then for hers. She didn't like getting yelled at. It hurt her feelings and made her cry, and then she got yelled at some more.

Lily was too afraid to move from where Shannon had placed her, so she just sat, shivering and crying on the toilet, until Brian barged in.

"What the hell are you doing? Get off."

He lifted Lily off the toilet and yanked her pants up.

"Ugh, God, flush next time." And he pushed her out of the room.

From then on, after every meal and glass of water, Shannon pulled Lily into the bathroom to do her business. She still made Lily wear diapers, but she soon stopped buying them because Brian said they were a waste of money. But that was okay, because she knew how to use the toilet.

Of course, she had to give up her pride when they kicked her out. Whenever she had to go, she would have to wriggle her pants and underwear down in plain sight and relieve herself somewhere on the ground next to the pole. But that was when she had enough energy to crawl a foot or so away. Sometimes all she could do was lie there and soil her pants.

But from what Ben was saying, it was all coming back to her.

"Then you throw the toilet paper into the bowl, and you flush." Ben guided Lily's hand to the metal handle on the side and made her push down. She jumped back at the noise, but Ben held her in place.

"Got that?" he asked. "And after, you come over to the sink and wash your hands." He guided her through the process. "See? More bubbles."

He opened the cabinet under the sink.

"These are called pull-ups, which is what you're wearing under your pants right now. I need you to come to the toilet when you have to go to the bathroom, but these will prevent any accidents. So put on a new one whenever you use the one you have on."

They looked like the diapers she used to wear. Lily looked up at him and nodded. Ben's mouth dropped open.

"And all this time, I thought I was talking to a brick wall."

Lily didn't know if that was a good thing or not, but Ben was smiling. She didn't smile back.

"I think this is a good time to start working on that mane of yours," he said, stroking her hair. Lily leaned away.

Ben brought Lily a chair from the kitchen and set it in front of the mirror so she could see everything that was going on. She bent her neck to see what Ben was holding, so he let her hold it and inspect it as much as she wanted.

"That's called a brush. That's how you get all the tangles out of your hair."

When Lily was through, he set it on the top of her head.

"I don't even know where to begin in this bird's nest."

He tried to pull the brush all the way through her hair, but it got stuck not even a couple inches down. Then he spent the next few minutes trying to detangle the brush from her hair. The only emotion Lily showed was a tiny wince every now and then. It was second nature for her, trying to hide her pain.

"Ah, there we go," he muttered.

He tried to tackle just the ends of her hair, but the only progress he was making was ripping out hundreds of strands.

Ben would say sorry, but proceed to tug on Lily's hair, pulling her head back with the brush. The chair almost fell backwards with Lily in it since she didn't counter Ben by leaning forward. Three times this happened until Ben pressed up against the back of the chair to keep it in place.

The fifth time the brush got stuck, Ben finally said, "I give up. Drastic times call for drastic measures."

He ran his hand over the length of her hair.

"I love long hair. I love this length you have it at. But," he sighed. "I guess it'll grow back."

Ben left the bathroom and Lily heard drawers opening and closing and rummaging coming from outside.

Left alone with the girl in the mirror, Lily studied her face. She knew Ben said it was her in there, but she was having a hard time believing it. Whenever she saw her face in puddles, the image was always warped and distorted. There was no way the girl in the mirror with smooth features and clean skin was Lily.

Although she could only see from the girl's nose and up, because of how low the chair was, she couldn't help but admire what was in her vision. The first time she looked at this girl, dirt and mud had been pressed into the creases by her eyes and on her forehead. Now, there were only faint markings, and Lily thought it could just be the grooves of her skin. Before, her hair had been so greasy and dirty that she thought she was a brunette. Now, though, a little bit of blonde was starting to show through. She touched her nose, surprised when the reflection copied her. Lily grazed over the deep circles under her eyes that were the color of the sky right before the rain came. She ran her hand over the bones of her face and her nose. When her hands came into her view, she stopped and studied those as well. Some of her fingernails were long and rough on the edges, others were short and stubby. The showers didn't wash out the dirt that was caked under her nails.

Ben didn't have dark circles under his eyes, or gross hair, or dirty fingernails. Lily wondered why she was so different.

"Found them," Ben declared, hoisting a sharp metal object. Lily sat on her hands, worried that she was caught doing something she wasn't supposed to. "Just pretend like you're in a salon. Like you're getting pampered."

Lily didn't know what that meant, but she didn't argue. She just tried to slow her beating heart.

"These are scissors, okay? I'm just going to cut your hair with these because it's too messed up to brush."

Lily followed Ben's motions in the mirror with her eyes. He took the scissors and stopped them on a spot near her neck.

"Is this good, here?"

He shrugged and began to cut. There was a small crunch as the scissors broke her hair and some of the strands fell on her shoulder. She moaned and whipped around to see what was going on, grabbing her hair in the back.

"Hey!" Ben yanked the scissors away from Lily so she wouldn't stab herself. "Stop, it's okay."

He took her shoulders and turned her around again. "Don't freak out. Don't turn around like that again. All I'm doing is cutting your hair, it won't hurt you."

He began to cut once more, and Lily had to restrain herself from whirling around. Her scalp tingled everywhere the scissors snipped. But gradually, as more hair decorated the ground, her head felt lighter and freer.

"And... all done," Ben said, finalizing her new haircut with one last clip. The hair on the bottom was slightly uneven, but now it reached just above her shoulders.

"It should be easier to brush and clean from now on."

Ben brushed the tangles out, and it was easier this time, because all the parts the brush kept getting stuck in were now on the floor. When her hair was as tangle-free as it was going to get, Ben helped her out of the chair. He stood her in front of him and gripped her shoulders so she could stand.

His eyes got watery. He gave a breathy laugh and wiped a tear away before it could fall too far. He lightly brushed a strand away from Lily's forehead with his finger before clutching her in a tight hug. Lily pulled away but he was suffocating her into his chest.

He buried his face into her new hair and whispered, "I'm so glad you're here."

Lily didn't hug him back—her arms hung at her sides—but she stopped pushing Ben away. Along with learning that not all human contact was harmful, Lily was figuring out how to read other people besides Brian and Shannon. Just like how she knew that Shannon had grown tired of her, she knew Ben needed to do this.

He pulled away. "I think I see some sparkle coming back to your eyes." He smiled at her, trying to fight through his tears. "C'mon, let's go eat."

He helped her stand up, but she pretended to fall to the floor. When her palms hit the tiles, Lily grabbed a strand of damp hair into her fist. She squeezed as hard as she could to keep it all together.

"Whoops, sorry, here let's get you up," Ben said.

Lily kept her hand closed as Ben grabbed her arms again and walked her to the kitchen so she could sit down.

"Just let me clean this up really quick and I'll be right out." He brought the chair out of the bathroom first, but retreated with a broom and a dustpan. While he was cleaning the floor, with his back to her, Lily slipped the strand of hair she was holding into the pocket of her jeans.

"Success," he said, smiling, with a dustpan full of loose hair. He dumped it into the trash, and dusted his hands off on his shirt. "Ready for breakfast?"

Lily gazed longingly at the trash can. She imagined her hair crawling out of it and connecting back onto her head.

He rubbed his hands together like Lily did when she was cold. "Okay then. I'll be right back."

He climbed the stairs, and at the top, he opened the door. The sound triggered her reflexes, so she turned around to see what was happening. Ben had disappeared, but the door was left open a bit. Sunlight was pouring in through a crack, and it drew Lily like a moth to a flame. She felt as though she hadn't seen the sun in months.

Ben came back and blocked the light from the doorway. His hands were full, so he kicked the door closed with his foot.

Lily again faced away from the stairs. Ben put two full bowls of cereal and milk down on the table.

Cereal, Lily thought. She knew the word for it because sometimes the crumbs at the end of the box were all she was fed after being banished to the backyard. Ben set the bowl—that was the same color as her shirt—down in front of her. His own bowl was the color of apples.

Lily's stomach was growling so loudly, it drowned out the pain in her teeth. Ignoring the metal object that was floating in the milk, she stuck her hands in the bowl to get as much of the sugary cereal into her mouth as she could before someone took it away from her.

"Lily!"

She froze mid-scoop. She didn't know what she did wrong, but she closed her eyes and waited for his fists to land. The food in her mouth was dribbling down her chin and the milk on her hands was dripping down her arms.

Ben jumped up and grabbed some paper towels to wipe the milk off. She resisted a little, not wanting him to touch her, but he held her in place and cleaned her up.

Lily leaned back in her chair and hung her head, sure Ben was going to punch her.

"Hey," he said softer. "Don't look so sad. You didn't know any better. You have a lot of learning to do. Now see, watch how I do it."

Lily lifted her eyes—not her chin—and studied Ben. He grabbed the metal thing in his bowl and scooped some of the cereal onto it. He brought the metal to his mouth and slid the food off. When the metal came back out, it was clean.

"See? You use the spoon to eat, not your hands. You try."

He nodded towards the spoon in her own bowl, so she picked it up. But she didn't pick it up how Ben did; she clenched it in her fist. Otherwise, she mirrored Ben as he brought the food to his mouth and they simultaneously ate their breakfast. Lily spilled quite a bit on herself and the table, but Ben still congratulated her.

"Good job. That's one less life skill you have to learn from now on."

He picked up both of their dishes and placed them in the sink. He came over to her chair and kneeled down beside her.

"I'm really sorry, Lily, but I have to go now. I didn't have that much time to prepare for you coming here, so I couldn't buy any groceries or anything. I'll be back in a couple hours, though, so I can make you lunch. And I'll have more food."

Ben gave her a quick hug. He got the blankets from her room and went upstairs. Lily twisted in her seat, hoping to see the light again, but the door was shut before the sun could peek through.

Ben closed the basement door and took his phone out of his back pocket. He'd had a few conversations with Amy in his head, updating her on what had been happening with Lily, but obviously she couldn't hear him. She needed to know what was going on if she was going to come home and be Lily's mom. And she would be great at it. She was such a good mother to Claire.

There was one day, before Claire was taken away from him, when everything seemed perfect. Amy had been making dinner, with Ben lurking around, pretending to help, but really he had been sneaking bites of food off the plates. Amy had smacked him with a towel and told him to get out of there, and that was when he had seen a little thief snatch something off the counter.

"Hold on a second, missy," Ben said. "Where do you think you're going with that?" He scooped Claire into his arms. "You were supposed to be in the living room watching TV."

She giggled wildly, holding a cookie in front of her rosy cheeks. She offered a bite to Ben, which he took gladly.

"You have been pardoned," he said around a mouthful of cookie.

Amy shook her head and laughed, carving knife in hand.

"Mommy doesn't approve," he whispered, loud enough for Amy to hear.

The doorbell rang then, and Claire's eyes lit up as she shoved the last bite of the cookie into her mouth.

"Can I get it?" she asked earnestly, crumbs sticking to her chin.

Ben put her down and she ran for the door. Seconds later, voices were exclaiming and coats were being taken off. Claire marched proudly into the kitchen with an entourage following.

"Jason!" Ben said, slapping the back of his best friend.

"Benjamin!"

"Oh here, Amy, let me help you," Jason's wife, Nicole, said. "All this food looks so good."

"No thanks to that one over there." Amy nodded towards Ben.

He laughed and put his hand on Claire's head, and she hugged Ben's leg. Jason had a similar situation going on, with his son hiding behind his dad's jeans.

"Ethan, don't be shy. You know Ben. And Claire? You guys play together all the time."

Ethan peeked around to look at Claire, but hid his face as soon as he made eye contact.

"Hey, Claire," Ben said, and she tilted her face up to him. "Why don't you show Ethan all the toys you opened last week for Christmas?"

Claire nodded and ran to Ethan, grabbing his hand and pulling him out of the room.

"Ethan better treat Claire right when they're older," Ben laughed.

As Amy and Nicole finished what they were doing, Ben pulled out wine. They sat around the table sipping from their glasses and reminiscing until the kids became too impatient for their food. The adults made their plates for them and sat them at a small table before eating their own dinner with compassionate glances at the kids even now and then. Laughter rang out and Ben's heart filled. He met Amy's eyes over his glass of wine.

Everything is right, Ben thought. *Everything is perfect.*

They all finished their dinners and went to the living room to talk—or at least the adults did. Claire and Ethan played a game of pretend. The TV was on the channel where they would see the ball drop, with a countdown in the corner of the screen. The kids ended up falling asleep—Claire in a green puffy dress over her clothes and Ethan with a cowboy hat on—but Ben woke them up when there was fifteen minutes left. They snuck out of view for a little while, and only came back when Nicole called to tell them that the ball was about to fall. While the adults were invested in the chaos on the screen, Claire and Ethan threw handfuls of ripped, colored paper into the air.

Everyone cheered and simultaneously said, "Happy New Year!" Amy and Ben kissed each other and lifted Claire in between them to kiss her too. The other family did the same. They all hugged each other. Everyone was smiling.

Ben wanted that moment to be frozen in time. Confetti scattered on the floor, people smiling, and a powerful atmosphere. It had been a new year. Anything had seemed possible.

Now, Ben squeezed his phone in his hand. Anything *was* possible, that was made evident not even six months later.

He gulped. He couldn't think of that right now. Not if he wanted to stay sane enough to work, not if he wanted to keep Lily safe. Ben hit his forehead with his free hand over and over again.

"Why didn't you stay outside with them?" he shouted at himself. "They were only five. You were the only one that could've stopped it and now he's—he's—" Ben couldn't even finish the sentence. "Jason, I am so sorry," he whispered. "I didn't mean to. I didn't mean to."

Ben squeezed his phone so hard that something beeped, bringing him back to his conflict with Amy in the present day. He was so mixed up with love and hatred towards her, and all these memories flooding back to him were just making him more confused. Ben wanted her here, and he wanted a perfect family. But how could he know if she would just take away this daughter too?

He couldn't stop himself. He pressed the call button. But before it could ring twice, he hung up and stared at the screen. Ben scolded himself for being so weak and he slid his phone back into his pocket. His shirt under his armpits was cold with sweat and he cursed himself all the way out to his car.

What is wrong with me? he asked himself over and over again on the drive to the gas station. Ben pulled into the deserted parking lot. He hated this place.

It wasn't as bad as it had been, though, because now he had something to look forward to. He had someone waiting for him at home.

Chapter Six

Lily shifted in the wooden chair. Her butt was starting to hurt from sitting there for so long, but she didn't really know what she was supposed to do. There was nothing for her to escape from anymore, now that Ben cut off her rope. Her hand instinctively went to her neck, rubbing it, pinching at the skin there, making it how it used to feel so she wouldn't forget.

She was afraid to stand, because she didn't know if she'd be able to get back on the chair if she needed to. But she didn't want to be up there anymore. She wanted to be on the ground. Her heart was racing, but she forced herself to slide out from behind the table and to the floor onto her hands and knees. She crawled a few paces away to the carpet so she wouldn't have to be on the hard ground, and laid down, exhausted.

"Purple, cereal, spoon, scissors, hair," she whispered. "Bathroom, bedroom, bowl, couch, kitchen."

She rolled over to face her darkened bedroom. A chill trembled through her body and the black room was pulled toward her by some unseen force until she was engulfed in the cold darkness. Lily was back in the yard, the rope scratching familiarly at her neck like a dog that had been waiting for its owner to come home.

Mailman appeared, lurking in the shadows.

"Long time no see, pal," he said. "What did I tell you? You'll never escape. You're tied to this basement like you were tied to the pole."

Lily hissed her words between clenched teeth. She didn't want the rope anymore. She wanted it off, away from her forever. A sob so aggressive it felt like it had been building for years forced its way up her throat, drowning her in its weight, and out of her mouth in a gasp.

She jabbed her fingers at her neck, her nails gouging the skin there and making the wounds bleed, but she couldn't get the rope off. It was melted into her neck. Mailman was right. She would never escape.

She was crying and choking on her words, barely able to breathe. Lily scratched herself over and over, but she was beginning to realize her fate. She wrapped her hands around her throat like they were the rope. Her fingers dug into the soft spots under her chin and she could feel her pulse pounding.

"You'll never escape," she told it.

Mailman continued to berate her. His voice was indistinguishable from her own and they spoke the horrible words as one.

"You'll never escape, you'll never escape, you'll never escape," Lily said. Mailman chanted the phrase with her, their volume growing louder until Lily's throat hurt. Then Mailman disappeared, and it was just Lily rocking back and forth, screaming at herself. Her hands documented every quiver of her throat, every jerk of her chin as the words cascaded out. They were bitter, lumpy, disgusting mud pouring up from her stomach, burning her throat, erupting out of her mouth. The foul words appeared as bile on the carpet in front of her face and forced her into terrifying silence.

Hours later and Lily was still in the same spot. A door opened far away and a cold wave of fear washed over her body. She was shaking so badly her fingers were blurs. She was shivering like she was still back in the yard, back in the cold.

There was a crash and then, "Lily, oh my God."

The voice jolted adrenaline into Lily, and her body stopped shaking. She forced herself to stay still, because if she didn't move, maybe she could be invisible. Maybe whoever it was would leave her alone. Her hands moved on their own accord, letting go of her neck and covering her mouth. She mouthed words into her palm.

Someone grabbed her shoulder and rolled her onto her back. Light was shining from behind him, casting the features of his face in shadows—but adding a halo around his head.

It was Ben.

Brian and Shannon weren't here anymore. It was Ben.

Lily let out a breath and it tasted stale, like it had been in her chest for years. No tears streamed from her eyes, but she blubbered and sobbed all the same.

"What's wrong? What happened? Are you okay?" Ben asked frantically. He tilted her head all around and examined her neck.

"What did you do..." he trailed off as he grabbed her hands. Lily followed his horrified gaze and saw the dried blood caked under her nails. "Oh, sweetheart, you're shaking." He took Lily's hands in his and squeezed them.

He brushed over her cheek with the back of his hand and smoothed her hair back before pulling her into a hug.

His voice was soothing when he spoke. "Nothing bad is going to happen to you. I won't let it. You hear me? I'm going to protect you from everything out there. You're going to be all mine and no one else's. No one's going to take you ever again."

But what he didn't seem to realize was that he couldn't protect her from herself.

After a few minutes, he stopped talking, and Lily stopped crying. Her breaths were jerky and uneven, but Ben pulled away from her, holding her at arm's length, and said, "Are we okay now? We're good?" He smiled at her. "Good. I want to show you what I bought. And don't worry, we'll clean that up later." He gestured to the spot where Lily was sick.

Lily was still on the edge of reality, confused. But Ben didn't look like he cared. He moved forward like it was no big deal. Was it a big deal? Lily didn't know. This kind of pain was only inflicted on her by someone else, never by herself. Maybe that was why it was better.

Ben helped Lily stand up so he could guide her to the couch. She took a few steps without him, using the couch to hold herself up, and tripped over her feet for the last two steps until she could grab the kitchen table. She slid around to a chair and crumpled in it.

"Hey, good job," Ben exclaimed. "That was great!"

He re-gathered all of the items back into the bags. That must've been what crashed before.

"I hope nothing broke open in here. This stuff was supposed to last you a week or more; I don't want to have to go back to the store. Oh, okay, we're good. Now make sure you don't eat it all at once."

Don't worry, Lily thought. Her days at Brian and Shannon's had trained her well; she had no problem making a small amount of food stretch over a long period of time.

Ben rambled as he pulled out each item. "I'm putting ham and cheese in the fridge, which you can make sandwiches with. And this is half a gallon of milk. You should have a glass every day, but it goes in your cereal, too."

He closed the fridge and said, "Everything in here has to stay in here, so you can't leave the milk or meat sitting out too long. It'll start to go bad if it gets too warm."

He moved onto the second and third bag. "These are crackers, which you can either eat with the cheese or by themselves. And chocolate chip granola bars. I didn't know what flavors you liked so I just got my favorite. And since you're my daughter, you probably like the same thing as I do." Ben laughed at himself, but Lily didn't see what was so funny. "Anyways, this is bread, which you make sandwiches with or you can eat it by itself. And you know what cereal is. I got you the same kind we ate this morning, because it looked like you enjoyed it."

He tapped the refrigerator shut and Lily stiffened in anticipation for the inevitable loud noise, but there was none. The door moved slowly and gently like it was closing through water.

"Oh, I almost forgot. If you're ever thirsty and you don't want milk, you can get water from either sink down here—this one or the one in the bathroom. Just fill up a cup."

Ben opened the door underneath the sink and said, "This is dish soap and there are towels right here to wash your dishes after you're done. I'll teach you how to do that once you"—Ben waved his hand around—"get used to things."

He put his fists on his hips. "Phew! Lots of information. Did you get it all?"

Lily blinked.

"Good. Every week I'll restock the pantry and the fridge, so you shouldn't ever be hungry. You can eat the cereal for breakfast and the sandwiches for lunch and dinner. I don't know exactly when I'll be able to come down and visit because I have to pick up extra shifts from now on. But you understand, don't you? I mean, I gotta work so we can eat."

Bread, milk, cereal, breakfast, lunch, dinner, Lily thought. She wanted Ben to leave. She had to dump the words into the air so her head wouldn't have to hold them anymore, but he was still talking.

"Last thing I have here," he said as he pulled out an object from the last remaining bag, "is an alarm clock. You can set what time you want to get up at, and it beeps so you wake up. And it tells you what time it is."

He let her hold it so she would know that it wasn't something to be afraid of.

"This is how you set the alarm. I'll do that right now for you, just watch." He paused. "Wait. Do you know how to read numbers? Do you know what numbers are?"

Lily didn't meet his eyes. He was mad at her, she knew it. She was supposed to know the numbers but she didn't and he was mad at her. He hated her and he was going to take her back to Brian and Shannon and she was going to be hungry again.

"Okay, well, I'll teach you to do that too…I guess." Ben said. He rubbed his eyes. "For the first week or so, I'll be down here to make sure you're awake and help you get used to the sound of the alarm."

Ben went to the cabinets and pulled out some of the food he just put away. This was it. He was going to take it all away and throw her out.

But instead of taking it away, Ben started putting it all together. And when he was done, he put it on a plate and slid it across the table, right in front of her.

So that's what he was going to do. He was going to mock her with food, with a sandwich, and right when she went to take a bite, he was going to take it away. She'd played this game before, with Shannon.

"Well, come on. Eat it. You have to be hungry—don't tell me you're not."

Lily sniffed and picked it up. She opened her mouth and brought the sandwich closer, slowly. Now. He was going to take it now.

But he didn't. He just sat across from her and watched her with one eyebrow raised. So she ate. She tore off piece by piece and Ben never took it away.

"So, um, I need to talk to you about something."

He didn't want her anymore. He was going to take her back to the yard. He was going to tie her up down here.

"I want to change your name." Ben crouched down next to her chair and patted her hand. He cleared his throat and shifted. "To Claire. If I keep calling you Lily, you'll always be reminded of who you were before you came here. I don't like that Lily reminds you of the backyard and those stupid drunks. It's so awful how they treated you." He shook his head in disbelief. "I don't want you to ever think about that yard, or the pole, or your old parents ever again. There's too many bad memories. What happened today? That'll just keep happening if you're always thinking of that place."

There was no way she could've expected that. But now she was worried. Her name was the only thing still connecting her to the yard. She didn't want to go back there or relive what she went through, but it was all she had. Lily didn't want to cut that rope, too.

"So, you're Claire now," Ben was saying. "Forget Lily, she no longer exists."

She could almost hear the crunch as Ben's words acted as a knife and sawed through the invisible rope.

"You have to show that you understand what I'm telling you," Ben said, more forcefully. "Your name is Claire. Not Lily. Do you understand? Yes or no?"

Lily ducked her chin. She didn't want to say yes, but she was too scared to disagree.

Ben huffed in satisfaction. "Good." He patted her knee. "Don't worry, we'll work on it."

He told her that he was going upstairs, and that she should try and entertain herself until he could get her some toys. He left, but she couldn't look up to find relish in the light from the door this time.

Her heart felt like it stopped beating. When it started to pump again, it was too large for her body. It squished her lungs together, so she couldn't get a good breath, and it crushed her stomach so it started cramping up. She bent in half and clutched her stomach to calm the monster that had taken over.

"Claire. Claire. Claire," Lily said in a frantic whisper, almost all other words forgotten. "Don't worry, Claire."

For the first few hours of his shift, Ben was alone at the gas station. Brian had shown up just as Ben was taking his lunch break, and Ben got out of there as fast as he could.

But now he was on his way back, and he was going to have to face Brian for however long their shifts overlapped. He was going to know what Ben did. He was going to know, just by looking at his face, that he was hiding something.

Ben turned off the engine in his car and sat for a second. He stared through the glass walls at Brian behind the counter. He was holding a phone to his ear, waving his arms as if the person on the other end could see him. Ben went inside and braced himself to face Brian's wrath.

"Shan, no, I didn't—I don't know. I don't know," Brian was shouting into the phone. He jerked his chin up at Ben in greeting. "Shannon, I don't know! She probably just ran off. Or died. Calm—shut up!" He threw the store's phone down into its holder on the wall, but it bounced out and clattered to the floor.

"Uh, what was that about?" Ben asked, slinking into the breakroom to put his stuff down.

"It's Shannon." Ben faced him again and Brian's head was in his hands. "A little while ago I was on the computer making a couple bets. I lost a bunch of money and then she was screaming at me that I was gonna kill us because now we can't buy food or anything. I told her that maybe if she got a job we wouldn't be so damn poor."

"Oh, man. That's…horrible." Ben was at a loss for words.

"That's not even the worst of it. She's been on my ass about everything lately, and just now she called me up and was screaming about how our"—Brian glanced at Ben—"our dog is gone and she's all upset about it. Somehow that was my fault too." Brian rubbed his temples.

Ben was speechless. So they did know that Lily was gone. And obviously Shannon was pretty angry about it.

"So, uh, what're you going to do? Are you gonna look for…" Ben cleared his throat. "Are you gonna look for it?"

Brian straightened up. "Probably not. I hated that thing anyways. Ate too much food, burned through too much money."

Ben's throat was tight. All he could do was nod. He went to a different part of the store so Brian wouldn't see how badly he was shaking.

For the next few hours, Ben avoided Brian the best that he could. Finally, Brian came to the aisle where Ben was cleaning and said, "Hey, kid, you're here a little longer, right?"

Ben jumped. They had been quiet for so long, he wasn't expecting a voice right behind him. "Mmhm," Ben said, without turning around. He didn't trust himself to say actual words.

"Alright, I'm outta here. If I don't come in tomorrow, assume Shannon ripped my head off."

"Ha."

"See you later, man."

Brian ambled away and Ben went to stand behind the counter.

"He doesn't care about her. At all. His daughter is gone, and he doesn't even care."

Ben flipped off the parking lot. "Lily is gone," he said, as if her name would conjure some sort of emotion from Brian, even though he couldn't hear him. "She's *gone* and you don't even care."

Out of nowhere, Jason came to Ben's mind. If only he'd reacted like that, completely unemotional, heartless. If only Jason hadn't cared, because then maybe Ben's life wouldn't have screwed up as badly as it had.

Years ago, Jason had been taking Nicole out to an anniversary picnic lunch, so he'd asked Ben to babysit. They'd decided that Ben would bring Claire over to Jason's house so the kids would be able to play in the pool he had in his backyard.

"My man." Jason had greeted Ben and smacked him on the back in a hug. He grinned. "Now I don't have to pay for a sitter."

"I'm not getting paid for this?" Ben had exclaimed in mock surprise. Claire tugged on Ben's pants. "You can go play with Ethan," Ben told her.

She wiggled in between his legs and squeezed past Jason into his house. He and Ben followed, and as he scrambled around the kitchen getting his things together, he rattled off instructions.

"Ethan has his bathing suit on, so he can swim if he wants. His floaties are in the shed out there, so if you're going to take them into the big pool, make sure he has them on. And could you be in there with them, just in case?"

"Of course. I'm not gonna dump them in the pool and go drink a beer somewhere. Although that does sound inviting..." Ben stroked his chin.

"Jason, I don't think we can ask Ben to babysit ever again," Nicole said as she came into the room. "Not if he's going to act like that."

"Hi, Nicole." Ben hugged her. Her floppy hat hit him in the face.

"Where's Amy?" Nicole asked, just as Jason said, "Oh, and there's cookies in the oven."

They looked at each other, and Jason continued. "Can you take them out when they're done? Should be about ten minutes."

"Sure can do. And she's out with her friends. I think one of them is pregnant again."

She smiled. "Good for her."

"You and Claire can have as many as you want," Jason said, still talking about the cookies, "just don't let my kid eat more than two. Got that?" he asked as Ethan and Claire ran into the room.

"Thanks for watching the kids, Ben," Nicole said.

"It's no problem. Claire was itching to see her boyfriend anyways."

Nicole raised her eyebrows.

"Daddy!" Claire said.

"Yeah, she's been talking nonstop about Ethan. How much she wants to come see him, that sort of thing."

"Nuh uh," Claire insisted. Nicole laughed.

Ben rested his hand on Claire's head when she ran up to him. She craned her neck to look at him and asked, "Can me and Ethan go outside?"

"Sure baby, just stay in the yard. Don't go near the pool."

She nodded and grabbed Ethan's hand to tug him out the door.

"It's not Ethan we're gonna have to watch out for, is it?" Jason joked.

Ben saw Jason and Nicole off and then it was just him and the kids.

He sat on the shaded porch and watched them run around the yard, disappear into the shed for a few seconds, then reemerge with a new prop for whatever game they were playing. Eventually, Ben realized they should be wearing sunscreen, and Amy's voice chastised him in his head. He ducked into the house to grab the sunscreen—and paused to smell the sweet aroma of baking chocolate chip cookies—and called Claire and Ethan over.

"Gotta put this on." They whined and groaned. "Do you want me to put it on or do you want to do it yourself?"

"Can Claire put on her bathing suit so we can go swimming?" Ethan asked, his voice as shy and quiet as ever.

"Ooh, can I, Daddy?" She bounced on her toes and clapped her hands, baring a big smile.

"It's inside the big pocket of our bag. Do you need help putting it on?

She shook her head and ran inside. Ethan took off his shirt and held out his hands for the sunblock. He was smoothing out all the white clumps when Claire ran out in her purple one-piece that had fish patterned all over it. Ben spread the lotion on her arms and legs, wiped it on her face—"Don't scrunch up like that."—and helped both of them put it on their backs.

Ben went to the shed to find Ethan's floaties, but they weren't anywhere he could see. He didn't look too hard, because he didn't really feel like getting in himself.

"Sorry, guys, but we only have one set of floaties. We can't go swimming in the big pool today."

Both of the kids' faces crumpled up, so Ben added, "But I saw a smaller pool in the shed that we can play in."

Ethan sniffled and nodded. Ben got it out and filled it up with water from the hose.

All disappointment forgotten, the kids splashed around in the kiddie pool.

Claire used a toy to scoop up dirt from the yard and water from the pool to make mud. "Here's a cookie for you, Ethan," she said.

"Oh sh—the cookies." He rushed into the house and the infamous smell of burnt chocolate hit him. He jabbed at the off button on the oven and opened the door, waving away the smoke that billowed out. He snatched a towel off the counter to get the pan, but it burned him through the fabric.

"Shit."

The pan of charred cookies landed on Ben's foot and clattered to the tiles. He scooped up the ruined cookies the best he could and was able to salvage a few, but his skin was still scorching. He ran his hand under cold water and lifted his foot to the sink to give it some relief, too. His skin was gradually relieved from the pain of the burns, and it was starting to feel relatively normal again.

Ben turned off the water and hopped in a circle on one foot, looking for the towel he discarded after it betrayed him. He wiped his hand and foot off and only then did he notice how quiet it was.

He couldn't hear the sounds of Ethan and Claire playing anymore. He limped over to the window and glanced out, and could only see Claire crouching over the side the kiddie pool. Tightness swelled in his chest and he ran outside.

"Where's Ethan?" Ben asked before he was even all the way out the door.

"He wanted to go swimming," was her simple reply.

The world stopped. Everything slowed down. Ben's heart exploded into a million pieces, sending shards all over his body and making it go numb. His eyes landed on a small body floating face down in the pool, arms spread like he was trying to fly.

"No," Ben huffed, hardly a word but something between a cough and a gag, already sprinting towards the water.

He leapt into the pool and fought to the surface. The splash blinded him and he spun in circles trying to find Ethan. His vision cleared. There. Ben grabbed him around the chest and lifted his face out of the water. He placed him as gently as he could onto the concrete beside the pool. His ankles were still dangling in the water when Ben pushed himself out of the pool next to him.

"Daddy?" Claire's voice was small, weaving its way through Ben's clouded mind.

He whirled around. She was taking small, unsure steps towards me. Ben shielded Ethan's body the best he could and said, his voice broken, "Not now, Claire. Go inside, grab the phone, dial 911. Tell them there's been an accident and they need to come right now."

She didn't hesitate, probably because of the scarily calm urgency in his voice, and, as an afterthought, Ben wanted to say, "Don't step on the hot pan," but couldn't make his mouth move.

Ben scanned every inch of Ethan's face. Ethan's mouth was slightly open and his eyes were closed. Ben had no idea what he was supposed to do.

"Ethan, wake up, please, oh my God." Ben's fingertips grazed his shoulders. "Come on, Ethan. Please."

"Daddy."

Ben turned and Claire was standing in the doorway, tears streaming down her face. She had the phone in a death grip by her ear.

"What is it, sweetheart?" Ben's throat was tight, his voice strained. His breath twisted around his throat, choking him.

"I don't know the address." Claire dissolved into a bawling mess.

Ben ran over and turned her away from Ethan. He hugged her hard, too hard, and took the phone. He told the police everything they needed to know while Claire sobbed into his shoulder. He let the phone fall from his hand.

Ben worked his fingers through Claire's hair, murmuring soothing words, but he couldn't stop staring at the small body laying by the pool.

Ethan had always seemed tiny, his timidity overpowering everything, but now he looked miniscule. Like Ben would need a microscope just to see the adorable features on his smooth face.

Even from this distance, Ben could see that his chest was no longer moving.

"Claire, baby, we're gonna go inside now. Okay? Come on, sweetheart, it's okay," Ben said, picking her up and carrying her inside. He set her down on one of the big armchairs in front of the TV and swaddled her up in warm blankets.

"Claire, I need you to sit here. Wait for Daddy to come back, okay? Don't come outside. Can you do that for me?"

She nodded, her blue eyes shining even more from the glaze of tears. Ben smoothed her hair back and kissed her forehead.

As much as he wanted to be Claire, huddled inside at no fault, he couldn't. He had to act as the adult and call Jason. Tell him what happened.

It was the worst thirty seconds of his life. Ben tried to end it with, "I'm sorry," but Jason had already hung up. Once again, he let the phone drop to the concrete, but he couldn't bring himself to care.

Ethan's body was still laying in the same spot. Ben had desperately prayed for him to have moved, even the slightest bit, but nothing had changed. His ankles floated in the water, bobbing up and down with the small current. Ben was too afraid to move him at all, even just to get his feet onto the dry ground.

Ben sat with him, holding his hand and trying to think of something else to do, how else he could help. It was like he had jumped back into the pool again. Tears were everywhere and he couldn't see. Confusion and panic were scrambling around, fighting for dominance, but all they were doing was screwing with his head.

The ambulance arrived. Paramedics rushed around Ben like he was a rock stuck in a river. Ethan was lifted onto a stretcher. A devastating cry pierced his ears and Ben looked up from where Ethan's body had just been. Nicole was bent over the fence that surrounded the yard and Jason was grabbing her shoulder, his face pulled taut. Nicole used the fence, then Jason for support as they made it through the gate. The paramedics wheeled Ethan past them, out the gate and into the ambulance. Nicole was grasping at Ethan's lifeless hands and the doors closed. The ambulance drove away, whining at cars to get out of its way and crying for the small boy inside.

Ben was left with silence. He hadn't yet moved. His knees were digging into the concrete, his head was down—staring at nothing—and his hands were open on his legs.

He stayed there for who knows how long, the sun giving a false impression of protection and comfort.

Something was missing.

Ethan, he thought. *No, Claire.* She was being so good, doing what she was told to do. Crises demand obedience.

Ben went inside to where Claire was on the couch, not even looking at the TV. She was staring at Ben, searching his face for clues that this nightmare was over. But he couldn't pretend nothing had happened. All he could do was hold her.

"Oh God, Claire, I'm so sorry." That was all Ben could say. Over and over again, while Claire cried into his shirt. "It's gonna be okay, Claire. Everything's gonna be okay." He had said it enough times to almost convince himself. But deep down, he had known it wasn't true. He had known even when he had first lifted Ethan out. He hadn't sputtered or gasped or anything. Ethan was gone.

"Um, excuse me?"

A voice near Ben snapped him back to the present. He swiped at his face when he noticed it was wet with salty tears. A lady was standing at the fridge.

"How much for a bottle of water?" She looked concerned.

"Oh, uh, one ninety-nine."

The lady grabbed one and came to the counter to pay. "Are you okay? You kinda drifted off there," she said as she rummaged through her purse for the money.

"Yeah, yeah. I'm fine. Sorry." Ben handed her back a penny.

"Okay, well, have a good night." She smiled sadly. Ben pulled the corners of his mouth up ever so slightly in return. He wished it was all just a bad dream.

The bells dinged, announcing the lady's exit.

Ben hadn't seen or talked to Jason since that day. Jason had called from the hospital, his voice stony and cold, to tell him the bad news. Ben could only keep saying how sorry he was, until his voice got caught in his throat and a sob came out instead.

"The funeral will be in a few weeks. Until then, I think I need to keep my distance from you," Jason had said. He'd sounded so defeated. Ben went to say sorry again, but was met with silence. Jason had hung up.

Ben and Amy had decided against attending the service, but he didn't know if that was more for his daughter's sake or his own. Amy had sat with him and rubbed his back while he sobbed.

Back in the gas station, Ben pressed the heels of his hands into his eyes. He needed something physical so he could put a source to the agony he was feeling inside, but he couldn't stop his head or heart from aching.

It was an oxymoron, that day, he thought. *The sun was shining, birds were eating out of the bird feeder, the wind chimes were making music. But then.... Bad things are supposed to happen on bad days, with bad people. Not on the sunniest day of the year with someone you trusted.*

Ben longed for a bottle to drown his sorrows in. He'd stopped drinking so excessively after Amy and Claire left, in hopes that his sobriety would draw them back, but now he was missing it. All these old memories he hadn't thought about in years—they hurt.

"Why didn't I stay outside with them? Screw those *damn* cookies."

The rest of Ben's shift was spent exchanging money with the few and far between customers and counting the small number of cars that pulled up and drove away filled with gas.

Ben wished he could do that. Just pull up to a station and be filled with energy. Filled with something to help him keep moving forward. To keep him alive.

He kept imagining that one of the cars would stop and Amy would come rushing out. She would burst in, the bells above the door ringing madly, and declare her forgiveness. She would pepper him with kisses and hug him until he melted in her arms. She would tell him everything was okay, that it wasn't his fault, that everyone forgives him. He would take her back home to see his new daughter, and she would bring Claire—the first Claire— and they would all be so happy together. Their life would be amazing; it would go back to the way it used to be. Except now they'd have two kids—sisters.

If he could convince Amy that this was a great solution—better than he'd ever imagined—his family would be whole again. It would be perfect.

Chapter Seven

"Claire, Claire. Don't worry. Claire, Claire," she whispered. Almost an hour later and she was still rocking back and forth in the same position Ben left her in.

Mailman had been taunting her for a while now. "How can he love you if he changed your name?"

Lily—Claire—glanced at him, but she was stuck in a loop of repeating her new name.

"Oh my God, would you shut up already? Why are you being such a baby over this? Nothing good ever happened in the yard, why would you even want to remember it? Quit whining."

She switched words. "Shut up, shut up, quit whining, shut up." She paused. Then, quieter, "Quit whining."

Why *was* she getting so upset over this? The yard had offered her nothing but starvation and suffering. She didn't like her yard, so why should she like who she was there?

"Mailman," she exclaimed. She never would've thought that he would be the one to actually help her. She looked around, but he had disappeared.

"Nothing good, nothing good, quit whining," she said, a little louder. And with a newfound sense of joy, "Claire."

She stretched her legs out and braced her hands behind her. How long had it been since she felt like this, like she was worth something? How long had it been since she felt real confidence? Had she ever?

With her shoulder digging into the wall, Claire stood on wobbly legs. Her knees almost buckled, but she caught herself, and took the first step. Her arms were straight out from her sides for balance, and she took slow, shaky steps on her own. Her eyes were round as she arrived at her destination—the fridge—and collapsed against it.

"Wow," she breathed.

She forced herself upright. She was thirsty, but she couldn't remember what she was supposed to do. Wasn't there something with a cup? She glanced over her shoulder. She didn't want Ben to get mad at her for using one of his cups without his permission.

"Water, water, water." Water came out of the sink in the kitchen and in the bathroom. She didn't know how to use this sink, so she ventured into the bathroom, where she had at least seen Ben turn it on.

She examined the tap. The water was supposed to come out of here. But how? She turned one of the little handles and jumped back as water rushed out. Her heart only fluttered once, though, and she stuck her face under the stream. Well, as much of her face as she could fit before it hit the back of the sink. She stuck her tongue out and lapped the water up like a dog. It was like when she was back in the yard and was forced to drink out of puddles. Claire's stomach involuntarily shrunk in on itself at the thought. She got sick a lot during the days that Brian and Shannon wouldn't give her water. And her tongue always tasted gross.

When she was content, she looked up. The girl in the mirror was different from the first—and even the second—time she saw her. She was like a whole new person, with her clean, shoulder-length hair and eyes that actually looked alive, not like they were sinking into her skull. The girl had long red scabs contouring her neck, and purple-grey bruises lining the underside of her chin. Claire liked that about her. They were the girl's personal rope. Claire thought that maybe she wasn't alone; maybe everyone has their own rope.

"Claire," she said to the girl, who repeated it back to her at the same time. She nodded in satisfaction.

She left the bathroom and wobbled back to the couch. She sat on the very edge of the cushion, so she wouldn't ruin anything.

Claire grasped at her neck so she could keep the rope away from her skin, but found nothing, so she just rubbed it instead. There was an odd sort of comfort in tracing her finger over the new scabs there. The already-healing wounds proved to her that she was able to overcome anything, whether it be walking or any injury inflicted on her. When her fingernails dug into the soft skin of her neck earlier, some of the distrust in herself trickled out in the form of blood, leaving confidence in its place. It wasn't much, but it was there, a tiny spark of something that could soon burst into a raging fire.

Claire's hands fell to her lap, she relaxed into the back of the couch, and she closed her eyes.

Not even a second later, her eyes popped open, and she was back in the yard. The house was floating away, spinning into oblivion, a small dot in the massive sea of blue sky. The grass grew, and wouldn't stop. First it was just over her ankles, but it kept going until it tickled her armpits and covered her eyes, so all she could see was green waving back and forth in the breeze. But it wasn't comforting, hiding her from Brian and Shannon. It was stopping her from getting away.

Something inside of her was screaming at her to run. She tried, but the mud latched onto her feet and wouldn't let her move. The tall grass turned into thorny vines and wrapped around her arms and stomach and neck.

Claire opened her mouth to yell for help, but her tongue was gone. She couldn't make any noise, because her throat, her lungs, her heart, were all gone, ripped away with the house.

Two hands slammed down on her shoulders. The mud was knocked off and the grass was severed from her body.

"I'm bringing you home," a voice growled.

Despite the hands holding her in place, Claire was able to turn in search of the source of the voice. But no one was there.

"I'm bringing you home."

Claire looked everywhere: left, right, up, down. But the grass was back, infinite in all directions, blocking the speaker from her view.

"Don't worry, Claire. I'm bringing you home."

The hands pulled Claire backwards through the tall grass, her neck snapping forwards and her teeth clanking together. Her feet scrabbled for purchase, but the mud, previously sticky and abundant, was falling away, and nothing was underneath her except for two outstretched arms.

Claire woke from her nightmare with a start. She was lying on her side, staring at the underside of the couch. She hoped with everything she had that she'd just fallen asleep, that her dreamland wasn't actually infested with fear and a horrible being that had every intention to take her away.

She sat up and rubbed her eyes.

"Couch," she said as she yawned. "Fridge, bathroom, water. I'm bringing you home. I'm Claire. Claire."

She stood up and walked around the basement, testing out the strength of her legs and ankles, mumbling words all the time. She only fell twice, and she had already forgotten her nightmare.

There was no way to track the days down here. She couldn't see the sun or the moon anymore, so she had no idea how much time had passed. She wandered into her room and bounced on the bed. Claire stiffened, vaguely recalling Brian roaring at her to get out of their room, so she had to take a second and remind herself that she wasn't there anymore. She was with Ben now. Claire laid on her back to watch the clouds, and tried to relax, but the top of the basement was in her way.

"Purple, last a week, bread, water. Cereal, eat with spoon."

The door at the top of the steps opened, so Claire slid off the bed and stopped talking. Fear pinched a small piece of her heart. She was getting tired of being so scared all the time, but she had no way to control it. Even just the sound of a door flashed her back to the yard, and she could only imagine Brian storming outside with a beer bottle in his hand, ready to strike.

Claire, Claire, Claire, she thought viciously. Her jagged fingernails were digging into the palms of her hands, grounding her, bringing her back to reality.

I'm Claire. Claire. Ben. Claire.

Ben appeared in the doorway of her room. He was holding her blankets, now clean, in his hands and he shrugged his shoulders.

"You wanna help me with these?"

He walked over and dropped the blankets on the bed with a huff. "I think it's time for you to learn how to make a bed."

Ben helped her put the sheets in the right place and showed her how to pull the comforter tight so that it wouldn't be wrinkly.

"Good thing you're a fast learner," he commented, almost to himself. "By the way," he said. "Did I hear you talking when I first came down?"

Claire tensed. Her shoulders rolled in a bit and she dropped her chin.

"Hm. I could've sworn I heard a voice." He screwed up his face like he was thinking and looked at her out of the corner of his eye. Lily kept her gaze locked on the floor in front of his feet.

"Okay, well, I guess I was wrong," he said, overdramatically. He knew she was lying, Claire had no doubt about that. "Anyways, do you wanna come see what I bought you?"

She didn't respond.

"Good, because I want to show you." Ben left the room and Claire figured she was expected to follow. She made sure to stay a safe distance behind him so he wouldn't be even angrier at her. When they reached the kitchen, Ben made a wide gesture with his arms and said, "Ta da!"

Claire didn't recognize the items that were spread out on the table, but her curiosity was sparked.

Ben was practically bouncing up and down as he explained to her what each thing was.

"This is paper, and coloring books, and crayons. You can color with these and draw pictures."

He picked up one book and said, as he pointed to the symbols on the front, "This says farm animals." Ben flipped through the pages, telling her what each animal was. "This one's a dog, this is a cat. There's a pig and a cow and a—and a bird? Why is there a bird in the farm animals coloring book? Maybe it's a chicken. I don't know, that's weird."

Claire knew the word animal. That's what she was, according to Brian and Shannon and Mailman. Deer and squirrels were animals too, but she didn't think she looked like those. She didn't think she looked like any of the animals in this book. How were they all animals if none of them were the same? Did that mean that ants and worms and other bugs were animals too? Claire shook her head to rid herself of the questions she couldn't answer and paid attention to what Ben was saying.

Ben picked up the second book. "This one's called mystical creatures. Let's see what's inside. There are unicorns, and trolls, and wow! Look, that's a dragon."

Claire stepped back when he showed her the dragon. The dogs and pigs weren't scary, but this animal was. She wouldn't want to color that page.

"Have you ever colored before, Claire?" Ben asked.

She shook her head.

"Okay well, come over here and sit down. I'll show you."

Claire did as she was told and Ben showed her how to pick up the crayon and to scrape it along the page.

Claire's mouth dropped open. She leaned forward to get a better look at the magic that was happening.

Bent told her the names of the colors as he pointed to the crayons.

"Red, like your shirt, orange, yellow, green, blue, purple, brown, black, and grey."

He twisted the grey crayon in his hands and averted his eyes to the table. He said, "I hope this will be enough to entertain you until I get some new toys for you."

Claire nodded. This was the most entertainment than she'd ever had, if she didn't count the boxes. Those were pretty fun for a while. She kind of wished Ben had brought those with them when he first brought her here.

Ben set the crayon down and said, "I should probably go now. Don't forget to eat dinner and be in bed by nine. Wait, did I teach you numbers yet?"

Claire shifted her eyes away from Ben's.

"I'll write them down for you." He grabbed the black crayon and a blank piece of paper.

He wrote the numbers one through twelve twice, saying them out loud as he wrote.

"Amy said something to me a while ago about how kids need routine, so I figure this should be routine enough, right? Okay, this is when you should wake up so you can shower and be ready for breakfast when I come down," he said, pointing to the first number seven. He wrote the same weird symbols that were on the front of her coloring books, saying, "Wake up...breakfast...," as he wrote.

Claire repeated each number in her head. *One, two, three, four, five, six—*

"I'll come down at eight every morning to give you breakfast," he said, pointing the number first, then the words. "This spells breakfast, in case you were wondering."

He told her, and wrote down, when she should eat lunch, dinner, and go to bed. The words and numbers scrolled through her head and got locked away in a place where she wouldn't forget.

Six, seven, eight, nine, ten, eleven, twelve.

Seven wake up, eight breakfast, twelve lunch, five dinner, nine bedtime, she thought. She said them over and over until they stuck.

One, two three, four five—

"So, pretty much the rest of the time"—he gestured to the numbers that didn't have words written next to them—"you'll have to yourself. My job doesn't really pay all that much, so I gotta get as many hours as I can so I can keep you alive." He chuckled, but Claire could tell that he was uncomfortable by the way he ran his hand down his head to rest on the back of his neck.

Six, seven, eight—

"I'll put this next to the clock in your room so you can look at it if you need to." When he came back, he said, "I'm gonna go upstairs now, so, goodnight for later. Mwah," he said as he leaned forward to kiss her forehead. Claire took a step back, but when he kept coming closer to her face, stood still and tensed until it was over. As soon as he had backed away, she swiped at the wet spot on her forehead. Ben ruffled her hair and said, "Don't forget to eat dinner and be in bed in a couple hours."

Nine, ten, eleven, twelve.

Claire peeked over her shoulder to watch him leave. She didn't see any light this time. And, even though Ben slammed the door behind him, Claire barely flinched.

"Seven, eight, breakfast, red, yellow, green," she said. "Dinner. Eat dinner. One, two, three..."

Claire stood up, her knees knocking together, and walked over to the pantry.

She said, "Bread," as she took out the package. Bread had been a main portion of her diet at Brian and Shannon's, and it usually had green or blue spots on it. The slices in this package looked clean and fluffy, and Claire's mouth started to water.

She didn't know how to open the bag, so she turned it all around in her hands and found a small tie at the top. She untwisted it, like how she used to untwist her rope if she went around her pole too many times, and the bag opened. Claire pulled out the top piece of bread and scarfed it down. She didn't want to eat too much and get in trouble, so she closed the bag without the tie and returned it to the cupboard.

"Eat dinner, eat bread, black, grey, blue."

Claire went to get a drink from the sink in the bathroom. When she finished guzzling the water, there was a pressure on her bladder. She remembered Ben's thorough instructions—and Shannon's harsh ones—and tried to carry out the task.

"Sit here, pull down pants, underwear, sit. Go, wipe, flush." At the last step, Claire screwed up her face and stretched her arm out so she could be as far away from the toilet as possible. She pressed down on the small metal handle and braced herself.

Claire opened her eyes, pleasantly surprised. The noise wasn't as scary as she remembered it being.

"Hm," she said, happy with her performance. "Good job."

The coloring supplies were still lying on the table. Claire picked up a crayon that was the color of her blankets. Some of the other colors rolled onto the floor, but she didn't notice.

"Pink."

Claire grabbed the crayon in her fist, like she did with the spoon, and slid a piece of paper over to touch the tip of the crayon to the page. She dragged her hand around like Ben had done.

"Pink." The paper had been white, but like magic, pink followed her hand wherever it went. She drew another line. "Pink." Claire stopped being timid and scribbled randomly. Big circles and jagged pink lines filled the paper. She clenched tighter around the crayon and pressed down as hard as she could to get the brightest color out of it.

Snap.

Claire opened her fist, palm up, so she could see the damage. The crayon was broken in half. Some little crumbles of pink wax were strewn across her hand, and its wrapper was torn.

Claire's face scrunched up. The strong sting of tears burned her eyes, and her nose was about to start running. She bit her lower lip so it wouldn't tremble.

But, with no one around, there was no need for Claire to hold back. Years of keeping her pain contained had built up, and she let out the loudest wail she could. Tears streamed down her face in a kind of salty waterfall. Her nose ran and the snot dripped over her lips, but she didn't care. Claire threw her head back and was almost choking on her own sobs. She had curled her fist around the crayon, but more gently this time, so she wouldn't break it even more. She hiccupped and sobbed and gasped.

Claire let herself cry for as long as she needed to. Once she calmed down to only a shaky breath every couple seconds, she let herself look at the crayon's corpse. It rolled out of her hand and onto the table, where it rested on its own creation.

Her shoulders still jerked every once in a while, but for the most part, her tears had dried in pink streaks down her cheeks. Now stone-faced, Claire grabbed the remains of the crayon and the drawing that caused it, and carried it into her bedroom. Mimicking a funeral, she opened the top drawer of the—of the—

"Dresser," she said. "Good job."

She put the paper and the broken crayon in the drawer as gently as she could. As an afterthought, she shoved her hand into the pocket of her jeans and pulled out the lock of hair she grabbed earlier, and put it in there as well. She closed the drawer and went to sit on her bed. She laid her head on the pillow, but didn't get under the covers or change into pajamas. She whispered, "Nine, bedtime, yellow, blue, purple, black, nine, bedtime," until the numbers on the clock matched the ones that Ben wrote on the paper.

Claire began to drift off into sleep. Right when she was on the brink of dreamland, adrenaline shot through her body. She forgot to put the crayons away. She leapt off the bed and ran to the kitchen. She shoved the crayons into the box, each facing a different way. Claire didn't know what Ben would do to her if she forgot to pick up after herself and she didn't want to find out.

She kept glancing up the stairs as she was desperately cleaning up. She knew, just *knew*, that Ben would open the door and see her out of bed. She imagined him stomping down the stairs and grabbing her, throwing her to the ground to beat her.

The vision scared her so badly that she had frozen. She put the last of the crayons into the box and bolted back to her room. She leapt back into bed and buried her face in the pillow. If Ben was going to beat her, she didn't want to see it. When a couple minutes passed and no punches landed on her, Claire tried to slow her heart that was beating out of her chest.

She took a deep breath, and before she could exhale, she was asleep.

Ben knew he could be overprotective sometimes. But he needed to be, if he didn't want something like what happened to Ethan to happen again. That was why Claire had to stay in the basement. That was why he had to change her name. If she was upstairs with him, or if she was still called Lily, anything could happen. Ben might accidentally hurt her, or worse, someone might take her away.

Once, months after Ethan had drowned, Ben was with Amy and Claire in their house. They had all lain low for a while, keeping out of the public eye when their story was posted all over the news. But spending all their time in a two-bedroom house had been taking its toll on Amy and Ben. Claire had made her own fun, like that time she had been singing some God-awful song at the top of her lungs.

She was striking random notes on her toy piano, belting out incomprehensible lyrics to an uneven tune. Ben was nursing a beer on the couch, taking swigs every so often so he wouldn't scream at her to shut up.

There was some football game on TV, which Claire kept blocking as she stood and danced around. One of Ben's old friends had told him, "They only get more annoying as they grow up," and God, was that true. Claire was five and discovering the wide range of her vocal cords. And she let Ben and Amy know all the time. Ben took another sip and squeezed his eyes shut.

"Ben!" Amy's voice was shrill.

Ugh.

"I've been calling you for the past five minutes." She was exasperated. But so was Ben. She would just have to deal with it. "What do you want for dinner?"

Ben rubbed his eyes. "I don't know." Claire was marching around the living room, still singing her made-up song, but now, every time she passed Ben, she would smack his knees.

"What?"

Smack.

Ben raised his voice. "I don't know." He opened his eyes and there was Amy, giving him one of her stares.

Smack.

"What do you want?" Her voice was tight. "Last time I made something you didn't like you called it garbage and stormed out of the room. So, what. Do you. Want?"

Smack.

"I. Don't. Care," Ben said, mocking her tone. He could feel the irritation ready to bubble over, so he finished the rest of the bottle.

Amy rolled her eyes. "Would you *please* stop drinking? It's the middle of the day."

Smack.

"That's it," Ben said. He grabbed Claire's arm. "Stop singing and stop hitting me!" Ben roared. He shook Claire and pushed her away. She landed hard on the floor and burst into tears.

"Ben!" Amy cried as she ran over to Claire.

Ben was shocked. Why did he do that? He was supposed to be protecting her from danger, not inflicting it.

He got off the couch and crouched near Claire, but she hunched away and Amy shielded her from him.

"Get away from her."

Ben reached out. "Amy, I didn't mean—"

"Don't you dare," she said, her voice trembling. "Get away." She picked Claire up and took a step back.

A jagged pain tore through his heart into his head. "Amy, please." He dropped the bottle. "I need to fix this."

Claire had wrapped her arms around Amy's neck like she was clinging to a lifeboat. Ben could see red marks around her wrist in the shape of fingers. From his own hand.

Amy had hugged her back, holding her away from Ben but close to her. They had retreated upstairs, leaving Ben a guilty mess.

It had been years since that incident, but Ben was still torn up about it. He had needed to protect Claire at all costs, and when he was unable to do so, he broke. That was what prompted him to spend a little extra to give his new Claire something nice. He had made the extra trip to the store to buy her some coloring supplies, despite barely having any money in his bank account. He had been so excited to show her that it didn't even dawn on him that she might not like it.

Claire had shown no emotion while he was flipping through the coloring books, when he knew any other little kid would be so happy. But as soon as Ben began to color, Claire's astonishment had been written all over her face. The way she had leaned over him to get a better look lifted his heart and all doubt was washed away.

When Ben was upstairs later, he wanted to share his happiness with the woman that used to make him feel this way all the time. He picked up his phone, and without hesitation, called Amy. The phone rang to voicemail, but he didn't bother leaving a message. He knew from years of being with her that she never checked her inbox. Ben tried calling her three more times that night, but never got a response. He came to the conclusion that she was already asleep; she wouldn't just be ignoring him. The past was in the past; Ben had changed. He was better now, he knew what he had to do to be a good father. Surely Amy knew that.

Chapter Eight

"Claire. Claire. Wake up."

Claire cracked open her eyes. Ben was standing over her, blurry through the haze of sleep. She rubbed the corner of her eyes to get out the stuff that gathered there during the night. Ben's hand was on her shoulder and he gave it a squeeze when their eyes met.

"Gotta wake up now. You slept through your alarm."

Ben pressed a button and the beeping stopped. Claire yawned.

"I have to leave soon, to go to work, but I left breakfast for you on the table. It's bacon and eggs." He turned his head slightly to look at the wall, like he was considering something. "I hope you're not vegetarian." He chuckled.

Claire stretched her arms above her head. Her back arched and her legs sprawled out, then, her muscles loose, she sighed.

Ben laughed. "Oh, and you know what I completely forgot about?" he asked.

Claire looked at him, not sure if he expected her to answer the question.

"I forgot to give you a toothbrush. See, you're supposed to brush your teeth twice a day, so I'm gonna show you how to do that really quick before I go."

He hooked his hands underneath her armpits and lifted her out of bed.

"Did you sleep in your clothes? You're supposed to change into pajamas when you go to bed."

Ben took her hand and led her out of the room. From what Claire could tell, the sheets were dry today. She could vaguely recall Ben waking her up to change her pull-up and go to the bathroom.

"This is a toothbrush, and you use it by putting this"—he picked up a tube—"toothpaste, on it." He unscrewed the cap. "You squeeze this to make the toothpaste come out, you put it on the brush, and scrub your teeth okay?"

Claire yawned again and scratched her arm.

"You'll understand when you actually do it. Okay, I'm gonna be late if I stay here any longer, so don't forget to take a shower, you remember how to do that right?" he asked. Claire sniffed and nodded, still not fully awake yet.

"Good. Oh, I got you some vitamins that I want you to take every day from now on." Ben went to the kitchen and Claire followed. "You just twist the cap to get it open. They're chewy, like fruit snacks. I didn't know what flavor you'd like, so I got the 'fruity variety,'" he said, squinting at the label. "Here, I'll open this for you."

Ben kissed her on the top of her head, said goodbye, and left Claire by herself.

"Breakfast, vitamin, brush teeth, shower," Claire said, repeating her schedule.

She sat down in front of the steaming plate of food. The bacon and eggs smelled amazing. Claire couldn't decide which smell she liked best: the soap or this breakfast. They were so wildly different, yet both so good. Claire thought back to how gross her backyard smelled, but found it hard to conjure up the memory.

"Eggs, bacon, eat breakfast."

Claire didn't know which part was the eggs and which was the bacon, so she crouched down to look at the food from eye level.

White and yellow lumps were all mixed together and spilling over onto the red rectangles. She grabbed a lump of the yellow with her fingers, disregarding the utensils next to the plate. She opened her mouth wide and put the lump on her tongue, pressing it to the roof of her mouth and spreading it over her taste buds.

She opened her eyes wide at the flavor.

"Good."

Claire liked these because they didn't hurt her teeth. She could swallow them with barely any chewing. She ate the rest with her hands, and when she finished, she turned her attention to the rectangles.

She wasn't as cautious with these, so she grabbed one and took a bite. They were even better than the eggs.

Claire devoured the bacon, with no regard to the pain in her gums, and licked the plate clean to finish.

"Breakfast, vitamin, brush teeth, shower."

Claire peered into the open container. There were a bunch of different colored gummies inside, and when she picked one up, it squished between her fingers. She popped it in her mouth and sucked on it at first, then bit down. The gumminess stuck to her teeth and felt like it was going to rip them out.

"Breakfast, vitamin, brush teeth, shower."

Claire was still tired as she walked to the bathroom and her legs and ankles were wobbly. She closed her eyes as she yawned, and accidentally ran into the doorframe. She made a small noise that could be considered a chuckle and rubbed her forehead.

She blinked at the girl in the mirror. She looked bleary and tired too.

Claire clutched the toothbrush in one fist and the toothpaste in the other. She tried to squeeze the toothpaste out of the tube onto the brush, but it wasn't working how Ben said it would. She peered at it. The cap was still on.

She used both hands to twist the cap off and pinched the tube so the goopy stuff inside spurted onto the counter. She scraped the paste onto the brush and shoved it all in her mouth. She scrubbed back and forth in one spot on her front teeth how Ben told her, but she didn't know how long she was supposed to do it for. After about ten seconds, she spit out the toothpaste.

Claire bared her teeth and the other girl did the same. The residue of the foamy toothpaste was on her teeth. She closed her mouth to swallow, and grimaced. Toothpaste tasted *bad*. Claire wiped her teeth and tongue clean with the towel hanging next to the sink and spit a few more times.

"Breakfast, vitamins, brush teeth, shower."

Now to take a shower. She pulled back the curtain and looked into the tub, waiting for Ben's instructions to come back to her. She pulled on and twisted the handle. Water was only coming out of the bottom spout. Claire hit her forehead to jog her memory on what to do next.

She thought back to what Ben had said before: "Pull up on the... thing."

She pulled it up and, sure enough, water began to stream out of the shower head from above. Claire had to jerk back so she wouldn't get wet.

She stuck her hand into the water like Ben did and imagined she was outside again, stuck in a downpour.

Claire stepped into the tub, fully clothed, and ducked her chin as the water pounded on her head: a gentle but much needed massage. The water flew off her arms and fingers, making their own little waterfalls.

There were two different bottles sitting on the shelf. She knew one was shampoo and one was conditioner—Ben told her about those, she remembered—but she didn't know which was which or in what order she was supposed to put them on.

She grabbed one of the bottles and tried to squeeze it into her hand, but her grip was so weak that nothing came out. She used both hands to squeeze the stuff out of the bottle and onto the floor of the tub, but as soon as the liquid came out, it was washed away by the water, leaving behind a thin trail of bubbles.

Claire huffed in frustration. How was she supposed to do this?

It occurred to her that if she stood a certain way, the water was blocked by her body and wouldn't hit a certain spot in the tub. Claire squeezed the stuff out in that spot and scooped it into her hand.

She held it triumphantly. But as soon as she lifted her hand up, the water splashed into her palm and washed it away.

Her shoulders drooped and her head fell back, and she groaned. Again, she went through the process of blocking the water, squeezing the bottle, and scooping it up, but this time, she covered her palm with her other hand, leaving the bottle on the floor.

"Good job," she said.

Claire worked the dollop of liquid into her hair, but the suds rinsed out as soon as they were formed. She held her hands to the water to wash off the slimy feeling and grabbed the bar of soap. The washcloth was hanging over the side of the tub, but Claire couldn't figure out how he got the soap onto it, so she rubbed the bar over her clothes and on her face and in her hair. She turned in circles under the stream to let it all wash off.

When she thought she was done, she twisted the handle the other way and the water stopped. She had trouble stepping out onto the floor. Her legs were heavy, way more than she was used to. Her foot landed hard back in the tub.

Something wasn't right. She used both hands to lift her first leg out of the tub, and did the same with the second. Claire was panting from the exertion.

She glanced down at her body where her clothes were being pulled down by the weight of the water. Ben wasn't here to lift her out of the tub this time. That was probably why she felt so different. The fleeting fear that she had forgotten a step was gone. She had done everything right.

Claire grabbed a towel and dried herself off like she knew she was supposed to, but it wasn't working as well as when Ben did it. Claire just shook her head and went to the bedroom for some better clothes. She grabbed a shirt and a different pair of jeans.

"Pink," she said. "Blue."

She took off her wet clothes that were beginning to stick to her skin and held up the dry ones.

"Umm..." Claire looked around for help, but no one was there. She stuck her head through the biggest hole at the bottom, but couldn't find the head hole at the top. She was stuck in the tangle of fabric with her face pressed against the stretched-out shirt.

Claire panicked. She waved her imprisoned arms, trying to get out, but she couldn't.

"Help," she moaned.

Just as she was about to succumb to her fate, the shirt slipped off her arms. The fabric hung loosely on her head like a tent. She ripped it off and threw it on the floor.

"Stupid."

She crossed her arms over her chest and defiantly looked away from the shirt. She took a deep breath and let her arms fall to her sides.

Claire didn't give up. That's not how she worked. If she started something, she would see it through to the end, no matter how big of a challenge. She taught herself to walk, she knew how to take a shower. She could get dressed. She knew she could.

This time, she kept calm, even when her head got stuck again. She freed her arms and used them to maneuver the head hole to her actual head. For a second Claire didn't think it was going to work, but eventually her head popped through the hole.

"That was great," she whispered to herself. Next she had to tackle the pants, but those weren't as much of a fight since she could see what she was doing. When she successfully dressed herself, she stood up straight and proud.

"One, two, three, four, five, six." She went over to the clock. For the first time in her entire life, Claire was curious about what time it was. She knew that Brian and Shannon constantly yelled about time ("I don't have time for this, I'm leaving."), but she didn't know what the numbers meant.

"Three, four, five, six, seven wake up, eight breakfast," she murmured as she went to the clock.

Claire pointed at the numbers written in crayon and said them in order as she dragged her finger along the paper. By matching up the time on the clock to the paper, she determined that it was nine o'clock. Claire panicked for a second, thinking she was supposed to be in bed.

But no, there are two nines that mean different things, and since she just woke up, she couldn't possibly be going back to sleep.

"Breakfast, vitamin, brush teeth, shower." Her agenda for the morning was completed, and now she didn't have to worry about anything until later that night. She stepped over the pile of wet clothes and sat on the couch, leaning back into the cushions. Claire completely forgot about the coloring books, and instead let her mind drift and wander. Without any interruptions, Claire's mind could go farther than it ever had before and she had no way to stop it. Like that one time she scratched her neck and choked herself, no one yelled or hit her to snap her out of it, and she kept spiraling into the depths of her imagination.

Claire thought about Mailman, and how it had been a while—nearly a whole day—since he'd come to visit. Not that she was complaining; she hated it when he came around.

Claire opened her eyes and scanned the room, making sure her thoughts didn't summon him. When she determined that the coast was clear, she closed her eyes again.

She thought of Brian and Shannon. She wondered if they missed her, or if they knew she was gone. She wondered if they were happy that she wasn't there anymore.

Shannon's voice echoed through Claire's head: "We would leave you here to rot." That phrase was the one that stuck out most to Claire, but she couldn't figure out why. Shannon had said plenty of nasty things to her, but that in particular hurt her the most.

She created a story in her head in which Brian and Shannon treated her as Ben did. She was still in the backyard, but allowed to roam free, rather than being tied up. They brought her food on the tray, but the food this time was cereal with a spoon, bread that wasn't green, and milk. They gave Claire all the time in the world to eat her feast, they didn't threaten to take the food away from her, and they stood there, smiling happily. She imagined that Brian ruffled her hair and Shannon kissed her on her forehead. Both of them grinned at her, but even in her fantasy, Claire couldn't force the corners of her own mouth to turn upwards.

Claire lost track of time while sitting on the couch. She replayed her made up story multiple times, yet not once did she wish that it would come true. The last thing she wanted was to be back in the yard. After a while, footsteps stomped above her.

"Goodbye, Claire?" she asked.

Her eyes followed the direction of the heavy footsteps, so she watched the door open and caught a glimpse of the light before Ben blocked it. He basically ran down the stairs with a big grin on his face and his hands behind his back.

"I snuck away on my lunch break to come spend time with you." Ben answered her question. "You hungry? I make a mean ham and cheese sandwich."

Claire tilted her head. Brian and Shannon were mean, but how could a sandwich beat her or tell her she's worthless? She didn't think she'd want to be around this sandwich.

Ben whistled as he got out all the ingredients. Claire peeked over the couch to watch as plastic rustled and two sandwiches were assembled.

"You have to come to the table to eat, though. I'm not serving you on the couch," Ben said, his voice sterner than before.

Claire sat at her normal spot at the table. To make room for the lunch plate, Claire had to slide the breakfast dishes out of the way. Ben scolded, "Claire, you have to pick up after yourself."

He picked up her breakfast plate. "I thought I told you, I like to have this place clean and orderly."

Claire recognized his angry tone and got defensive. She thought, *No, no. Ben didn't say.* Oh no. She made him mad again.

"What're you shaking your head at me for? I know I told you. You have to start taking responsibility for your actions."

This wasn't good. This was how Brian's voice used to get right before he exploded. Ben was going to yell at her. He was going to hit her.

"Make sure you wash those, and these plates we're using now." Ben groaned and put his head in his hands. He rubbed his eyes. "You don't know how to do that, do you?"

No. Ben didn't say, she thought again. She was begging with him in her head. She didn't want him to be mad at her.

Ben sucked in air through his teeth. "I had no idea you would be such a challenge for me." He said it with a smile, but Claire knew it wasn't genuine.

Ben rubbed his head and the back of his neck. "Ahh, I didn't mean that," he said. "You know I didn't mean that right?"

Claire hesitated, but nodded.

"Good, okay. I didn't mean that." He seemed to be reassuring himself more than her. "Well, come on then. Dig in."

She waited until he pushed the meal towards her, then scarfed it down as quickly as she could in case he wanted to take it away.

"Hey, slow down. Don't eat your food that fast."

Claire looked up and bread, meat, and cheese all smashed together dribbled out of her mouth. She did it again. Why did she keep messing up?

"Ugh, Claire." Ben stood up and grabbed a paper towel. He wiped her face with it and pinched it between two fingers to throw it away.

"You're gonna get sick if you keep eating like that. You might choke."

Claire knew it was her fault, the way his attitude changed so suddenly. She was the one doing things wrong, which was why he was frustrated and mad at her.

They sat in silence after that, with Ben picking at his food and Claire with her head down at her almost empty plate.

Ben shifted the food to the side of his mouth, and said, "You can finish that, you know." He pointed with a nod of his head.

Claire put the food in her mouth and chewed slowly and deliberately, to show Ben she was capable of following directions and that she didn't need to be reprimanded.

"Good, now you need to wash these," Ben said. "First you clear everyone's plates and put them in the sink."

Claire listened intently, waiting for the next instruction. Ben didn't say anything, but raised his eyebrows and jerked his head towards his plate. Her mouth rounded in an O. He wanted her to do what he was saying as he was talking. She jumped up and put his plate on top of hers.

"Careful. Now put the plug in the hole in the bottom of the sink. Or wait, maybe you should've done that first, whatever. Turn the handle so the water will come out hot."

Claire tried to turn the handle one way but it wouldn't budge.

Ben sighed. "Other way."

Claire turned the handle the other way and lifted up. Water came pouring out and filled the sink.

"Now squirt some soap in there. The soap's under the—yeah in that cabinet."

Claire did as she was told.

"Now take that dish rag there and get some bubbles on it. Just scrub away. Once all the dishes are clean you rinse them off in the other side of the sink and put them on a towel to dry. Oh yeah, I forgot that too. Get the towel out first and lay it out on the counter, then you can put the dishes on there to air dry. When they're not wet anymore, you put them back in the cupboards where they belong."

Claire's back was to him. She froze, because her arms were elbow deep in the sudsy water. Was she still supposed to get the towel out, even though her hands were wet?

"Okay, I guess I'll get it for you."

Claire was already moving hastily so that Ben wouldn't be angrier than he already was, so when she was trying to finish up, with the last plate in her hand, she was a little too aggressive. She went to put the plate on the towel but it flew out of her hand and clanked against the others.

"Careful," Ben scolded.

Claire shrunk in on herself and fixed her mistake.

"Okay, good. Thank you for doing that."

Claire nodded with her head still low and returned to the table.

"Speaking of thank you, do you know the magic words?" Ben asked. "If someone does something nice for you, you say thank you, like I just did. If you want something from somebody, you say please. And if you do something wrong, you say sorry."

Claire wondered if these rules don't apply to adults, since Ben didn't say please when he told her to do the dishes, and Brian and Shannon never said sorry. But maybe they never apologized because they never did anything wrong. Claire hadn't even thought of that.

Sorry, she thought, directed at Brian and Shannon. All this time she thought they were mean, but they weren't doing anything bad. *Sorry.*

"You understand?"

She nodded.

"So what do you say since I made you a sandwich?"

Thank you, she thought.

Ben raised his eyebrows at her again. "I said, what do you say?"

Thank. You, Claire thought with more intensity, as though he would be able to hear her thoughts if she thought it louder.

Ben sighed. "Okay, listen. At some point you're going to have to start talking to me. You're a smart girl. I know you can."

Claire wrung her hands under the table. Lying didn't feel good. Even though she didn't really know if not telling the whole truth counted as lying, her stomach was still turning.

"God, I hope you're retaining all of this information. I know it's a lot to learn in a short period of time, but soon you're gonna have to do this all on your own. Claire? Are you even listening to me? Do you know what I'm saying?" Claire went to nod, but Ben waved a hand in front of her face, which made her flinch backwards and grimace.

"Okay, whatever." Ben waved it off. "Since you washed the dishes, I'll put these away for you. What do you say?"

Thank you.

Ben put the food away and rummaged around for a few seconds.

"Wait, Claire, have you been eating the snacks at all? I mean, I know it's only been a day or so, but still, you must be hungry," Ben said. His voice softened when he said, "Oh, Claire, I'm sorry. I just want you to be…I don't want to see anything bad happen to you. And that includes seeing you starve to death with a cabinet full of food right next to you." The corners of his mouth twitched upwards. "I bought this food specifically for you, and you won't get in trouble if you eat it. I won't be mad. I'm not gonna hurt you."

Claire's hands were red from the friction of wringing them through each other. She still wasn't sure what kind of person Ben was. He would get exasperated with her as easily as Brian and Shannon, but the next second he would be back to normal again.

He hugged her. Claire made no move to hug him back.

"I only have what's best for you in mind. I just want you to be safe. And happy. So, I have a gift for you."

He told Claire to close her eyes, which she did without hesitation. There were some rustling noises behind her.

"Now, open them!"

A stuffed animal was sitting on the table in front of her. She reached out to touch it, stopped, and looked at Ben for permission.

"Go ahead," he whispered excitedly.

She grabbed the teddy bear around his stomach and brought it to her lap. She stroked his soft fur, rolled the pad of her finger over his marble-like eyeballs, and touched his felt nose. She loved the color of the bright red ribbon that was tied around his neck. Claire thought he was adorable.

"Don't you love it? As soon as I saw him I thought of you." She looked at Ben, who was grinning wildly. The smile fell and he stuck his lower lip out in a pout.

"I don't get a smile, even for that?" His shoulders dropped dramatically. "Fine," he said. "So, what're you gonna name him?"

Claire only knew a couple names. *Brian, Shannon, Ben, Claire, Lily.*

She didn't want to name it Brian or Ben, but the only other names were for girls. And she couldn't call it a girl name because Ben kept calling it a "him."

"Okay, fine, don't tell me." Claire was afraid Ben was mad again, but he was smiling. "I thought you'd like some company, is all. For when I'm not here."

He went to the bedroom to look at the clock on her nightstand. "Oh no. Like now, for instance. I have to go back to work, or I'll be late. Don't forget, you can color, and eat the snacks if you want. Mwah." He kissed her head. "Bye, Claire."

Bye, Ben, she thought.

After he was gone, Claire took the bear into her bedroom. She put him on the nightstand, right beside the clock. She walked away, but, as an afterthought, went back to him. She picked at the knot that held the bow in place and loosened the ribbon, crumpled it up in her hand, and put it inside the drawer with her other treasures. Claire knew what it was like to have something around your neck all the time, and she didn't want anyone, or anything, to feel that way too. She huffed in satisfaction, left the room, and turned out the light.

Things with Claire were going well. Ben had only a miniscule touch of fear that he was going to get caught left in his heart. There hadn't been mention of her on the news, there were no missing-person posters around town, and her name didn't pass anybody's lips.

"In what world would a mother and father hate their child so much that they didn't care when she went missing?"

Ben's fingers itched to try Amy again. He had already called a couple times that day, and didn't want to seem desperate, though he was. He wanted to share his love with her. He wanted to be a family again.

Ben punched her number on the screen and brought his phone to his ear. He paced and tapped his foot as he listened to the automated ringing. Just as he was about to give up, the ringing stopped with a click.

He stood straight up and cleared his throat. "Hello?"

"Ben!" Amy's voice floated through the phone. Ben thought she sounded delighted.

"Amy, it's so great to hear your voice—"

"Stop calling here.

Ben blinked. "What?"

"You have to stop calling me."

"Amy, no," Ben said, flustered. "I have to tell you something."

"What?" she snapped. Ben closed his eyes. He could picture her face. "Ben, what is it?" Amy didn't sound as curious as she did impatient.

"Come back," he whispered. "I need you here with me."

Amy sighed on the other end. Her voice was tinny and metallic. "Ben…"

"No, Amy, I'm serious. Come home. Be with me again. We'll be happy."

"No."

"Come on, just listen—"

"I am listening. But I can't come back; I would never come back. Not unless I was absolutely crazy."

Now it was Ben's turn to be fed up. "And why not?"

"How do you expect me to? After what you did to me and Claire?"

Ben scoffed. "But Claire's fine now."

Amy paused and Ben could almost see the gears turning in her head. "How would you know how Claire's doing? Have you been seeing her? You know you're not allowed to do that."

Ben waved her off. "She's here with me right now, and let me tell you, she loves it here. She loves me."

There was some shuffling, a muffled, "Claire?" coming from the other end, then Amy's voice, clearer again, "Ben I don't know what you're talking about, but stop. Stop calling me, stop making up stories. Just…stop."

There was another click and then, silence.

Ben stared at his phone in disbelief. "You didn't even try," he shouted. He chucked his phone on the couch and it bounced off onto the floor with two dull thumps. He kicked the couch and stomped on his phone, but with only a sock on, he didn't do any damage.

Ben stormed into the kitchen where his eyes landed on the shopping bag on the floor, empty except for the receipt. Ben picked up the small piece of paper and read it over.

"See, Claire. I'm better. I give you presents." He dropped the receipt back into the bag. "Even though I can't afford them."

Ben had gotten angry with Claire downstairs. Everything she was doing was endangering her life. She could've choked on her food the way she was eating it and she didn't seem to care that he was teaching her valuable life skills. She even threw the plate down on the counter. What would happen if it shattered and she cut herself when Ben wasn't home? He couldn't stand idly by and watch her make all these mistakes that could harm her.

But to make up for his agitation, he gave her a teddy bear with a pretty bow around its neck. It had cost him nearly three dollars, but he figured she should have something that reminded her of him and all his lessons while he was away.

"I'm a good father," he said, looking at the closed basement door. "I am."

Chapter Nine

Claire was sitting on the couch, her face burning in shame from what happened the night before. A couple days had passed since the gift of the coloring supplies, and she had gotten bored of coloring on the paper. She tried to color on the table, but it didn't seem to have a great effect. So she took her crayons to the white walls of the basement. She scribbled for a while until her hand slipped and the crayon made a mark it wasn't supposed to. She tried to wipe away the mistake with her finger, but it didn't come off. Claire stuck her finger in her mouth to wet it and scrubbed at the crayon mark. It still didn't come off. She would just have to accept that she had messed up.

Ben had come downstairs to eat dinner with her. When he saw what she had done, he reprimanded her. The fear of being beaten, at this point, only scrolled through her mind as an afterthought; it was no longer her biggest concern. She just didn't want to disappoint him. He licked his finger like she did to rub it off. When it didn't go away, Ben said, "Ugh."

Sorry, Claire thought.

He went to the sink and squirted some dish soap onto a paper towel, then ran it under the water for a second. He came back to the wall and scrubbed away the mess. Little by little, Claire's masterpiece was destroyed.

When the wall was relatively back to normal, Ben sat her down at the table and sternly said she can't do that anymore. He said he won't punish her this time, but if she does it again, she should expect consequences. She was finally feeling consistently full and her bruises and scars were fading, so she really didn't want to endure any punishments that would bring them back or empty her stomach. She didn't let herself touch the crayons for the rest of the night, even when Ben went back upstairs.

Claire thought it was weird how Ben told her before he actually punished her. Brian and Shannon would never warn her in advance; some days she just wouldn't get something to eat, or she would be beaten especially hard. She never had any way to prepare for it or try to fix what she had done wrong. And another thing: Ben told Claire the mistake she made. He told her which rule she had messed up so she wouldn't do it again. Brian and Shannon wouldn't even tell her what any of their rules were.

Claire tried to make herself feel better by listing all the things she'd learned since Ben brought her here.

"Eat breakfast, take shower. Color. Crayons are pink, red, blue, green, yellow. Numbers are one and four and six and ten. Wake up at seven."

Over the past couple days, Claire had gotten better at being able to wake up to an alarm, although Ben still had to help her sometimes. But now she could brush her teeth, shower, and sometimes she went to the bathroom in the toilet. She was still wearing pull ups, which she had to change once or twice a day.

The first few times Claire took a shower by herself, she left her sopping wet clothes in a heap on the floor. Ben didn't discover this until a few days after, and he asked her what they were.

Claire just shrugged in response.

"I think those are clothes. Why didn't you put them in the hamper like I showed you?"

He went to pick them up, but when he found the ones on the top were damp, he dropped them.

"Did you have an accident?"

Claire shook her head.

"Then why are these all wet?"

Claire pointed to the shower.

"Have you been showering with your clothes on?" Ben laughed. "Claire, you're supposed to take your clothes *off* when you shower!"

He picked up the pile of clothes and dumped them into the hamper in the corner of the room.

"Claire, Claire, Claire, you crack me up."

Claire almost smiled at that. Her mind was filling up with good, happy memories, pushing out the old, bad ones. Mailman hadn't really visited her since she'd been down here, and despite the minor mistakes here and there, Claire was proud of herself.

But now Claire knew what it was like to be bored. She had definitely been bored at Brian and Shannon's before, but that was different. Back then there was nothing to do but stare at the sky and fear for her life. She didn't know that there were so many things to do, like color and walk around. Now that she knew what it felt like to have fun, she didn't like sitting around and doing nothing.

She didn't want to pick up the crayons yet, because it was still too soon after last night. She figured she should give herself the day off from coloring so there wouldn't even be an opportunity for her to draw on the walls.

Claire was laying on her back, staring at the motionless ceiling. It was far less fun to watch the sky when she couldn't see the clouds moving. She shut her eyes and pretended she was back in the yard.

A slight breeze hit her cheek and ruffled her hair, and at the same time, pushed the clouds a little closer to their new destination.

Claire switched the image in her head so she was staring at the vast openness of a starry night. Those nights were her favorites, even though she liked the clouds. Guessing where the next pinpoint of light would break through the pitch blackness and flicker on and off was calming.

But, the fantasy was shattered—as usual—when Brian's voice pierced the night, "Lily!"

Claire bolted upright, panting. She curled up, her arms and legs protecting her vital organs.

Stop, it's okay, she told herself.

She unfurled almost immediately.

"It's okay. It's okay."

She let her breathing slow and her heartrate return to normal before she stood up. She needed to walk around, to get the vision out of her mind.

Claire decided she wanted to explore. Being mentally back in the yard made her feet itch even more for adventure. She walked in and out of each room in the basement, but there was nothing she hadn't seen before. She circled the entire basement twice before stopping in front of the stairs.

"Stairs," she said. This was the one place that she hadn't seen yet.

Claire looked quizzically at the mountain in front of her. She bent her knee so that her foot could reach the step. Somehow the motion came naturally to her. She tried to push her leg straight again, so that she could reach the next stair, but it was harder to do than she expected. She grabbed the railing on the wall and put most of her weight on it. Claire was sideways, completely dependent on the wall to hold her up, but her leg was straight. She brought her other foot up next to the first one.

"Good job." She looked down behind her. She was a whole foot taller now. She took a deep breath in, puffing up her chest, and held her head high. It seemed different, somehow, looking at the basement from a new angle.

Claire turned her attention back to the task at hand. She repeated the process she had with the first step and managed to climb. At each stair, Claire glanced behind her to mark her progress. When she was almost at the top, she turned around and could no longer see all of the basement since the overhang was in the way. She put her foot on the last stair.

The stairs were her Everest, and she had just reached the peak.

Claire rested her hand on the door handle. The devil on her shoulder was urging her to open the door, but the angel was reminding her of the consequences Ben had told her about.

The devil won and Claire pushed down on it—ever so slightly—and half expected some sort of alarm to go off. Without removing the pressure, she glanced around. When nothing happened, Claire pressed down a little harder. There was a little click under her hand.

When the handle wouldn't go down anymore, Claire shifted her weight forwards. The door creaked as it cracked open. Not a lot of light met her as it opened, but it was enough to blind her for a second. She was so adjusted to artificial bulbs that the dim light from the setting sun hurt her eyes. Claire couldn't move. She was glued to the floor, gazing at the world outside the glass door. There were so many trees out there, like the ones behind the fence in the yard. About half of the sun was showing above the leaves on the trees. Claire reached her hand out. She could almost touch it. She was so close…

"Hey!"

Her eyes barely adjusted and hand still on the handle, Claire blinked rapidly. Because of the sun shining in from behind it, Claire could hardly make out a dark figure striding towards her.

Mailman, she thought. *Bad idea, bad idea.*

Claire yanked the door closed and the momentum almost pitched her backwards. She caught herself on the railing and saved herself from a drastic fall. She tried to go back down, but the motion was different than going up, and she couldn't figure it out in time.

The door whipped open behind her.

"Claire!"

Claire was startled by his booming voice, and her heel slid off the step. She fell a few feet down, and she cried out, tears wetting her face. She let herself slide on her butt down the stairs until she hit the bottom. She pushed herself off the floor to run away, but Ben's hand clamped down on her arm before she could get very far.

"What do you think you're doing?" Ben yelled. He clenched her other arm in his fist. The only coherent thing that Claire could think of was how Brian had shouted the same thing at her back in the yard.

"Didn't I tell you that the only rule was to stay off the stairs? And especially not to open the door? Huh?" Ben held her arms right below her shoulder and shook her back and forth. He didn't stop until he realized that Claire was gasping and sputtering and shrinking away from him.

Ben let go of her arms and stared at his hands. He held them in front of his face as though they were separate from his body and he couldn't believe what they had done. Claire took a couple steps back and hugged her arms around herself. She was trembling.

"Claire—" Ben reached out to her, but she flinched. His hand stopped and fell to his side.

"I, uh, I didn't mean to. Okay? I didn't—I didn't mean to." Ben's words reached Claire's ears, but he was only muttering to himself. "I never mean to."

Claire stayed where she was, but was still shaking. She didn't look at him.

"Don't—don't do that again," Ben whispered. Claire couldn't tell if he was talking to her or himself, but she nodded vigorously. Ben ran up the stairs. The door slammed and Claire dropped to the floor in a ball.

Claire rocked back and forth with her face pressed into her knees, so her tears fell onto her legs and her words were muffled.

"Don't do that again, don't do that again, don't do that again."

She ruined it. Now Ben was going to take her back to the yard, for real this time. He hated her. He was going to stop feeding her and he was going to keep hurting her like that. He already hurt her tonight, what was stopping him from doing it more in the future?

It was all her fault. She was always the problem. She was always bad. It was her fault that Brian and Shannon hated her, and it was her fault that Ben wouldn't want her anymore.

Later that night, when Claire looked at the clock and it said eight followed by a four and a five, she brushed her teeth. Ben hadn't come down for dinner, so Claire had eaten a couple pieces of bread. She was brushing her teeth when the basement door opened. Her body cringed automatically, but she continued to scrub back and forth so Ben wouldn't yell at her.

She stared straight ahead into the mirror, but could see out of the corner of her eye that Ben was leaning against the doorway.

"Hey," he said.

Claire didn't respond, but she was done brushing, so she put the toothbrush down.

Ben looked at it, with his brows furrowed. "Uh, did you have any toothpaste on that?"

Claire mentally scolded herself for forgetting.

"Don't worry, you're fine. Just squeeze the stuff out of the tube onto the brush first next time."

Ben's voice was a lot calmer than it was earlier that day, but Claire still had reason to be afraid. His mood changed all the time. She kept her chin and eyes down, and stared at his feet. She willed him to move out of the doorway so she could pass.

"I came down because I'm going to put a lock on the outside of this door. Okay? It's just in case you get in trouble again, which I don't expect you to, but I'll need to something to punish you if something like this happens again," he said. He pulled out some weird looking objects and loud noises started happening. Claire threw her hands over her ears.

"Sorry, forgot to warn you. This might be loud!"

When the loud noises stopped, Ben showed her what he did.

"I put a lock on this door on the outside. You flip this part up and slide it over and then"—he jiggled the handle—"you can't open the door. See?"

Ben grabbed all his tools and said, "And I wanted to say goodnight. So, uh, goodnight."

Ben walked away from her and up the stairs. After the door closed, Claire let out a big breath she didn't realize she was holding. Ben hadn't kissed her before he left this time. Claire didn't know if that was good or bad.

Claire went to inspect the new lock on the bathroom door. She flipped it and slid it how Ben did, and sure enough, the bathroom door wouldn't open. She slid it back to its original spot so she wouldn't be locked out. She hoped Ben wouldn't lock her in there. She hoped *she* didn't lock herself in there.

She shivered and walked away from the lock. She didn't want to look at it anymore.

Claire went to her room to sit on her bed until the clock turned to nine. She didn't turn on the light.

"Nine, bedtime," she said.

The glowing numbers blinked to a nine, so Claire lay back on her pillow. She didn't change into her pajamas or crawl under the covers.

She was shivering from both cold and fear, so she curled up and wrapped her arms around her knees. She squeezed her eyes shut and whispered, "Don't do that again, goodnight, don't do that again, goodnight."

Eventually, she fell into silence, but couldn't fall asleep. She opened her eyes again and the numbers changed, from nine to ten, ten to eleven, and eleven to twelve. Claire wasn't even close to sleeping.

In the cold and the almost complete darkness, Claire was back in the yard again. Terror made her heart explode, leaving very little in her chest to pump blood and keep her alive.

She was laying by her pole, shivering, the rope abrasive against her neck. Her clothes were ripped, dirty, and stiff, and the shadows that the tree created were darker than normal. The wind was blowing hard, and her hair stung her cheek where it hit her like a whip. The darkness was so great that the only visibility was to the fence; anything past the metal wires had been swallowed by the blackness. Mailman's dark figure appeared. He started by shouting incomprehensibly at her, but his words started to take form: "Don't do that again."

Adrenaline shot through Claire's veins, and she opened her mouth to yell at him to stop, but either the wind was stealing her words or she couldn't speak at all.

The rope around her neck tightened, cutting off her airway and leaving her short of breath.

"You'll never escape," Mailman shouted over the wind.

Claire scratched at the rope, trying, and failing, to wedge her fingers underneath so she could get some air. The rope squeezed her like a python with its prey and Mailman cackled over the tornado-like winds.

Claire opened her mouth to scream, but no noise came out. The wind grew louder until the only thing she could hear was a deafening whistle. She released her grip on the rope to protect her ears from the horrible sound. The darkness was closing in, ready to swallow her as it did everything else in the world.

All the while, Mailman roared with laughter in the background.

Claire?

The sound of the wind had not decreased in intensity, but she was sure that she heard a voice.

Claire, wake up!

She squinted in the darkness to see where the voice was coming from, all pain in her head and throat forgotten.

Claire!

Claire gasped and sat up straight in bed. The dark figure of a man was standing next to her, and a noise of distress escaped her as she tried to scramble backwards.

"Hey, no, it's me. It's Ben. You were having a nightmare; you were screaming. It's okay, I'm here now. It was just a dream."

Claire's breathing began to slow, but she didn't let her guard down.

"It was just a dream, you're awake now. Nothing's going to hurt you."

Ben reached out to Claire to comfort her, but she jerked away.

When Ben spoke, he sounded hurt and betrayed, "Claire."

Claire closed her eyes before tears could escape.

Ben. It's Ben, she told herself.

She scooted closer to him on the bed, and he cautiously touched her shoulder.

At that loving gesture, Claire melted and collapsed into his arms. He wrapped his arms around her into a hug and whispered comforting words into her hair.

"Did I do this?" he asked. But Claire couldn't answer.

After a couple minutes of rocking her, Ben stood Claire up and led her to the bathroom to go. He helped her change into pajamas for the night, but in her dreary state, still recovering from her nightmare, she couldn't understand what was happening. When she was back in bed, he played with her hair. Claire relished the good feeling.

"I can sit with you until you fall asleep. I mean, if you want," Ben offered.

Claire nodded slightly, and she didn't know if Ben saw. But he stayed where he was anyways. He lifted the covers over her and continued to stroke her hair. She used the warmth of his hand on her head to ground her in reality. She wasn't at Brian and Shannon's anymore. She was safe here. Ben got mad sometimes, but that was her fault. All she had to do was not make him mad. She looked at the clock. It had a two on it.

It made Claire feel bad that Ben was awake this late at night. She tried to fall asleep so that he could too.

The next thing she knew, there was a loud, rapid beeping noise.

She blinked the sleep out of her eyes and saw that Ben was gone from the side of the bed. The room was dark—the only light trickling in was from underneath the door. The closet door was slightly ajar, and the darkness was even deeper in there. Claire rolled onto her back so she wouldn't get sucked in by it, spread her arms wide, and just listened to the harsh beeping. The alarm whined for a long time.

This is your new life, it told her. *There's no more yard, no more pole, no more rope.*

"Yes," she said. This was a safe place. There was nothing to be scared of, as long as she didn't make Ben mad. She had to be the best Claire ever.

Finally, she rolled over and pressed the buttons until one of them stopped the cry of the alarm clock.

"Seven, one, three," she read off the clock. "Seven, wake up."

Claire let her legs dangle over the side of the bed. She swung her bare legs and feet back and forth. She flexed her toes and rolled her ankles.

"Wow," she murmured. Claire had never really thought of it like this before, but all she had to do was tell her feet to do something, and even before the thought was fully formed, they were doing it. She told her arms to lift her hands to her face and her fingers to bend and straighten. The next thing she knew, she was standing.

"Wow."

Claire didn't even have to tell herself to stand up—she just did it. She couldn't get over at how much control she had over herself. She looked down and made her toes curl in the soft carpet.

As Claire walked to the main room of the basement, she focused on every step. She told her brain to lift her leg, bend her knee, and place it down on the ground again.

"Up, down, up, down."

In an awkward sort of march, Claire made it to the bathroom. The bright lights flooded the room as she flipped the switch, and Claire had to close her tired eyes before they burned out.

She squinted at the reflection in the mirror. There was a new girl there this time. Claire and the girl in the mirror lifted their hands at the same time. Both of them reached out towards the other and their fingers touched. Both girls leaned forward to see, but there was a small gap between their fingers.

Claire's face fell. She made a sad sort of noise in her throat and she separated her hand from the other girl's, who did the same. Why couldn't she touch her? Claire wondered why she hadn't seen this girl before.

"You're never going to get out," Claire whispered to the other girl, repeating Mailman's words to her from earlier. But the girl in the mirror whispered it back to her. Claire jerked away.

"No." Her voice was louder this time, but the other girl said it back with the same force. The other girl's eyes grew wide and she shook her head.

"No!"

Claire ran into the open door behind her as the girl in the mirror did the same.

"You're never going to get out," the girl in the mirror yelled, her voice hoarse.

"Stop." Her vision blurred as tears stung her eyes. "Stop!"

Claire sobbed loudly and that was all she needed. She bolted out of the bathroom, not waiting to see what the other girl did.

The basement was still dark, save for the single spotlight in the kitchen, but Claire could hardly see from the tears that made her nose stuff up and eyes glisten. She squeezed her eyes shut, not allowing any to actually drip down her face. Claire didn't want to cry anymore; she wanted to be in control.

So, just like how she did when she flexed her fingers and moved her toes, Claire told her brain to stop her eyes from crying. She willed the tears away and replaced her mind with words.

"You're never going to get out, you're never going to get out."

Her hands balled into fists without her telling them to.

"You're *never* going to get out."

Her eyes still shut, she stamped her foot.

"You're never going to get out. You're never going to get out."
Say other words. Stop!

"You're never going to get out, you're never going to get out!"

Claire screamed in frustration. Her voice sounded like the girl who was in the mirror. It was rough and scratchy.

"Claire?"

Claire shut her mouth at once and snapped open her eyes. Her fists unfurled and her foot stopped throwing a tantrum.

"Are you...are you okay?"

Ben stood at the top of the stairs, staring down at her. He was peeking around the door as though he were afraid. In another situation, Claire would've found it amusing that he was scared of her and not the other way around.

"I heard you screaming, I got worried. I was in the shower so I couldn't hear very well..."

Claire shook her head so fast, her neck cracked.

"Are you sure, I could've sworn I heard a voice coming from down here." Ben disappeared for a second and reemerged from behind the door with food in his hands. "You don't have to lie, you're not going to be in trouble for talking. Actually, I think you'll be rewarded if you do."

Ben reached the bottom of the stairs and set the food down on the table. He flicked a switch and glanced upwards as the lights exposed everything in the room. He looked at her sideways.

"But, if you can't do it," Ben sighed, "I guess I'll just have to tally that with the other things you're unable to do."

Claire blinked, momentarily distracted from her mental pain.

If Ben noticed her increased interest, he didn't show it.

"Yeah, I mean, I had high hopes for you, but...." He took a sharp breath in through his teeth. "I guess that's just something you can't do."

Anger bubbled in her chest. How dare he say that she can't do something?

Ben seemed disinterested now. "Oh, don't be upset, lots of people can't speak. Like some older people who are sick, little babies. Don't worry if you can't, I never thought you would."

Claire pursed her lips together and furrowed her eyebrows.

I can, she thought.

"Don't get mad, Claire, it's okay. I get it, this is just something that's too hard for you."

Stop. I can.

Ben raised his eyebrows high. "If you're really saying you weren't the one talking down her, then I guess you just can't do it."

"I can."

Ben's eyebrows raised even higher. "What—what was that?"

Claire coughed and tried to make her voice clearer. "I can."

"I'm sorry, I really can't hear you." Ben took a step towards her and cupped his hand around his ear.

"I can talk. I can." Claire spoke as loud as she could, but it was still soft.

"Oh, so that *was* who I heard yelling down here earlier?"

Claire nodded.

Ben shook his head slightly, and blinked. "What? I couldn't hear that."

"Yes. I...yelled...earlier," Claire said, using his words.

Ben's face broke into a wide grin. He ran towards her and scooped her into a big hug. Her feet lifted off the floor and she was bouncing up and down as Ben jumped in excitement.

"Claire! My Claire can talk. She speaks!"

Claire almost smiled at how happy she was. Ben was so excited, it made her feel proud of herself, like she had actually accomplished something. She felt bigger now, not as small and weak. Ben put her down and knelt down in front of her, a huge, goofy grin on his face.

"I don't think you understand, I am *so* happy right now."

Claire couldn't make herself smile, though, so she just stared at him. He sighed contently, his face settling down from the excitement.

"Have you been able to talk this whole time?" Ben's voice sounded slightly betrayed when he asked her this, although Claire couldn't say why.

She nodded, then corrected herself. "Yes."

"If you could talk, why haven't you? I've been wanting to hear your voice forever." He tucked a strand of hair behind her ear. "Oh, who cares? I'm happy you finally did. Better late than never, right?" Ben squeezed her shoulders, but not to hurt her; it was out of pure affection.

Claire was uncomfortable at how long he was looking at her for, so she averted her eyes and fixed them on a spot in the kitchen.

"I'm sorry." Ben chuckled, but it sounded forced. "I'm just remembering. This makes me feel like—well, there was this one time, I let her out of school early one day—I said she had a doctor's appointment—and we went to the movies and the mall, and I let her pick out all the clothes she wanted. It's stuff like that, like this"—he gestured to Claire, then the whole basement—"that just makes me feel so good inside."

She didn't know what he was talking about. Ben wasn't even looking at her anymore. His hands were still on her shoulders, but he was fixated on a spot over her head. He sighed.

"Amy had to mess it all up. She said I was a bad father. She said I didn't know how to raise a child, that I was horrible with kids. But now you're here. And I'm not doing too bad a job am I?" The grin was back, and he was nodding ecstatically.

Claire nodded back at him, but wasn't sure what she was agreeing with.

"Good, now, time for breakfast."

Ben and Claire ate breakfast together, sitting across from each other. He let her have peace while she was eating, but as soon as she cleared the dishes, he started firing questions at her.

"What else can you say? Do you know a lot of words? Do you want me to teach you some more? Or do you know how to say sentences? I can teach you that too. You never answered me from before, why didn't you say anything earlier?"

Claire had her back to him and her lower arms were submerged in soapy water. She shrugged. She knew why she hadn't talked before this. It was because whenever Brian and Shannon heard her, they would beat her and scream at her to shut up.

"C'mon. I know you know why. Just tell me."

Claire paused. She opened her mouth, but since she hadn't intentionally spoken in over a whisper for a long time, no sound came out. She cleared her throat and tried again. "You little brat, don't say another word. Shut up or I'll beat that stupid little mouth of yours right off."

Ben didn't respond to that. She finished washing the breakfast dishes and put them on the towel to dry. She pulled out the drain from the bottom of the sink like she was supposed to. The basement was quiet except for the sound of the water gurgling down the drain.

Claire wiped her hands on her shirt and turned around. She blinked at Ben. He was staring at her with some sort of emotion covering his face like a mask. Claire thought he needed to stop showing what he was feeling so much if he wanted to survive. She knew all about that. If she showed her anguish through crying or screaming or lashing out, she was met with an even harsher response.

"What did you say to me?" He asked this in such a way that Claire couldn't tell if he was mad at her or not.

Claire quickly backtracked, meaning to explain that she wasn't saying that to him, she was simply answering his question, but she could only stutter. She had no words of her own to use, and she couldn't think of anyone else's either.

Ben stood up and strode the one step it took to reach her. "I said, what did you say to me?"

"I—uh, I didn't—no," she stuttered. "No, Brian. And Shannon." Claire surprised herself. That was the first time she's ever said their names out loud, and they felt strange on her tongue. They kind of tasted bad too.

"Brian, your dad? And Shannon? What about them?"

"You little brat, don't say another word. Shut up or I'll beat that stupid little mouth of yours right off." Claire repeated herself, begging with her eyes and pleading for Ben to understand.

"Do you mean, they said that to you?"

Relieved, Claire nodded. Ben's eyebrows raised slightly and his lips parted, like he wanted to say something, but he didn't.

"Your parents. They actually…they told you that?"

Claire nodded more vigorously, thankful that he knew what she was saying, but not seeing why this was such a big deal.

"What else"—Ben cleared his throat—"What else did they tell you?" He collapsed back in his chair, but Claire stayed standing by the sink.

Claire almost chuckled at the question. Where did she even begin? She brought her hand to her face to think of some of their memorable quotes. She tapped her chin, trying to decide which she should say.

"Do you want me to kill you? No one will ever want you. Your lightbulb's gone out." Claire had no emotion while restating these. But Ben did. His mouth opened farther as his eyes grew wider.

"No. They didn't say that. Did they?" He sounded disbelieving, but Claire didn't know why. She nodded.

"Oh, Claire, I am so sorry. I knew they hit you and hurt you, and that's bad enough in itself, but God, telling your own child that you want to kill them? What could even bring you to that point?" Ben hid his face in his hands. "I am so glad I rescued you from there. Now I know I did the right thing. You would've died out there. They didn't care about you at all. But I do. Claire, I care. I love you. You know that, right?"

Claire didn't know why he was making this such a big deal. They said stuff like that all the time; why did it matter now?

But she nodded anyways.

"Good, good," Ben said as he turned his head. He clapped his hands together to clear the air. "I wanna hear you talk more. It's been so long. What else can you say? Not the bad things, is there anything good you have in there?" He tapped her on the top of her head. The smile was returning, growing on his face.

"I, uh..." Claire didn't know what to say.

"Can you say hi Ben?"

"Hi, Ben."

Ben did a little excited kicking motion with his legs.

"Can you say—oh, I have an idea." Ben spilled the crayons out and they tried to run away, finally free of their prison.

"What's this color?" Ben asked, holding up a red crayon.

"Red."

"And this one?"

"Purple."

"So close. It's blue. But this is great. How about this?"

Ben continued to hold up colors for her to say, some of them she knew, but others she mixed up or forgot.

"Good job. Oh my God, this is amazing."

Ben led her around the basement, asking her if she knew the names for different objects. She knew almost all of them, but the ones she didn't know Ben told her. She filed those away for later.

Claire couldn't figure out at first why she trusted Ben enough to be able to talk in front of him, but then it hit her. The words had been building up inside of her for years and years, and to finally be in a place where she could feel them roll off of her tongue with no threat of injury, her mind and mouth worked together to release everything that was built up inside.

When they ended up on the couch in the living room, Ben couldn't stop smiling.

"You are so smart. I didn't know if you were understanding anything I was telling you, but you've proved me wrong. I can't believe you can remember pretty much everything I say. I'm gonna have to be more careful around you aren't I?" He laughed to himself. He checked his watch. "Oh, shoot I have to leave soon. My shift doesn't start 'til nine today but I better get a move on."

He grabbed the back of her head and pulled her closer to him so he could kiss her goodbye. He kissed her forehead, then stroked her hair.

"Did you take a shower this morning?"

Claire shook her head no and a chill ran up her spine when she heard the whispers of the girl in the mirror in her head.

"Okay, well make sure you do that. You can change out of your pajamas if you want, too. And brush your teeth. And take your vitamin."

Claire couldn't help herself. The morning's events and the praise that came with them bubbled up inside of her. It made its way from her heart to her mouth. The happiness didn't stop there; on its journey to her brain, it tugged the corners of her mouth upwards into a gigantic smile.

Her teeth were broken and crooked and yellow but she didn't care. She was tired of being sad all the time. She finally knew what it meant to be happy, and she wanted to show the world.

"Claire," Ben exclaimed happily. "You *can* smile. Today is the day of new experiences for you isn't it? You've come so far from where you were when I found you."

His words of encouragement made her beam. Her cheeks hurt from the strain of the grin, but she didn't care. The last time she had to use these muscles must've been years ago. Being this happy made her feel warm inside.

"You know, I'd love to see that more often."

He waved goodbye to her as he went upstairs. Although alone again, Claire's smile didn't fall.

Ben knew he overreacted sometimes. He knew that he could be overbearing. But he had to be if he wanted Claire to be safe. She had to stay down in the basement, away from things that could hurt her. Ever since the day Amy ripped his first daughter out of his life, he had felt unfulfilled, like he needed to sufficiently protect someone he cared about if he wanted to feel like he had something to live for.

When Amy ran away with their daughter, Ben was not only guilty, but terrified. She could get hurt out there, and he wouldn't be able to help at all.

"Ben, stop! Don't touch her," Amy had yelled.

The taste of old beer rested on his tongue as he had slurred, "Get out of the way."

Amy had her arms splayed in front of Claire. "No! I won't let you hurt her!"

She was crying, her face red and tears and snot mixing together over her lips. Claire was behind her, a perfect mirror image, clutching her mother's shirt.

"I couldn't hurt her any more than she already is. Look at her knees." Amy didn't turn, but Ben glanced down. Claire's knees were scraped and bloody from when she fell on the playground earlier that day. "You did that to her. I need to fix it. Help her."

"I said no."

The alcohol was lazily swirling through Ben's veins, so it wasn't his fault when it made his fist connect with Amy's cheek. Claire wailed and Amy screamed and Ben wanted them both to be quiet. He lurched towards Amy again, but she stepped backwards and he almost fell over. By the time he righted himself, she was almost out the bedroom door. Claire was behind Amy's arm span, so there was no way Ben could dart in and grab her.

"Ben," Amy said carefully. "We're going to leave. You're not going to follow us. You understand?" Her voice was considerably calmer than it had been seconds before. Ben's brain was cloudy. He knew what the words meant, but it didn't sound real.

"No you're not. You're staying here" Ben said. "Claire needs someone to keep her safe."

Ben finished the bottle that was in his other hand. It thumped as it hit the carpet of Claire's room.

"No." Amy shook her head. "We're leaving." The two of them continued to back up in unison. "Claire, run down to the car. I'll be right there. Go!"

"Mommy!" Claire wailed.

"Now!"

Claire hesitated for only a moment, staring into Ben's eyes one last time, then bolted.

"We can't keep living like this." Amy was speaking to Ben again.

Ben curled his fingers into a fist again. "You're not going." He stepped towards her, she took a bigger step back. Fear flashed over her face, but before she could run away, he grabbed her wrist. She made a noise in the back of her throat and tried to get away. The beer loosened his grip a bit, but Ben tightened his fingers and yanked her towards him with both hands. Ben didn't sound like himself when he spoke next, but it gave voice to the menace raging inside of him.

"Go ahead and leave, bitch, but you're not taking Claire."

"You were about to hit her a couple minutes ago!" Some of her spit landed on Ben's face, so he reached up to wipe it off. With only one hand on her now, Amy bent over and twisted and pulled on her arm to free herself. "You don't do that to someone you love." She tore herself out of his grip and started pummeling him with open hands. Ben leaned back, hands covering his face, until the blows stopped.

He opened his eyes and saw her skid around the corner and down the stairs. He didn't chase after her.

"I wasn't..." Ben said to the empty room. "I wasn't going to hurt her. I was going to help."

A stab of guilt nearly split his brain in half. He clutched the sides of his head, willing for it to stop, and dropped to his knees. The image of her face, sobbing and begging, was tattooed on the inside of his eyelids. He had hurled the empty bottle on the floor against the wall and it had shattered.

"Come back," Ben had shouted. But only screeching tires had responded.

Chapter Ten

The day went on as usual, except now the corners of Claire's mouth were nearly touching her eyes. Her cheeks were aching from smiling so hard, but now that she knew how, she didn't want to stop. She wandered around the basement, talking to herself, but she didn't repeat any of Brian and Shannon's words; she only said Ben's of praise.

"This is great. You have a beautiful smile. You're so smart." Claire was starting to believe this more than ever. Mailman was forced to the deepest parts of her mind, so far away that she could hardly tell he was there anymore. He hadn't spoken to her in a while.

It was almost time for Claire to go to bed, and she had completely forgotten to take a shower after Ben left. She didn't want Ben to be mad at her, since it was so nice when he was happy. She glanced up the stairs as she passed to make sure Ben wasn't there, and scurried into the bathroom. She turned the handle and closed the door gently so it wouldn't make a lot of noise. Claire was sick of doors being slammed all the time.

"You're supposed to take your clothes off when you shower," Claire said, using Ben's words from before to remind herself.

Claire went to throw off her clothes, but she hesitated because they were so comfortable. The grey, baggy sweatpants were soft and warm, and she was wearing a long sleeve pink shirt, but one sleeve was rolled up to her elbow, and the other was so long it covered her hand. She giggled at how disheveled she was.

Claire was making a show of not looking into the mirror. She didn't want to see the girl who crushed her spirits and made her scared. Claire turned her back to the mirror and walked sideways to the shower.

She fiddled with the knobs for a few seconds, and pushed her shoulders back in pride as warm water came out of the shower head. Claire peeled off the pajamas she had been wearing all day and stepped into the stream. She loved the feeling of the water cascading down her shoulders and over her head, and almost missed being outside. When she was in the yard, despite the rope around her neck, she felt free sometimes. She was so close with nature, and the stars were just out of reach, as though if she could've stood up she could've grabbed one and floated away forever. Claire missed watching the clouds and imagining that she could stand on top of one, having the sky take a deep breath and blow her far away from the house. Claire missed the trees and the sounds they made. She missed the animals that would walk or scurry up to the fence if she stayed still long enough. She missed the feel of what little grass there was in between her toes, tickling her cheek, or sliding effortlessly through her fingers.

It was a good thing that there was water washing over her face, because otherwise, Claire would've known that she was crying.

She turned her face towards the source of the stream one last time before shutting the shower off. She stood, shivering, in the cool porcelain tub as somehow a breeze reached her all the way down here and made the hair on her arms stand on end. She crossed her arms over her chest, ripped open the curtain, and stepped into the cooler air. Claire wrapped a towel around herself before drying off as fast as she could manage. She got tangled in her shirt for a couple seconds, but her clothes were on and she sighed contently at their warmth. As soon as she was dressed, Claire screwed her eyes shut because she didn't want to look in the mirror, but when the girl over there didn't say anything, Claire peeked open one eye.

The mirror was completely fogged over. Claire could hardly see the reflection since it was so cloudy. There was a faint outline of the girl, but the edges were all blurry and hard to make out.

"Are you okay?" Claire whispered. She took a step towards the mirror. The girl didn't say anything back, but she stepped closer too. Claire reached a hand out to touch the mirror, and the fog disappeared where she made contact. She snatched her hand away. Three little circles where her pointer, middle, and ring finger touched were clear, and Claire could see through. Claire brought her eye down close to the circles, and was met with the other girl's face right next to hers. Claire jerked back, but now she was curious. She put her whole hand on the mirror, splaying her fingers out, and sure enough, the fog vanished there too.

Claire swiped at the glass, making the clouds go away and leaving streaks and thin lines of water in their place.

The girl in the mirror was just standing there. Her arms were hanging by her sides and her head was tilted. Her face was partially blocked by a streak that went right across her head, but Claire could tell she was looking at her.

"Are you okay?" Claire asked, and was shocked to hear the girl ask her the same question.

Claire nodded, and so did the girl.

"What's your name?" they both asked.

"Claire," Claire said.

The girl on the other side shook her head.

But Claire insisted. "I'm Claire."

The other girl still shook her head.

"I *am* Claire, I am."

"No. I'm Lily."

A cold finger dragged down Claire's spine, and she ran out of the bathroom so no more icy hands could reach her. Claire willed

Ben to come downstairs so she wouldn't have to be by herself down here with Lily.

"I am Claire," she said, partially to reassure herself of her identity, but mostly to break the deafening silence in the basement. Claire could almost hear Lily in the bathroom, shouting that she'll never escape, and that Claire was trapped, just like her, forever.

Claire covered her ears to silence Lily's voice that somehow made its way inside of her head.

"La la la la, la la la la," Claire hummed with no recognizable tune, to drown out the defeated voice of Lily crying out, desperately pleading for Claire to listen. Or maybe she was trying to save Claire before it was too late.

"Hey I have a gift for you." The click of the handle turning from the top of the stairs and Ben's singsong-y voice abruptly cut off Lily's helpless cries.

Claire brought her hands away from her ears, but kept them close by, to make sure that Lily truly stopped her wails of despair.

Ben's footsteps stomped down the stairs until he reached the last two, which he jumped off of, landing on the ground floor with a thump and a grunt.

Ben looked excited and he had his hands behind his back. He strolled over to Claire, who was sitting at the table, and shrugged.

"I got you a little something since you did so well this morning."

Claire looked up at him with hopeful eyes. Ben shifted his weight a few times.

"Well, aren't you going to ask what it is?"

"What?"

"Ta da." Ben brought his hands around front.

Claire leaned forward to see what was in his hands. A rectangular red package was sitting on his open hands. There were white squiggles on it, which Claire could only assume were words. She really wanted to learn how to read.

"Do you know what this is?"

Claire shook her head.

Ben gasped. "You've never had candy?"

Claire shook her head again, her confusion stirring excitement within her. She hadn't, but now she really wanted to.

"Well come here then. You don't really have a childhood until you get sick from eating too much of this stuff."

Claire stood up and went to Ben as he ripped open a small corner of the package.

"Hold your hands out in front of you, palms up."

Claire did as she was told, and Ben titled the bag. Out poured a couple of orange, green, and red balls. The candies were the colors of her crayons.

Claire glanced up at Ben again, unsure of what to do.

"You eat them, like this." Ben picked out his own candy and chewed it. "Mmm, I haven't had these in a long time."

Claire dumped them all into one hand, and pinched a red one between her fingers. She inspected it and Ben nodded at her encouragingly.

She placed it onto her tongue, rolling it around in her mouth for a while to savor the flavor. She moved it to the back of her mouth and bit down with her back teeth. Cold pain shot through her gums, and she brought her hand to the side of her face to help. She unwillingly grimaced when the half chewed candy scratched her throat as she swallowed.

Ben's shoulders drooped. "You don't like it."

Claire shook her head. She couldn't find the words to explain why she looked upset, so she opted for popping one of the orange candies into her mouth. She didn't chew this one, instead, she waited for it to get mushy and soft so that she could crush it with her tongue against the roof of her mouth and swallow it easier.

Ben nodded like he understood. Claire finished eating the other orange and green balls that were in her hand, and she marveled at the little colorful dots the candies left on her palm.

"I'm really glad you like these; they were my favorite when I was growing up, when I could get my hands on them." Ben chuckled, eating another one. Then his face grew serious. "You do like it here, don't you? I'm making things okay for you, right?"

Claire nodded enthusiastically.

Ben's eyebrows came together as he nodded. "Good, good. 'Cause I like having you here. I like seeing how much you've changed."

Claire tilted her head at him, because she didn't understand what he meant.

"When I first was in your yard, I looked into your eyes and there was no light behind them. There was no shine or twinkle that every little kid who's discovering the world should have. But I guess that makes sense, because you didn't have much of a chance to discover anything." Ben rubbed his hand along the back of his neck, his trademark for when he was nervous or uncomfortable. "But now, I can see the light coming back. You're curious and excited about things, how a kid should be."

Claire smiled at him, but kept her lips together and didn't show her teeth.

Ben cocked his head at her. "You can talk to me you know. You don't have to be quiet all the time anymore."

Claire looked down at her feet and nodded.

"I'm gonna make a rule. Starting tomorrow you have to start saying stuff out loud, like please and thank you, remember those? I'm gonna stop buying you gifts and stuff if you don't start talking to me. Okay?"

Claire nodded.

Ben sighed, but said, "Do you need to get ready for bed? I'll wait so I can tuck you in."

Claire brushed her teeth, but that was all she had to do before going to sleep. She made her way into the bedroom, where Ben was already waiting, and climbed into bed.

"It's so awesome to see how much progress you've made in such a short period of time. You're so smart, and you definitely don't get it from me," Ben said.

Ben tucked the blankets around her and kissed her forehead.

"Oh, and I put the candy into the cabinet, just be sure not to eat it all at once," Ben said, winking at her. "Sleep well, alright?"

Claire only nodded in response. Ben smiled sadly, not showing his teeth like how he did earlier. He flicked the switch to turn the lights off, and he was nothing but a shadow in the doorway. The door closed behind him and Claire was left in a comfortable silence.

She waited until the door leading to the upstairs closed, then grabbed the stuffed bear off her nightstand. She hugged it close to her chest, tucked under her chin, and closed her eyes to go to sleep.

The next few days went by in a blur. Nothing eventful really occurred; Claire woke up, went through her morning routine, then colored or daydreamed until it was time to go to bed. Claire was living in luxury now, and she couldn't even fathom how she used to tolerate her yard.

She finished off the rest of the candy, she practiced speaking the new words and phrases she'd picked up, and she started to learn to change her clothes when she needed to. Claire was settling down in the basement with her trust and love for Ben growing with each day.

He had restocked the pantry and fridge and took up her clothes to wash a couple times. Claire had gotten enough control that she deemed herself capable of not wearing pullups anymore, and she hadn't had an accident yet.

All the while, Ben had been coaxing Claire into talking more. When he was putting snacks in the cupboard, he asked her what she says since he was doing something for her. She said thank you, and he beamed at her. Ben asked her basic questions, like, "What are the magic words?"

Claire would respond, "Please and thank you."

"What do you say if you do something wrong?"

"Sorry."

Ben only asked her questions that she should know the answer to—only stuff that he taught her. He would point to something, whether it be in the basement somewhere or in one of the coloring books and she would have to name whatever it was he was pointing at. Ben would constantly have her repeat sentences, and he tried to make them more complicated as she learned to better control her tongue and the sounds that came out.

The best thing of all, in Claire's opinion, was that Ben always told her how well she was doing, and how proud of her he was. He would gush about how smart she was and how fast she learned. Every time he complimented her, Claire couldn't help herself. She would smile from ear to ear.

Of course, she forgot to do things every now and then. Sometimes she would forget to put the dishes away after she washed them. She didn't always wash her hands or flush the toilet after going to the bathroom. Her clothes would often never make it to the hamper; they would lie on the floor after Claire took them off. Ben would get mad at her for stuff like that. He would never hit her like Brian did, but he would scold her and wag his finger. Claire never liked getting in trouble, but she found herself laughing inside whenever he would point his finger and wave it up and down in her face.

The girl in the mirror, Lily, still bothered her every now and then, but Claire had found ways to ignore her, or at least drown her out. Claire could rattle off the numbers on the clock and what they meant without having to look on the paper, and she could name the color of a crayon or any object at the drop of a hat. Claire was learning and expanding her mind, but then Ben brought something that threw her a curveball.

"Books," Ben said happily one day at breakfast. "I saved up my money so I could buy you some, and here they are."

The books had large fonts and lots of pictures. Ben left them in a stack on her dresser so that she could get to them whenever she wanted, but Claire hadn't worked up the courage to open them yet. They were all she had been silently pleading for in the past few days, but she could not force herself to pick them up. They mocked her from their position on her dresser, calling out from across the room when she was trying to sleep and whispering when she picked out her clothes for the day. Claire didn't want to disappoint Ben by not being able to read, so her solution was to not look at them at all.

A couple weeks later, Claire was coloring late in the day. Every time she picked up a new crayon, she would say its color out loud before using it.

Claire had adapted to her new way of life. She got food and water when she was hungry and thirsty and she entertained herself when she was bored. It was easier for her to remember the things she needed to do every day, like picking up her clothes, flushing the toilet, and washing the dishes, but sometimes she got lazy. For instance, as she was coloring, dirty dinner dishes waited to be cleaned in the sink.

Whenever she messed up or did something wrong, she had an underlying fear that Ben would find out and hurt her. But this fear wasn't bubbling at the surface anymore. Instead, it was deep in the crevices of her brain, just a tiny stone in the mountain of her mind. At the thought of her mistakes, though, she glanced over towards the couch. Heat rose to her face, flooding it with red embarrassment.

Earlier that day, Claire had been sitting on the couch. But when she stood up, she began to pee. She hadn't been wearing pullups since she learned how to use the toilet, so this was a shock. Unable to stop, she stood, frozen still, until she was done. She scrunched up her face and cried. Claire kept standing in her spot, not exactly sure what to do. Her pants and underwear were soiled, and there was a damp spot on the carpet now. She glanced around, but, of course, there was no one to help her.

Claire had swiped at her face, annoyed with herself for crying. She made herself calm down and think about this rationally. After she wet the bed all that time ago, Ben made her take a shower, then he washed the sheets.

She ran into her room, ripped off the dirty pants to throw them in the hamper, and grabbed new ones. She washed herself off, and could see Lily out of the corner of her eye, following her movements, but Claire ignored her. When Claire had redressed herself, she went back to the couch and smelled something gross. She grabbed some nice smelling dish soap and squirted it on the damp spot on the carpet. Claire got a towel from the bathroom and tried to sop up the mess, with little success. She tossed the towel in the hamper, along with her clothes, and went back out to the living room.

She stared at the spot from up close and from far away. From certain angles, you couldn't even tell it was there. But she knew that Ben would find it somehow and be mad at her. Claire determined that the only option was to move the couch over it. Luckily for her, it was a cheap piece of furniture, and not that difficult to push. It took her a while to do, and she had to take a lot of breaks, but Claire was able to move it the couple inches forward that she needed to cover the stain.

"Sorry."

She patted the back of the couch, nodded her head once, and turned on her heel. That was when she'd sat down at the table and began to color, in order to forget everything that had just happened.

"Will Ben come down today?" Claire asked to the empty basement. She looked up and around as though she expected an answer, then shrugged. Ben's visits downstairs had become sparser over the weeks. Sometimes she wouldn't see him all day, since he would drop off her breakfast before she got out of the shower and he wouldn't come down for dinner.

Claire finished coloring the dog on the page purple with green spots. There were only a few pages left to color before the book was full.

"That is paper, that is crayons, table with chairs, bathroom and mirror." Although Claire was confident in her speaking abilities, old habits die hard, and she was a broken record with some words.

As she glanced around the room, naming objects, it struck Claire that she hadn't seen Mailman in forever. Without thinking, Claire grabbed a piece of paper off of the stack and the black crayon out of the box.

"Black crayon," she said, and put the wax to the paper. She started with the head, a circle that she scribbled completely black, save for an evil, red smile on his face. The body was short and squat, much like how she remembered Brian's being. She added two thick arms to the side and two legs to stick out the bottom of the figure. She pressed down hard with the crayon to color in the figure all black. This crayon didn't break like the pink one did.

Claire stared at the paper, sure that she had drawn an accurate representation of Mailman, and the cold finger returned, with another long nail to scrape down the knobs of her spine. She tensed up, almost too scared to look around, fearful that her drawing had summoned Mailman. She whipped her head around, but he was nowhere to be seen. Claire huffed, triumphant in his disappearance.

Over the past few weeks, Ben had brought Claire more toys, her favorite being the small dolls with big smiles and perfect hair. Ben also brought her a two-story dollhouse and a tiny doll car. He said he got them at a garage sale for his daughter a long time ago.

"When you're playing with these, you can make them walk around and talk to each other. You can make them act out scenes or conversations, or whatever you can think of, really," Ben had told her. "This would also be a great way to practice your sentences, instead of just talking to yourself."

Claire played with the dolls all the time. She named the boy doll Brian, the girl doll Shannon, and the smaller girl doll Lily, after the girl in the mirror. But if Ben was downstairs while she was playing, she couldn't call her Lily. He got mad when Claire said that name.

Speaking of her name, after Claire began to talk more, Ben would ask her what her name was. He was shocked that she never called herself Lily anymore. That name was only a character now, portrayed by the girl in the mirror and the doll. She imagined it like a cloud on a windy day: barely even forming before the breeze would make the wisps of white disperse.

Claire left the picture of Mailman on the table and she slid to the floor, feeling the chill of the kitchen tile seeping through her socks. She went to her dollhouse, which was balanced on the edge where the carpet met the tile. She glanced inside to see how her little family was doing.

The dollhouse was tall, and it had a bathroom, three bedrooms, a kitchen, and stairs just like her basement. But the Lily doll didn't live in the house with the Brian and Shannon dolls. Claire crawled around the house to the backyard where the Lily doll was laying on her back. Claire bent the doll at her waist so she was in a sitting position, her torso making a right angle with her legs.

Claire grabbed the Brian doll. She bounced him up and down as she walked him to the backyard.

She made her voice deep and threatening as she made the Brian doll yell, "Lily, if you don't shut up, I'll make you shut up."

"No food for you, brat," Claire made the Shannon doll say, and then pretended like Shannon spit on Lily.

Claire had a great idea. She grabbed the Mailman picture off the table and brought him to the backyard to play with him as if he was a doll.

Claire made her voice deep and gravelly, much like Brian's, and said, "No one will ever love you. You're trapped forever."

Claire shuddered and a sense of dread washed over her, as though the cold hand was about to grab her from behind. She glanced over her shoulder—to confirm that no one was there—but she stopped playing. The presence of Mailman sucked all the fun out of the game and replaced Claire's joy with fear.

When she was scared of Brian, she noticed, he caused a physical reaction, like when she curled up and shook from terror. But Mailman made Claire's mind freeze, rather than her body. Her brain would stop functioning and she could do nothing to make him go away or to stop him from tormenting her. With Brian, there was nothing she could do. He was bigger and stronger than she was, and if she tried to be defiant, he would hurt her. But with Mailman, it was frustrating. He never physically laid a hand on her, but the mental distress he caused was unbearable. Claire looked back at whenever he visited, and determined that she should've been able to make him go away.

Mystified that she had that thought, Claire dropped all the dolls to the floor, except for the Mailman picture. Claire was done being scared of him. She marched into the bedroom, opened the drawer with the pink paper and the lock of hair, and put Mailman inside. She closed the drawer with finality, and the cold hand retreated. She brushed her hands off like she finished a dirty job, turned on her heel, and stormed away.

Ben came up from the basement and clicked the lock behind him. There had never been a lock on the door before, since Ben was so sure that Claire would never try to climb the stairs, but after her curiosity got the better of her one time, he had it installed. It had burned a pretty big hole in his wallet, but it was worth it to keep his baby safe and here with him.

For some reason, all of Ben's old, terrible memories had been striking him at random times. Whatever it was, his brain digging up the depths of his past had caused him to crave a drink once again.

"Come on, I know I hid you somewhere," Ben mumbled. After he had made the decision to quit drinking, he had thrown out almost all of the liquor in his house, save for one or two quarter-full bottles. Ben was shoulder deep in a cabinet, blindly rummaging around, when his hand struck gold. He wrapped his fingers around the warm glass and maneuvered it towards him.

Ben unscrewed the cap and took huge gulps. He cringed as the warm liquid hit his tongue and winced when it burned his throat. Ben put his hand to his neck and coughed. It had been a while since he felt that, and it was strangely comforting despite the whispers of bad memories it brought.

He swished the remaining liquid around in the bottle. He went to the living room and slumped on the couch, barely registering the stupid sitcom playing on the TV. He shifted his eyes left, where the front door would've been if he was still in his and Amy's old house.

The last day he'd lived there was awful. Ben had been alone, wearing a dirty white t-shirt and boxers, and drinking excessively. The front door had flown open and banged closed, with Amy stomping into view and disappearing upstairs. Ben had wiped his face and followed her, taking the stairs two at a time.

His heart inflated, thinking that she had come back to be with him, but burst when he saw Amy yanking clothes from hangers and stuffing them into a suitcase.

"You...came back," Ben said, the bottle still hanging from his hand. He couldn't seem to shake himself free.

"No, Ben, I didn't. I'm just here to get our stuff." She shoved past Ben out of the closet and lifted her suitcase into the hall.

Ben stared at the disaster she left behind. His clothes were all over the floor, shoes thrown out of the way, everything crumpled into a ball. He was dumbfounded.

"What the hell was that for?" Ben shouted and stormed into Claire's old room. Amy was shoving Claire's clothes into Claire's pink suitcase and her toys into her ratty backpack. Amy whirled around and got right up in Ben's face.

"That was for abusing my daughter."

"*Your* daughter? She's mine too."

"Not anymore," Amy mumbled, but not before Ben shouted, "And *abused?* I never abused her."

"You know what?" she said, struggling with carrying all the stuff downstairs.

"What?" Ben asked, trailing behind her, making no effort to help.

"I'm not going to explain myself anymore. I've tried. You don't listen," she said, slightly out of breath. "Ben, I know Ethan's death was hard for you—"

"Don't you even start."

"I have to. It happened and it was your fault and that's horrible, but that doesn't mean you get to go around hurting and scaring a child. *Your* child."

"I was protecting her," Ben growled.

"No." Amy set down one of the bags to open the front door and Ben ripped it open and dumped the contents on the floor. Claire's dresses and skirts fell everywhere.

"Where is she, huh? Where's Claire? What'd you do with her?" Ben took another swig of the bottle and threw it to the floor. It shattered. The liquid inside bloomed in a dark stain like a splash of blood. "Dead, isn't she? She's dead because you didn't let me keep her safe."

"What are you talking about?" Amy said, dumbfounded. She put the other bags on the porch and gathered everything up again, not minding that broken glass was mixing in with all the clothes. A small twinge of guilt poked Ben's stomach like the shard of glass he stepped on, but the alcohol rushed to cloud it.

Amy held one of the bags by its handle and awkwardly balanced the others on top. She hurried out to the car and threw the stuff inside. She tried to get in the driver's seat, but Ben had followed her and slammed his hand on the door in front of her face.

"Where is my daughter?" Ben roared, spit flying onto her red, wet face. He slammed his hand down again but stepped around Amy and yanked open the side door.

He crawled inside, calling for Claire. She wasn't in the middle or back seats.

The car started.

Ben hurried out and tried to open the driver's side, but it was locked. He pounded on the window, but Amy was backing down the driveway.

"You better bring her back to me. She's mine too. Claire, I'll save you!" Ben was screaming at air, since Amy had already screeched away.

Ben dropped to his knees, already running out of steam. He crawled off the driveway to the grass, onto a shady spot under a tree, and sobbed into his arm.

"She's dead, she's dead, she's dead," he moaned. He repeated this mantra until he passed out.

That night, Ben came to and crawled inside. There was a message on his machine from someone who apparently knew Amy, but he didn't recognize the number. The lady had said that Amy would be moving away and if Ben attempted to follow or find her that the police would have to get involved. She had said that someone would be by soon to grab the rest of her and Claire's stuff.

Ben had cradled the phone in his arms and sunk to the floor, crying for the daughter he couldn't protect.

Ben downed the last of the bitter alcohol inside the bottle. He had torn himself off the hard floor and packed up his stuff that night. He had taken what he could, and headed out to find a park bench to sleep on.

Ben looked back at the TV and tried to conjure up a good memory he had with Amy. Failing that, he glanced around his miserable excuse for a house.

"What a dump." The carpet was mangy and brownish-grey, when it was supposed to be white. The walls were drab and boring and the wood looked like it was rotting. Everything had a brown tint to it, almost like a filter had been put on his life to reflect his inner self. Ben groaned and slouched back into the couch.

Chapter Eleven

Days turned into weeks, weeks turned into months. At some point, Ben had brought Claire a calendar and showed her how to mark off the days. She flipped the pages two times before Ben taught her how to read—either in the mornings, when she was still rubbing the sleep out of her eyes, or in soft voices at night after dinner. After teaching her the alphabet, and all the sounds that went along with each letter, they read picture books—the kind that only had a few words on each page.

Eventually Claire could sound out the names of the months on her calendar. The one at the top of the open page said March. After a couple more flips of the pages, when the top said July and the basement was warmer than it had ever been, Claire could read long sentences. She could get through books without Ben's help, and she would proudly show him whichever one she completed so he would bring her some more. Reading was her new favorite pastime and she constantly begged for new material. Sometimes Ben got mad at her for asking so often because he didn't have enough money, but other than that, he was happy that she was reading and learning.

Ben brought her books that he called "nonfiction" and they were all about bugs and animals and plants. Most of her stash was fiction, which Claire learned meant made-up. These were about things called "schools" and "malls," "neighborhoods" and "playgrounds." Most of these stories made her laugh because they were so absurd. Ben explained to her that kids actually go to school to learn, they go to the mall to hang out with their friends, and they run around on the playground. Claire pretended that she believed him, but she knew he was making things up. None of those things were real; he was just trying to trick her.

As the months went on, Claire craved knowledge. It was better than candy, it was better than bacon and the scent of soap. She wanted to keep learning and reading and reaching more goals and achievements.

When the calendar was on the last page, and proudly declared the word December, Ben circled the box with the number fourteen.

"Since we don't know your real birthday, I'm just going to say that the day you came here is your birthday," he had said. "This is the second December you've been with me, Claire. Did you know that?"

Claire didn't and said so. She also didn't know what a birthday was, but she wasn't about to admit that.

Ben said, "We didn't do anything for your birthday or Christmas last year because you were still getting used to everything. But look at how far you've come since then. When you came here, you could hardly hold yourself upright. Now look at you. Wow."

Claire beamed and hugged Ben. She surprised both herself and Ben by initiating the affection.

Sure enough, when the circled day arrived, Ben came lumbering down the stairs with a few wrapped boxes teetering precariously in his arms.

"These are for both your birthday and Christmas, since they're so close together," Ben had said.

"What are those?" Claire bounced up and down on her toes. "Presents!"

Ben set the boxes down in front of the couch and beckoned Claire to come sit next to him. She obliged, and Ben said, "You have to tear off the paper to get to the gift part."

Claire looked at him expectantly, waiting for his permission. "Go ahead," he laughed.

Claire squealed as she opened her gifts. She got a bunch of candy, some new books and toys, and a calendar for the next year. Claire was smiling and laughing the whole time.

"Thank you, thank you, thank you," she said as she tackled Ben in a bear hug.

"You're welcome, you're welcome, you're welcome!"

Claire ripped open one of the bags of candy and Ben said, "Don't eat it all at once!"

Claire turned her head towards him, her mouth so filled that her cheeks puffed out. She giggled and some of it dribbled out. Ben teased her and she joked right back.

Ben told Claire that the gift part was over, but she still had another treat coming. He apologized for not having a cake, "But I brought you a donut. With chocolate frosting."

Claire scarfed down the donut and got frosting smeared all over her hands and face.

"You're getting so old aren't you?" Ben said after he chuckled at Claire's mess. "Nine years old, wow." Claire smiled her toothy grin at him. Ben surprised her again by telling her that he took the day off work, and they spent hours together reading and playing.

As more X's filled up the pages on her calendar, Claire began to notice some things. For one, she was losing some of the teeth that hadn't already fallen out—which worried her at first, since they left a bloody hole in their absence—but Ben assured her it was completely normal. But her gums didn't hurt as badly as they used to, and she could chew normally without anything bothering her.

By the month of June—which was her favorite because the picture of the puppy was the cutest—Claire realized that she could reach things on higher shelves without standing on the counter or on a chair. Some of her pants were too short and rode up on her ankles, but she didn't think that really mattered since it was hot down in the basement and she wore shorts and t-shirts all the time.

Claire continued to mark off each day in the calendar as it passed, and she circled her "birthday" so she would have something to look forward to.

Two weeks before her birthday, Claire was listening to Ben's footsteps walk around upstairs. She waited until they faded away and a door to shut before she began to eat her breakfast. She couldn't say why she waited like that, but it became a habit for her, much like brushing her teeth and taking her vitamins.

Claire had just sat down in her usual chair and arranged her plate and utensils to eat when there was a small movement in the corner of her eye where the floor met the bottom of the cupboards. There was a small scrabbling noise, but she couldn't locate the source.

Her searching eyes found the culprit: a small, grey rat. Claire recognized the animal from her nonfiction books, and almost stood up to go towards it. But even the small twitch of her leg that made her pajama pants rustle caused the rat to be on red alert. Both the rat and Claire froze. She held her breath, praying that it wouldn't be so frightened that it would run away. The small animal returned to exploring the bottom of the cupboard, no doubt smelling the food within. Claire continued to hold still, weighing her options on what she could do. Besides her, Ben, and the occasional bug, this rat was the only life form to see this basement in the past couple of years. Claire didn't want it to leave.

She very carefully slid out of her chair and around to the other side of the table, her eyes boring holes into the rat the whole time. It paused as it heard her moving around, but soon accepted her as a new extension to his environment.

Claire reached over to the box of crackers that was sitting on top of the counter. She lifted the cardboard tabs and reached inside the plastic bag. She winced at the sound of the crinkling plastic, but managed to grab a couple. The rat stood still, one paw in the air and ears perked towards the ceiling. Claire sat still for a minute or so, to let the rat be comfortable again. She got down onto her hands and knees and set the cracker on the smooth kitchen tiles, lightly pushing it along the floor towards the rat. Its nose twitched wildly.

Claire brought her hand back and waited to see the rat's reaction. At first, he stayed frozen, as if he couldn't be seen. But then, paw by paw, he made his way to the treat. He reached the cracker, sniffed it for a second, and snatched it off the floor. He chewed the square edges off by spinning the cracker around in a circle. Once it got small enough to shove in his mouth, he did, and Claire laughed as it stretched out his cheeks.

The sudden loud noise startled the rat and he bolted, but Claire didn't see where he went. She wondered if he was living down here with her, and if so, for how long, and where. She decided she liked the rat with mysterious origins.

The entire ordeal reminded Claire of the situation with the deer back when she was in the yard. But this time, Brian wasn't here to interrupt, and Claire was successful.

"I have a new friend." She glanced into the bathroom, hoping Lily in the mirror had heard her exciting news, and hoped that Mailman could hear too, wherever he was.

Over the next two weeks, Claire fed her new friend, whom she named Tommy after her favorite character in her favorite book. She kept Tommy a secret from Ben, though, and hoped that Tommy knew to stay hidden from him. Claire didn't think that Ben would like her new friend.

Claire's birthday came along, and she got some new books and another donut. Ben joined her for breakfast this time, and waited until she was done eating before he commented.

"You know, you're a whole decade old."

Claire's eyes widened comically and Ben had to laugh.

"What does that mean?" she asked.

"It means that you're ten years old. You're almost a third of my age."

Claire's jaw dropped. She didn't feel that old.

The rest of the morning went well, and Ben stayed with her an extra hour. When he got up to leave, he ruffled her hair and said, "Happy birthday, Claire. Sorry I have to go to work today, but I have a big surprise for you later." Usually when Ben said he had something for Claire, he was excited. He didn't look happy this time, though. He bent down and kissed her on the head. "You understand don't you? I gotta work if we wanna live." Ben ran his hand down the back of his neck.

Claire nodded, because she was used to being alone, but she was anxious for what Ben was planning.

After Ben left, Claire distracted herself from her curiosity by reading her new books. She also kept an eye out for Tommy, but he was nowhere to be seen. She hoped that he was alright.

Two chapters into the book, Claire was lost in the story. It was about a young boy who was angry at his parents, so he ran away. His parents were beyond worried about him, so when he returned home, they were loving and accepting and happy to see him.

She put the book down in her lap when she finished it. The story made her think of her own parents. She hadn't thought about them in a long time.

"Do they miss me?" she wondered aloud. "Would Brian and Shannon be happy to see me?"

Claire decided that she probably didn't want to know the answer.

Later in the day, Claire was playing with her dolls, and there were footsteps and faint voices coming from above her head. Her back was to the door, but she clearly heard it open. She figured it was Ben, coming to give her the surprise, but she wanted to be funny and scare him when he came down, so she ran to hide before he could see her.

She stood behind the wall of the stairs, just in front of her bedroom door.

But instead of Ben's footsteps falling on each step, an unfamiliar voice spoke: "Benjamin, I am too old for stairs, don't you know that?"

Claire's breath caught in her throat. Who is that? And who's Benjamin? Is that Ben?

She heard a different voice stutter, and it kind of sounded like Ben. He sounded like he was trying to come up with an answer.

The first voice answered its own question. "Of course you don't. You've never put others in front of yourself, why would you start now?"

Then Ben spoke. "Um, we don't have to go down there, I guess." She could imagine Ben's hand making its way to the back of his neck.

"No, no, you want me down there, I'll go."

"Here, dad, let me help you."

"What did you call me?"

Claire gulped on Ben's behalf.

"Sir, sir. I meant, uh, sir, I can help—"

"When have I ever needed your help, Benjamin?"

Ben stuttered once again, and Claire was beginning to think her fearless father was scared of this new man.

Slow and heavy footsteps landed on each stair, with a few grumbles of protest mixed in.

"Woah, don't fall," Ben said suddenly.

"I did not give you permission to touch me."

"I didn't—I just—"

"Just wanted to kill me is all."

Finally, the new man reached the basement floor with a sigh. From her point next to the wall, she could see the back of his head was light and had brown spots, with only a thin layer of grey hair covering it. The man was wearing a tweed jacket with patches on the elbows and tan pants, but despite his formal appearance, was wearing white tennis shoes with orange stripes on them. Between his grumpy tone, his rudeness towards Ben—or Benjamin as the man preferred to call him—and his eccentric clothing, he gave off a bad impression on Claire.

She inched backwards until she hit her bedroom wall, then slid quietly through the open doorway into the darkness. She stood behind the wall there, and didn't want to come out. She didn't understand why Ben had brought this terrible man into her basement, where no bad blood had ever passed the doorway.

"Now why did I get dragged down here?" the man asked, sighing as though this was going to ruin his life.

"Well, sir, you said you wanted to meet your granddaughter. Or, I mean, wanted to make sure she was real before you gave me the money," Ben replied. Claire stiffened. She knew Ben was talking about her. She prayed that he wouldn't make her come out.

"I still don't understand why you would willingly pass on *your* genes. Unless she wasn't planned…"

"Dad—I mean, sir. She was planned. And wanted. For the happiness and stability she would bring to our lives." His voice, a little softer, floated back to her ears. "They were your genes first anyways."

"Excuse me?" The man, who Claire guessed was Ben's dad, sounded as if he were going to rip Ben's head off.

"I didn't say anything, sir. Uh, Claire? Can you come out here for a second?"

Claire's eyes grew wide. How could he betray her like that? Ben, of all people, should know that Claire had never interacted well with mean people.

"Claire, come here." His voice was firm.

She gulped and squeezed her eyes shut, wishing the situation away. Unfortunately, Claire's wishes never really come true. Seemingly out of nowhere, a hand grabbed her arm and yanked her out of her room, and she let out a small cry. Her eyes snapped open as Ben leaned in really close to her face and hissed, "Don't make me look bad. We need this."

Ben straightened up just as they rounded the corner, face to face with Ben's father. He had even less hair in the front than he did in the back, the only wisps being above his ears and the eyebrows on his forehead. The old man squinted as he scrutinized her. His face was droopy around his mouth, where the corners of his lips were pointed as far down as they could get.

Ben contorted his face into a smile and said, "Claire, this is my father, Walter, er, Mr. Walter, to you. He's my dad, your grandpa. You need to treat him with respect."

Claire, uncomfortable with the way Mr. Walter was staring at her, dropped her gaze to the floor, and nodded.

"What is this?" Mr. Walter spat.

Ben's grip tightened on Claire's shoulder. "This is Claire, your granddaughter."

"How old is she? She doesn't look more than five."

Offended, Claire's head snapped up. But all of the anger drained from her mind and face when she saw Mr. Walter's evil expression. Claire was helpless, and looked to Ben to defend her.

"She's—she just turned ten, sir. Today, actually, is her birthday."

But that seemed to be the wrong thing to say. Instead of wishing her a happy birthday, or at least lightening up at the mention of the special occasion, Mr. Walter's face turned stormy.

"All these years. All these *ten* years, and you've never bothered to introduce me to your daughter? And now"—he scoffed—"the only reason I get to see her is because you need some cash. I cannot believe you, denying me the right to meet my own kin."

"Well—"

"Well what?"

"Sir, don't take this the wrong way, but... Amy...she was the one who didn't want you over," Ben said. He sounded sheepish, but the way he was gripping Claire's shoulder made her believe that he was simmering underneath the surface.

Mr. Walter had not lost any aggression or volume. "And why is that?"

"It's nothing, really. I don't want to fight—"

"Oh, so now you don't want to fight. What about all those times when you were younger? Arguing with me was your favorite pastime," Mr. Walter shouted, but around the same time he said the word "fight," Ben raised his voice and yelled, "No, I don't want to fight. I just want to visit with both of you and make up for lost time."

Both men finished their arguments at the same time, and a heavy silence fell over the room. Ben let go of Claire's shoulder, and she automatically retreated to the safe space behind his legs.

Mr. Walter was the first to speak again, his voice no less menacing than before. "I told you to drop that woman the moment you brought her home to meet me. I told you to get rid of her; I knew she'd be bad for you." Mr. Walter's hand curled into a fist. "Amy, was her name? Where is she now? I'm gonna go give her a piece of my mind."

"Sir. Don't be mad at her. She had every right to wish that you not meet Claire and I had to respect that."

"Oh, Benjamin, don't you talk to me about respect. I spent my entire life as a single father trying to get you to respect me and others and you never listened. How am I supposed to believe that suddenly you've changed and—"

"Sir, stop," Ben yelled. Fear drenched Claire from head to toe. Mr. Walter reminded her a lot of Brian, and the fact that Ben was yelling at him made her think Ben was about to get punished really soon. "Sir," Ben continued in a lower tone, "listen to me."

"Do not order me around. I am still your father. Now tell me why your wife refused me the chance to meet my only granddaughter."

"I was just about to." Ben said something under his breath, so quiet that not even Claire could hear what he said.

"Don't mumble at me. Speak up."

"She thought you would be a bad influence. Or something. She thought you would make me 'worse,' whatever that means, and she didn't want you teaching Claire your ways."

"My ways? My ways are what teach the able-minded how to be presentable citizens in society."

"Yeah, well, look what 'your ways' did for me." He took a deep breath and tried to be calmer. "Listen, sir, she knew you wouldn't agree with the way we were raising our daughter, so she wanted to cut you out. You wouldn't even know what you were missing."

"So not even mentioning the fact that you had a child is the correct way to treat your father? I had no idea," Mr. Walter said dramatically, and Claire knew he was being sarcastic. "Amy has no right to believe that I would do anything to jeopardize a child."

"Sir, we're not like you. We didn't want to raise Claire like an adult when she was still young. We didn't want her to grow up being afraid of making a mistake or just being herself. We wanted her to have free range of her interests and hobbies, and we would support her the whole way."

"If that's a bash on my parenting style—"

"It is! Of course it is. After Mom died, you raised me like I was in the military. Only I wasn't. I was eight years old, and terrified of doing something wrong should I get reprimanded by you."

Mr. Walter straightened his back. "I only did that for your own good."

"No, you did it because you were mad at the world for taking away Mom, and you took your aggression out on me. Amy didn't want that for our child."

Mr. Walter opened his mouth, but Ben beat him to it. "No, don't say a word. Amy didn't want you turning Claire into your second little recruit."

"Amy, that—you know what? Where is she? I'd love to have a chat with her," Mr. Walter said, cracking his knuckles. Claire winced at the noise.

"No, sir. She's at work. She won't be home till later. Can't we just enjoy dinner with what little courtesy we have left for each other? You and Claire can talk, and we can have a nice, family meal, then you can see how amazing she is and help us out a little."

The starkness in Ben's voice sent a chill down Claire's spine. Already, she was the center of the men's problems, and she didn't want to spend another minute with Mr. Walter. He made Ben angry, and angry Ben was never a good thing. It brought him too close to acting like Brian when he was mad, and that brought nothing but misery.

"What time period do you think we're living in? Nobody has nice family meals anymore," Mr. Walter mumbled.

Ben threw his hands up in exasperation. "Won't you be civil then, for my sake?"

Mr. Walter looked like he wanted to argue, but he just grumbled to himself.

"Sit down, sir. Claire, you too. Sit," Ben ordered, pushing Claire into the line of fire.

She stared, wide-eyed, up at Mr. Walter.

"We're eating down here?"

"Yes, sir, so you can take a seat."

Mr. Walter stomped over to the table and yanked out a chair. Claire's chair. The one she always sat in. She whimpered and tugged on Ben's pant leg, but he sighed and shook his head. "You gotta choose your battles, and this...this isn't one of them. Pick a different chair."

Claire scrunched up her face like she was going to cry, but she managed to hold it in.

"Good girl." Ben mustered up a weak smile. He gently pushed Claire towards the kitchen and went upstairs to prepare the food.

She picked the seat directly across from Mr. Walter, who sat with his hands folded in front of him on the table.

"This place is a mess," he said, acknowledging Claire for the first time all night. "Don't you ever clean up around here?"

Was she supposed to answer? More than ten seconds had passed and Mr. Walter was still looking at her with his eyebrows raised.

She opened her mouth to say something but now she was flustered and could only make little noises in the back of her throat.

"Claire, you can speak to your grandfather," Ben said as he came back downstairs. "I put the burgers on the grill, so it'll be a couple minutes."

Mr. Walter didn't seem to hear him.

"Hello? Anybody home?" Mr. Walter asked as he waved a hand in front of Claire's face.

She swallowed hard and still could not speak.

Mr. Walter turned to Ben. "Is she slow?"

Claire turned to Ben. His lips were pursed into a tight line, and his face was getting increasingly red.

Finally, Ben said, "Actually, she is very bright. She can read amazingly fast, and she can memorize almost anything. In fact, I think she's documenting everything that's happening as we speak."

Once again, Mr. Walter squinted at her. "She doesn't look it, though."

"You know, I'm going to check on the burgers." Before he left, Ben crouched down and whispered in her ear, "If you're dumb, then Mr. Walter crapped himself while he was screaming at me." Claire smiled and laughed a little, which made her feel better.

If it was even possible, Mr. Walter looked even meaner. "No secrets, Benjamin."

But Ben didn't respond. He went upstairs, leaving Claire with the monster that was Mr. Walter. She didn't want to interact with him at all. She wanted him to leave her and Ben alone. Claire stared at the table even though she could feel his eyes boring into her.

Claire flicked her eyes up. It was at that moment that she noticed Tommy scrounging around under the cabinets for his daily snack. Her eyes widened. A sick feeling crept into her stomach, and she thought she was going to puke. If Mr. Walter was horribly rude to his own son—threatening Ben, who is a good foot taller—

then what would he do to a creature who is far beneath him, both physically and mentally?

"What is it?" Mr. Walter asked.

I have a name, Claire wanted to say, but didn't. She kept her mouth shut.

Mr. Walter began to turn in his seat. "What are you looking—"

"Fresh, hot burgers, ready to eat," Ben called. Momentarily distracted, Claire took her eyes off Tommy and Mr. Walter faced forward again.

When Claire wrenched her eyes away from the food that was making her mouth water, she scanned the floor for Tommy. But he was gone. Claire breathed a sigh of relief, but she also felt bad for him, since he probably would've really loved this meal.

"Hamburgers? You couldn't have been a little classier, Benjamin?"

"You'll eat it or you'll starve," Ben said in a sing-song voice. Claire looked down at the plate that was being slid in front of her to hide her smile.

Ben set out ketchup, mustard, lettuce, tomatoes, and onions, but Claire didn't like all that extra stuff, so she didn't put any on. She picked up her burger and was about to dig in, but Mr. Walter scoffed.

"Do you not let her add the other ingredients? I'm ashamed, Benjamin, she is stick and bones. The child needs to eat." Then, to Claire, "Put toppings on your burger. Don't let them go to waste."

Claire glanced at Ben, unsure of what to do, but he was staring at his own food. Claire guessed he was done arguing for today.

Choose your battles. She swallowed any anger or disgust she had and lifted the top bun of her burger. She grabbed a tomato by its slimy outer ring and tried to hide the grimace on her face. She piled on lettuce and onions, and finished by squirting both ketchup and mustard on top.

"Are you going to sit there and stare at it all day, or are you going to eat it?"

I'm going to shove it in your face, Claire thought. But she complied with his wishes and picked up her burger. Content, Mr. Walter did the same, after piling his high with toppings as well. Ben followed suit, and soon they were all eating their dinner. Except, Claire was only pretending to. Whenever Mr. Walter wasn't looking, she'd loosen her grip on the burger and let a couple toppings slip out onto her lap. She ate the rest of the hamburger, but she had to deal with the red and yellow sauce that had already soaked into the bun.

Ha, you don't even know, Claire taunted in her mind. She tugged on Ben's sleeve and pointed to the napkins, and he gave her one. She pretended to place it in her lap, but actually picked up the toppings and curled it into a ball. She put the full napkin on top of her now-empty plate and stood up to clear it. She threw away the napkin and rinsed off the plate, waiting for the rest of the dishes to be done before washing it.

Mr. Walter sat back in his chair.

"Did you enjoy it, sir?" Ben asked, finishing up his own food.

"You know what, Benjamin?" Mr. Walter started, and Claire thought that he was actually going to be nice. "That was the worst burger I've ever had." She was wrong. "It was a burnt hockey puck. I don't know how you managed to mess even that up, but I should've known you'd find a way."

Ben's shoulders tensed up. Claire thought he looked like a bomb about to explode.

"This has been a great dinner Benjamin, but I'm afraid I really must be going. And after this, don't expect any help from me." Mr. Walter's eyes narrowed as he glared at his son. He braced his hands on the edge of the table and pushed his chair back forcefully, and it screeched as it scraped across the tiles.

Mr. Walter stood up, straightened his coat, and turned to go up the stairs.

"I'll show you to the door."

"I can find it, Benjamin. I'm not an idiot."

Both men headed upstairs, Ben following Mr. Walter like a sad puppy. Claire was left in the basement alone, but she could faintly hear their voices from up above.

"If you can't even cook a burger right, how did you expect to raise a child?"

If Ben responded, it didn't reach Claire's ears.

Something bad must've happened, because Mr. Walter screamed, "I helped you as much as I could when you were younger so you just need to come up with that money on your own!"

A far-away door closed loudly and Claire shrank in her seat. Mr. Walter was so similar to Brian, it was scary. And she couldn't help but feel as though what had happened was all her fault. She lost all confidence she had when in the presence of people like him.

Claire glanced around the basement, sure that her old parents or Mailman or Lily in the mirror were going to come and get her. Claire scrunched her face up and brought her shoulders to her ears as defense against the monsters in her life. She frantically began to say words, but it mostly came out as just gibberish.

A couple minutes passed before the door to the basement was opened again. It shut quietly and Ben slugged downstairs. He slid into his chair, propped his elbows on the table, and dropped his head in his hands. His shoulders were shaking slightly, which usually meant that he was laughing. But Claire couldn't find any humor that he could've taken from this night.

Claire didn't want to bother Ben, so she cleared his and Mr. Walter's plates and washed them, along with hers, in the sink. When she finished, Ben's shoulders were no longer bobbing up and down, but his head was still buried in his hands. Claire wanted to cry; her fearless leader had been broken down by just one man. She went over to Ben and moved his arm out of the way so she could crawl on his lap.

Ben jerked a little when she did this, but he wrapped his arms around her, engulfing her in warmth and comfort. Claire couldn't help but notice this was the first time she had willingly gone to Ben for consolation, but she liked it. She liked the way he rested his chin on her head and how his hands were rubbing her back. She liked the way that he rocked back and forth and how he hummed an unrecognizable tune under his breath. Claire turned her face so she could be buried in his shirt and breathed in the familiar scent of him.

After a while of this, Ben pulled away. His eyes were red-rimmed and glossy, but he tried to smile for her.

Ben cleared his throat. "You are so lucky you could escape all that," Ben said, jerking his head towards the direction of the door. "I had no one to rescue me. And don't you worry. He won't help us out, but that doesn't mean we're not gonna be okay."

Claire nodded in agreement, but just eased herself farther into Ben's lap. She didn't really understand what he meant, but frankly, she didn't care. All Claire knew was that she finally had a home, that she finally had someone that loved her and cared for her.

No one rescued me, Lily shouted from the bathroom.

Every muscle in her body tensed. If Ben noticed, he didn't show it.

No one rescued me.

Claire flicked her eyes around the room. Could Ben hear her?

No one saved me. I'm still here. I'm still trapped.

Ben slid Claire off his lap, kissed her head, and said goodnight. Absentmindedly, Claire repeated the word, and stared into the bathroom. She barely registered the door closing behind Ben, or his unintelligible screams from above.

Now that he was gone, Lily was able to speak aloud. "I'm still trapped."

Claire crept into the bathroom to make sure Lily was still in the mirror. She was, and she looked more terrified than ever.

"Help me. I'm still trapped," the girl in the mirror said.

"I can't. I don't know how." Claire averted her eyes from the reflective surface.

"I'll always be trapped," Lily said, and Claire met her eyes. Claire's breath got caught in her throat. "*You* will always be trapped." Her palms were sweaty and she clenched her fist. "No one's rescued us." Claire's knees almost gave out. "We're in here...forever."

"She'd been with me for months...years. I kept her hidden for so long. Why did I have to mess everything up?" Ben tore at his hair. "He never would've given me money, why did I even ask?"

After Claire had begun to read and demand more from him, Ben had noticed a dramatic dip in his bank account. The job he was barely holding on to contributed basically nothing to his savings, despite the insane amount of hours he was racking up. Ben had finally cracked and called his father for money, hoping that if the man saw Claire, he would fall in love and do anything to help out.

But he hadn't changed. He was still the rude, loud man that cared so much about appearances he resorted to violence to keep his family in line.

Ben's father had taken to beating him and his mom—though he called it "necessary punishment"—even in the weeks leading up to her death. One day, Ben had been in the backyard when his father shouted at him from the house.

"Benjamin, come here. Now!"

Ben had lifted his head from where he was crouched in the yard and hadn't hesitated running to obey his father's command. He ran inside to stand in front of his father. He'd had to tilt his head all the way back because even though he was seven years old, he was smaller than average.

"Why were you playing in the mud when I have *repeatedly* told you not to?" his father demanded.

Ben shifted his weight from foot to foot and tore his eyes away from him.

"Answer me dammit."

Ben's voice sounded squeaky compared to his father's. "I wasn't playing in the mud."

"Don't lie to me, boy."

"I'm not!" Ben insisted.

"Excuse me?" His father somehow grew even taller.

"I'm not lying. Sir. I wasn't, I swear."

"Then would you like to explain to me why you were sat in the backyard and why you are standing here with dirt caked under your fingernails?" He yanked Ben's hands up in front of his face.

"Sir, I wasn't playing in the dirt," Ben pleaded. "There were worms all out on the porch from the rain and I was building them homes again."

Ben's father crouched down so he was eye to eye with him. His face was calm, but Ben knew there was a storm brewing beneath the mask. But when his father spoke again, he wasn't expecting the severity that was thrown at him.

"What have I told you about being in the yard? You *do not* take your shoes off, you *do not* put your hands near the disgusting ground, you *do not* play with worms. You are ruining this family's image with every blade of grass you disturb. Do you understand me?"

Ben had to resist the urge to wipe away the spit that had landed on the corner of his mouth and right above his eye. He had to stand at attention whenever speaking to his father, and moving without being dismissed was fatal.

Ben's father removed his belt and snapped it between his hands.

"Walter." Ben's mom stood in the doorway, her favorite purple bandana wrapped around her head, wiping her hands on a dish towel.

"Go away, Lucille, I'm about to knock some sense into this boy." Ben's father snapped the belt again.

"Walter, if you so much as touch a hair on his head—"

Ben's father turned on his heel and stormed towards Ben's mom.

"Mom!"

His mom faltered and fell against the wall, using it for support as her knees gave out.

Ben's father shoved his mom into the connected room. All Ben heard was his mom cry out, then his father came back.

"You know the drill."

Ben had tried to mentally distance himself from the belt that was whipping his backside, but it had been hard when he was still sore from the last beating he had received.

Ben, after recounting that memory that he'd tried so hard to forget, stomped his feet on the floor and aggressively flipped off the front door with both hands.

"You ignorant bastard," Ben shouted at no one. "Why did you ruin my childhood? Why did you mess up my head?" Ben hit the couch so the noise would be concealed by the cushions. He whipped around to face the front door. "You never helped me, you only ever punished me. And for what? Even now, you don't give a *shit* about me. There's nothing I can do to make you proud, and you don't even care. Well, neither do I. Don't ever come back." By the end of his speech, Ben was screaming, almost foaming at the mouth. "I don't need you! We don't need you!"

Chapter Twelve

For the next few days, Claire was shaken by the hostility of Mr. Walter and the desperation in Lily's voice. But her jumpiness soon wore off as she lost herself in stories and played with Tommy.

By that point, she had a couple X's marked off in her calendar on the page that said January. On this particular day, Claire set out the crackers for Tommy again. His little nose emerged, twitching and moving from side to side.

Claire wanted to pick him up. She was desperate for living contact besides Ben. All she wanted to do was pet him, and she thought Tommy trusted her enough to let her do so. His little paws brought him closer and closer to the food, and he snatched it up, twisting it around until he could make it an acceptable size to stuff in his mouth. Before he could run away, Claire reached behind him and grabbed him under his stomach.

Tommy started twisting and wriggling, trying to get free, but Claire kept a tight grip on him.

"Ow!"

Pain shot down her finger like lightning. She let go of the rat to tend to her wound, and Tommy scrabbled for purchase as he hit the floor, scurrying away. Claire was too busy scrutinizing her finger to notice.

There were two little holes on her finger from Tommy's teeth.

"Tommy, that hurt," she whined. She cradled her hand near her body and she sat on her knees on the floor. Her eyes pricked with tears, she stretched her jaw in a silent scream. Recently, the only thing she had to deal with were minor discomforts; this was like that time Brian had torn her shoulder out of its socket, then shoved it back in place. It came with no warning, no time to prepare.

She mustered up the courage to look at her hand again, and sure enough, two spots of blood had appeared. The wound puffed up, making her finger look fatter than the rest. Small stabs of pain shot through her finger which made it feel like she was being bitten over and over again. The door opened upstairs, so Claire ran to her bedroom and shut the door.

"Don't come in," she yelled, trying to control the shakiness of her voice.

"Okay, I'm just giving you some breakfast," Ben called back. "I'm going to work, see you later."

"Bye," Claire said, but it was so quiet that she didn't think Ben heard. When she was sure that she was alone again, she let out a sob. She couldn't tell which hurt worse, the bite on her finger, or the fact that her only friend betrayed her. She sat in her room for a while, mourning over her hand and the loss of a friend.

Claire had to be really careful with her hand for the next few days. It wasn't hard to hide from Ben since he hardly came down, but it was getting so much worse. The swelling and redness hadn't gone down at all, and now there was some white stuff leaking out. Claire's shoulders fell. She didn't want to tell Ben, but she had to.

The next morning she decided she would show Ben her finger and he could figure out what to do about it. He stomped down the stairs with a plate of food and Claire could tell that he was already aggravated about something. But she also knew she couldn't wait any longer.

"Uh, Ben?"

"Yeah?" Ben rubbed his temples.

Claire brought her hand from her lap and lifted it to show Ben. His eyes grew wide and he grabbed her wrist.

"Oww."

"What the hell is this?"

"I don't—I don't know." Although Tommy was mean to her, she was hoping they could still be friends, and she wanted to protect him.

"You don't know? Claire, this looks infected. How long have you hid this from me?"

"A couple days…"

"A couple—oh my God this looks serious."

Ben's voice was concerning Claire. She had assumed that he would just give her some medicine and a bandage and she would be good to go.

"Shit, this means I have to take you to a doctor doesn't it? I can't take you outside. Claire, why'd you do this to me?"

Claire opened and closed her mouth, desperately searching for an answer.

"You know what, fine, I'll take you. Who knows what will happen if I don't."

Ben was scaring Claire with his seriousness towards the situation. She almost expected him to laugh it off, tell her she was overreacting. But the way he was treating this bite made it sound like she was going to die.

"Go get dressed, grab your coat. Get your shoes too, I'll go start the car," Ben ordered. But before he could leave, Claire had to ask a question that had been burning a hole in the back of her mind since he mentioned the word doctor.

"Why haven't you taken me to a doctor before?" Claire's voice was quiet because she didn't want to make Ben even more annoyed.

"Because before this you've never needed to go."

She cocked her head. "But I've been sick before, and in my books, when people get sick, they go to the doctors."

"But you've never been seriously sick. Now go get dressed."

"If doctors are real, does that mean schools and malls and playgrounds are real too?" Claire wasn't even asking Ben directly, she was just wondering out loud, but Ben still answered through grinding teeth.

"Yes, they are."

"Why don't I go to them then?"

This question sent Ben over the edge. "Because you're mine! Only mine. If you're anywhere but here someone might take you from me, that's why!" His face was burning red and his fists were balled up. "The only things you'll ever need to learn come from me and your books. Don't ask me again."

Claire made herself as small as possible. "But—"

Ben slapped her across the cheek. Her head snapped to the side and her mouth dropped open as her fingers grazed the red handprint that was surely forming on the side of her face.

"Ben—" she tried again. But her former savior, the only person in the world that she could trust, grabbed her by the arms, just below her shoulders, and began to shake her. Claire swore something was rattling around in her head as she tried to keep it still.

"You. Are. Mine. Only. Mine," Ben shouted, each word punctuated by another shake. "I'm not going to let you be taken too!"

Claire once again tried to take up the smallest space she could. She began mouthing words and her eyes were closed, so she didn't see if Ben was appalled with himself or satisfied, but she did register when his hands left her arms.

"We'll go after you eat," was all Ben said before he promptly left the basement.

Claire stood at that spot, in shock, for what felt like hours before she crumpled to the floor in a heap.

"Claire, you better be ready to go in ten minutes," Ben yelled from upstairs.

Claire had managed to rip herself off the floor and change her clothes, and she was in the kitchen, finishing up a bowl of bland cereal. She could see her reflection in the spoon, so she held it up to her face. The image was upside down and distorted, but Claire could see that the red handprint on her face was gone. She knew that she had bruises on her upper arm, so she wore a long-sleeved shirt to cover it.

She flinched when the door opened. "We need to leave now, or we'll be late."

She didn't hear the door close again, and assumed Ben had left it open for her. She went to the stairs to climb them for only the second time in her life. This time around was slightly easier—her muscles remembering the motions she needed to use—but it was still slow going. She was only halfway up the staircase when Ben reappeared in the doorway. His sudden appearance frightened her, and she almost fell backwards before she caught herself on the railing.

Ben rolled his eyes and stomped down the few stairs it took to reach Claire, and grabbed her by the sore spots on her arm. She whimpered, but he didn't seem to notice. He pulled her through the house, not allowing her eyes to adjust to the natural lighting, so the small glimpse of the outside world went by in a blur.

They went through another door and Claire, for the first time in two years, felt the contrast of the sun's heat fighting for control over the biting wind. She reveled in the feel of nature surrounding her again, and she wanted to take a moment and pause, to breathe in the clean scent of winter and hear the crunch of a new frost under her feet. Claire wanted to lay on the ground again, capturing its heat and transferring it to her own body while breathing in the crisp air that almost scratched her throat. She wanted to bask in the fact that she was a completely different person since the last time she was outdoors. But Ben didn't seem to notice or care. He just lifted her up into the side of a car, which she had read about in her books. Grumbling to himself, he closed the door loudly behind her.

Ben got in his side of the car. "You're not wearing a coat."

Claire looked down at herself. She didn't know she needed one.

He stormed away and came back with a puffy pink coat. He threw it at her and told her to put it on.

Ben started the car and Claire jumped when vibrations electrified her seat. She shoved her arms into the sleeves so her hands would be free to hold on to something. She glanced out the window as they started to roll backwards, and whipped her head around to see how Ben was handling this. He was acting like this was completely normal, so Claire tried to calm down too. They stopped rolling backwards and Ben twisted the wheel in front of him. The car lurched forward, pressing Claire against the back of her seat. After a couple seconds, the car stopped abruptly, throwing Claire forward and almost hitting her head on the dashboard.

"Ugh, put your seatbelt on," he said. He pushed Claire back into her seat with both hands. He leaned over her head and pulled out a long black strap that he connected with the bottom of the seat. Claire tugged at it, wanting it off, but Ben reprimanded her.

"Stop that, it's supposed to be there."

His voice was gruff, and Claire didn't like it. She didn't like this new Ben that had taken over. She kept her hands in between the seatbelt and her body so it wouldn't touch her, but did so subtly, so Ben wouldn't see.

"And when we get there, don't even think about causing a scene, alright? Behave yourself. Don't scream, don't run, we're gonna get in and get out. Got that?"

She swallowed hard and nodded. She tried to watch out the window as the car wheezed and whined towards the doctor's, but the constantly changing scenery made her dizzy, and she had to look down. She was desperately curious about the car, the roads, and especially the doctor's, but she was too terrified to ask Ben anything. The last thing Claire wanted was for Ben to snap at her again.

Finally they arrived at the doctor's office. Ben stopped the car, turned off the engine, and walked around to Claire's side of the car. He ripped open her door and unhooked her seatbelt. He didn't even wait for her to climb out by herself; he grabbed her arm and pulled her out of the car. The cement underneath her shoes jarred her legs.

The walk inside the doctor's office was longer than that of the basement to the car, so Claire's eyes had time to adjust. She could see birds, and other cars, and grass, and trees. She wondered if those were the same trees she could see from her yard. Subconsciously, Claire tried to wriggle free of Ben to go explore. She wanted to hear the swish of the grass up close again, and she wanted to feel the dirt seeping through her fingers and toes.

"Hey," Ben hissed. "What did I tell you? Behave."

Claire couldn't help herself; she shook her arm to get herself out of Ben's grip.

"Quit fooling around," Ben yelled.

"Is everything alright?"

Both Ben and Claire stopped battling each other to turn around. A woman was standing behind them, worry etched all over her face.

Ben smiled, although to Claire it seemed to be more of a grimace. "Yes, we're fine, thank you. She's just scared to get a shot today."

A shot? Claire's eyes widened as she looked up at Ben. *What's a shot?*

The woman laughed and walked in front of them to hold the door open.

"Don't worry," she said. "It'll be over before you know it."

Ben said thank you to the woman and led Claire through the doors to the empty waiting room. He gripped her hand as he signed her in, he squeezed her shoulder as he sat her down in a chair, and put his arm over the back of her seat to ensure she didn't go anywhere.

"Don't cause a scene. Don't tell anybody where you live or about your old parents. Don't scream," Ben whispered fiercely just as a woman with a tired looking baby on her hip walked in.

This made Claire stop and think. She wasn't planning on screaming, but now she wondered if there was something she was supposed to be screaming about.

Claire kept fidgeting, shifting around to cross her legs or adjust the way her arms were positioned. She was sitting on the edge of her seat so she wouldn't be touching Ben's arm when she felt pressure on her bladder. She stiffened. She didn't want to have to ask Ben to go, but she couldn't hold it in.

"Um, Ben?"

He didn't hear her.

"Ben?"

"What?" he snapped.

"I have to go to the bathroom."

Ben rolled his eyes.

"Claire?" A pretty woman with short blonde hair like Claire's stood in a different doorway than the one they had come in.

"She has to go to the bathroom," Ben told her.

"Oh, no worries. It's right through that hallway." The woman pointed them in the right direction and Ben followed Claire back.

"Hurry up."

Claire grunted and went inside, grateful for the privacy. She flicked the lock on the door, turned around, and gasped.

Lily was here. She was right there, in the mirror. How did she get out of the basement?

"Why are you here?" Claire asked.

"Same reason you are."

The two girls let that statement sink in. All need to go to the bathroom was gone, and Claire reached her hand out to touch Lily's.

"Come on, they're waiting." Ben rapped three times on the door.

"Are you out?" Claire asked, ignoring Ben for a second. "For good?"

Lily shook her head.

"Neither am I."

Her hand fell from the mirror. She flushed the toilet to pretend like she went and turned the faucet on like she was washing her hands.

She threw Lily one last apologetic look before joining Ben again. He took her back out to the waiting room, and the nurse was still waiting patiently. She took them to a different part of the office.

"Okay, sweetie, I'm going to need to get your height and weight, so if you'll take off your shoes and coat for me," the nurse said and adjusted the scale to get it ready.

Bewildered, Claire used the wall as support as she slid off her shoes.

"Now just stand up here, there you go. Stand up really straight for me." The nurse was nice, and Claire liked her.

The nurse wrote something down on a clipboard that she was holding, and said, "If you'll follow me, you'll be in room two today."

Ben kept his hand on Claire's shoulder the entire time, except for when she was standing on the scale. She wanted to shake him off and tell him to get away, but she couldn't. He'd already told her a million times not to make a scene. She relented with imagining herself running away from here, rolling in the grass outside and living amongst the trees.

"Claire, you can sit right up there for me."

Claire stepped on a stool and sat down on a high table that had thin paper spread over top of it. As she sat down, the paper crinkled and ripped. Claire froze, sure the nurse was going to be mad at her for messing up her room, but the nurse didn't seem to hear or care.

The nurse started asking Ben questions and she wrote down all the answers. Claire glanced around at her surroundings while the attention was off of her. The room smelled strongly of the hand sanitizer Ben kept in Claire's kitchen downstairs and it made her scrunch her nose. The walls weren't plain like her basement's were. These walls were mostly white, but they had a stripe of blue running across the middle, and there were pictures of dancing elephants and bunny rabbits who looked like they were at the circus.

Claire was acutely aware of every little sound the paper underneath her made when she moved, so she tried to stay as still as possible. But that became hard to do when the nurse started coming after her with a bunch of tools. Claire tried to squirm away as the nurse held out a bag-looking thing with a ball on the other end.

"Claire, let the nurse do her job," Ben scolded.

So she sat still again, but the nurse did her best to console Claire. "All this is going to do is check your blood pressure. I'm going to wrap it around your arm and start squeezing this, which will make this tighten." The nurse explained everything that was happening as she did it, so Claire was a little more at ease.

"Very good, Claire. Now I have to listen to your lungs." Again, the nurse explained everything she was doing, and even let Claire listen to her own lungs when she was finished.

The nurse finished up her routine checks, writing things down the whole time, and said, "You did so well, Claire. The doctor will be in shortly to check on that nasty cut, okay?" Claire nodded and smiled at the nurse.

Claire was fascinated that the nurse was writing down so much stuff about her. She didn't know there was so much to know or that anybody cared to know it. Claire didn't even think Ben knew what her favorite book was, but this nurse met Claire for the first time today, and she cared enough to know Claire's height and weight.

But as soon as the door closed, Ben groaned. "Why do people have to be so happy all the time, it's annoying."

Claire frowned at him, but he couldn't see since he had his eyes closed and his head leaned back. Claire wanted to say, *At least she was nice to me,* but thought she would get in trouble if she did. So, she settled with humph-ing and crossing her arms to glare at the opposite wall.

They sat in silence for the few minutes it took the doctor to come in. When he did, Claire instantly liked him. He had a full beard and smiling eyes. He had glasses that were small circles perched on his nose.

"Hello, how are we doing today?" he asked.

Before Claire could answer, which she was going to do since she felt so comfortable here, Ben spoke up. "Oh, we are doing *marvelous.*" Claire could tell he was being sarcastic, but couldn't figure out if the doctor had noticed. He was still smiling, but it had faded a bit.

"Alright, well, what is the patient's name?" the doctor asked.

Ben didn't answer this time, so Claire cleared her throat and said, "Claire."

"Does Claire have a last name?"

"Uhh…"

"Bohler. It's Bohler," Ben said. "Silly, you know your own last name."

The doctor chuckled, which made Claire assume he didn't see the look Ben shot her.

The doctor rubbed his hands together. "Okay, let's do this. Claire, where does it hurt?"

Claire showed him the bite on her finger, and he took her hand. She was amazed at how soft his skin was.

"How'd this happen, Claire?" He looked up at her. He seemed genuinely concerned, and Claire didn't want to lie to him. Her words clumsily struggled to jump off her tongue for a few seconds before she looked at Ben for help.

"You don't have to be shy, Claire." Ben pressed his fingers into his eyes again. "Some animal bit her when she was playing outside. I don't know what it was; I was too far away to see."

The doctor nodded. "Well, this is nothing serious, just a small infection. I'll go get you a sample of some antibiotic cream, and I want you to put it on with a bandage for a week, okay? I'll write you a prescription too," he said. He scribbled something on a small piece of paper and handed it to Ben.

The doctor was smiling again, holding out his hand for Claire to shake. "Pleasure doing business with you."

Claire noticed that his eyes crinkled up in the corners when he smiled, and it made her feel warm inside. She was pretty sure Ben's never did that.

The doctor nodded to Ben and they followed him out of the room. Ben had to stop at the desk to do something that Claire didn't understand, but as she was standing there, her eyes barely over the edge of the counter, the other receptionist held out a small basket full of different colored suckers.

"Take your pick sweetheart." The lady smiled at her as Claire picked the red one.

"What do you say?" Ben asked, not looking up from the paper he was signing.

"Thank you."

"You are very welcome."

Claire smiled at her. She liked the doctors. Everybody was so nice.

Ben clutched her hand once again and led her out to the car. Neither of them said a word as they pulled into the pharmacy and got her prescription. Claire stared in wonder at the shelves and shelves of stuff, and almost drooled as they approached the stacks of candy by the register. But Ben just pulled her along, not feeding her curiosity.

Back in the basement, Ben spread the cream on her finger and wrapped it in a bandage. The whole time, he was muttering to himself. "So close, the damn doctor probably knew what was going on. I knew we shouldn't have done that, your finger would've gotten better on its own. That doctor needed to mind his own business. If we got caught it would've been your fault."

Claire so badly wanted to tell Ben, *This is your fault. You're keeping me here when there's a whole world out there.* She kept her mouth shut, though. Ben was the one who taught her how to be respectful, but here he was being rude.

He threw the bandages and the tube of cream on the counter and stormed upstairs.

"As usual," Claire said. She sighed and glanced around her basement. "This is smaller than it used to be. The walls are closer."

Claire stood up and walked around. It only took her three strides to reach the bathroom, then three more to reach the couch. Four strides to get to her bedroom, then two to get to the stairs.

"It's so small." She pushed her hands out to either side of her. She was feeling claustrophobic, but didn't have the word to describe it. "Help!"

The walls were closing in on her.

"You can't get out," Lily shouted from the bathroom.

"You're starting to sound a lot like Mailman," Claire yelled back. That shut Lily right up.

The air was getting harder to breathe, and Claire's head was starting to pound.

"I want to get out," she shouted.

The walls stopped moving in.

"I need to get out."

The walls bounced back to their original position.

"I have to get out," she whispered.

Ben had to miss a day of work to take Claire to the doctor, and he was even shorter on cash now that he had to buy her prescription.

Ben pummeled the steering wheel, accidentally honking the horn. He pulled into the gas station parking lot and braced himself for a long day; he had to make up for the time he'd missed.

Henry was finishing up his shift when Ben arrived, but their times overlapped about an hour, so Ben was stuck with cleaning around again.

"Man, you're wound up so tight, you look like you're about to explode. How long you working today?" Henry asked.

"Till eight."

Henry whistled through his teeth. "So that's why I couldn't get another shift in today? Come on man, we all need the money."

Ben sighed. "It's complicated. I don't have anything to fall back on. I'm literally running on my last fifty dollars. I need this next paycheck, and I need it to be loaded."

Henry rolled his eyes. "So do I. You can't take up all the shifts just because you think you're above everyone else."

"I'm not trying to start any trouble," Ben said, honestly not sure why Henry was so angry. "I'm just trying to keep myself alive."

"It's not like you have a family to provide for. I have a girlfriend. And a kid on the way."

Ben was shocked. He never would've thought someone would want to have a baby with the brute. "Oh, I didn't know." Ben had to shove down his rising anger. He had a child to provide for too, but it wasn't like he could tell Henry that.

"Of course you didn't. You're so self-absorbed you don't realize that other people have problems too. Other people need money, Ben, so get over yourself."

Ben kept his mouth shut. There were so many things he could've said, but he didn't want to get beaten on by the man.

Henry craned his neck to look around the store. He dropped his voice. "Just take some from the register. Leave the shifts open for the rest of us."

Ben was appalled. "I can't do that."

Henry rolled his eyes again. "I do it all the time. You really think they watch us that closely over here? They have better things to worry about." He nodded towards the camera above the counter.

Ben was still wary, but he was considering it at this point. He had no other choice. Henry left and the customers were few and far between. The sun dropped lower and lower in the sky, until

Ben couldn't see outside anymore, and only his reflection stared back. His shift was almost over, so he knew it was now or never.

He opened the register and flipped through the bills, pretending like he was counting. He kept glancing up at the fish eyed camera that seemed to be peering into his mind and reading his thoughts. His heart jumped up to his throat as he pretended to drop the stack of bills. He shot one last look at the camera and bent down to sweep up the money. Ben crumpled some bills in his hand and gathered the others into a pile, which he replaced in the register. He kept his hand loose and casual, but made sure the stolen bills didn't fall out. Ben desperately shut down the store and didn't even breathe until he was back in his car.

His heart was still throwing itself against the walls his ribs created to hold it in place, but Ben was already speeding away.

Chapter Thirteen

The basement now, in Claire's opinion, was drab, boring, and way too confining. Even in the yard, she had more room than this. She hardly realized it, but she was slouching now, like the walls and ceiling really were closing in and she needed to make herself fit.

"Why is Ben keeping me here when the whole world is just outside?" Claire asked Tommy. She hadn't thought she would ever see her friend again, but he was obviously as lonely as she was, since he continued to visit her every day.

"This basement must be huge for you. That's probably why you keep coming back. Your house is too small, so one day you went exploring and found this giant new world, which also happens to have food." Claire pushed another cracker towards him. "How did you escape? Isn't there someone back home that wants you to stay with them?"

As if her words made Tommy remember, he turned and ran away. Claire sighed.

She heard the click of the handle turning above.

"Breakfast is here," Ben declared. He was in a much better mood than before, but he still wasn't being his normal self. Claire grunted. She was still annoyed with him.

"Okay, Mrs. Grumpy pants, maybe cinnamon rolls can cheer you up."

Claire raised the corners of her mouth to what she believed could pass as a smile. She didn't want to be down here anymore. She wanted to be out in nature, at the doctor's, anywhere but down in this cellar. At this point, she would even consider going back to the yard if she was given the option.

"Alright then. I'm going to work. See you later." Ben waved goodbye from the stairs, not bothering to kiss her goodbye, but he hadn't done so in months.

Claire had a suspicion about Ben when he left every day. She ran over to the stairs and peeked around the wall, just as Ben was reaching the top.

Ben turned the handle and pushed the door open with no hesitation.

"I was right," Claire whispered. Whenever Ben would leave, as soon as the door was closed, Claire could hear a faint little *click,* so she assumed he was locking it. But if he locked the door when he came *down*stairs, he would need a key to get back out.

She had just watched Ben open the basement door from the inside without using a key for the second week in a row. That had to mean that he never locked it when he came downstairs.

"This is perfect."

Claire looked at the half eaten cracker on the floor, and a plan started to formulate in her mind.

Ben thought he would win father of the year with the treat he bought for Claire. He was able to splurge a little bit and buy her cinnamon rolls, but she was acting strange. He chalked it up to her just being tired; he couldn't dwell on it for too long. He had something more concerning waiting for him at work.

The manager of the gas station, Mrs. Johnson, was leaning against the counter, head bent in conversation with Henry.

When Ben walked in, they both stopped talking. Mrs. Johnson straightened up and cleared her throat.

"Ben, would you come into the back room with me please?" she said, waving for Ben to follow. The bells above the door hadn't even stopped jingling yet. Ben shot a questioning—and slightly worried—look at Henry, but he wouldn't meet Ben's eyes.

"What's going on?" Ben asked as soon as they were in the back.

Mrs. Johnson folded her hands in front of herself. "We received an anonymous tip to check the cameras from yesterday, so we obliged. Although there was no sound, we very clearly saw you pocket some money from the register. This is completely unacceptable, and with your recent actions—not showing up for your shifts, arriving late, leaving early—leads us to the only practical solution. I'm sorry, but we're going to have to let you go."

Ben opened and closed his mouth and stuttered, unable to defend himself.

"Here's this." She held out a slip of paper. "Your paycheck from the last three days you worked." Ben knew they were all the same size, but this check seemed too small, too thin. He scanned it, hoping that it was strong enough to hold a solid amount of money, but the dollar amount scrawled in pen proved otherwise.

Mrs. Johnson ducked her head as she passed Ben on the way out of the breakroom. Ben followed soon after and made eye contact with Henry, who averted his gaze just as quickly. He was wiping the counter. With a dirty rag.

"Anonymous tip," Ben spit out as he passed him.

What did I ever do to him? Ben thought as he stormed out to the car. *I took a shift away from him? Oh boohoo. He's always complaining about not wanting to work, but the moment someone takes it away from him...*

Ben jabbed his keys into the ignition and squealed out of the parking lot into the road. At a stop sign, he stared at the numbers on the piece of paper. It wasn't even two hundred dollars. Ben got home but couldn't bring himself to go visit Claire. His anger had dissipated and was replaced with a sinking fear in his stomach.

"What the hell am I gonna do?"

"You know Tommy, right?" Claire asked Lily, who was trapped in the mirror like how Claire was stuck in the basement.

Lily nodded.

"He's gonna help me get out of here." Claire was bouncing up and down on the balls of her feet.

Lily looked confused. "How is that going to work?"

Claire was talking so fast out of sheer excitement that her words were stumbling over each other. "I'm going to put him in the bathtub and when Ben comes and give me breakfast, I'm going to beg that he gets him out. Ben will go into the bathroom and I'll close the door behind him, put a chair under the handle—someone did that in one of my books. I'll lock the door, then, I'll run."

A smile cracked through Lily's somber expression. "If you get out, that means I'll be out too."

Claire nodded enthusiastically. "It's perfect."

"What if Tommy bites you again?"

Claire bent down and rummaged through the cabinets under the sink. She popped up again, with a bucket in hand. "I'll use this. I'll put it over him and scoop him up."

But Lily, being her typical self, looked wary. "If you do this, and it doesn't work, Ben's going to kill you."

"That's why it has to work the first time."

Lily bit her fingernails.

"Don't worry. I'm going to get us both out," Claire assured her.

The next day, Tommy showed up as usual. Claire fed him a cracker and told him, "I'm going to need your help later."

Claire tested the theory of the chair under the doorknob. She grabbed a kitchen chair and dragged it across the tiles to the closed bathroom door. She wedged it underneath and tried to move the handle, but it wouldn't budge. She also tried the lock on the door. Ben completely forgot about that punishment the day after he installed it. She smirked. Everything was falling into place.

She practiced getting the chair under the knob so she could do it quickly when the time arrived. She pretended like she was capturing Tommy in the bucket by using the stuffed bear Ben got her so long ago. Claire jogged a couple laps around the basement, hoping to build up some muscles in case she had to run a long way.

Finally, the day arrived. She had been planning this moment for a week now, and her heart wouldn't stop pounding.

Eight o'clock rolled around, but Ben didn't show.

"Maybe he's going into work late," Claire said.

But he never came down to give her breakfast.

"He's probably at work now, he'll come down for dinner."

All day, Claire pumped herself up for the big escape, making last minute preparations and running around the basement. But Ben didn't come downstairs.

"No big deal." There were some times when he wouldn't come down at all. This was just one of those days.

But the entire next week, Ben never opened the door. He was nowhere to be found, and Claire was getting worried. She had marked off eight days on her calendar and he still hadn't brought down more food. She was almost out, and could barely afford to give Tommy his daily cracker.

Ben skirted his eyes over the basement door. He hadn't been down there in days. He couldn't muster the courage to tell Claire that he lost his job.

He was just about to go out again to try and find work, but he had to look more presentable. He was searching for better clothes to wear, but couldn't find any that didn't smell like a dumpster. Ben only had a little less than a hundred dollars to keep himself alive at this point, so he couldn't afford to waste water with showers or washing clothes.

Ben straightened up and was glad that he couldn't see himself in the mirror. He couldn't afford electricity either. The lights were off, so all he saw was a shadow of a man staring back at him.

"You disgust me."

He haphazardly put together an outfit that smelled the best and left the house to find a job. Somehow, though, he found himself in front of a liquor store, and the next thing he knew, he was carrying a six pack. He didn't even wait until he was home to start downing the beer.

It was already starting to get dark outside, which didn't coincide well with Ben's slight intoxication. He basically fell into his house and ran into nearly everything in his path. He didn't turn on the lights; not because of the electricity, but because he really didn't want to have to see himself right now. He crumpled onto the couch and stared at the blank TV screen. Ben kept glancing over at the basement door. He knew what he had to do, he just had to be brave enough to follow through with it.

On the tenth day without Ben showing, Claire had eaten all the food, and was guzzling water to try and trick her stomach into being full. She had to spend the day hunched over in a ball because her stomach kept pinching her. Two times already she had run to the bathroom to be sick, only to dry heave until her eyes were about to pop out of her head.

She definitely noticed she wasn't as tolerant to hunger as she used to be. Not like when she was in the yard. Curled up on the couch with her hands clutching her stomach, Claire was transported back to more than two years ago, when she was dirty and starving all the time.

Claire didn't understand how she ever lived that life. She could only move a couple feet from her pole, and she couldn't even fully stand up until Ben brought her down here.

She was torn between her brain, which was telling her to leave this basement and get a real life, and her heart, who said to stay with the man who rescued her from her horrible old situation.

"This isn't rescue," Claire mumbled.

"Take it or leave it, this is the best you're going to get."

Claire froze. She would know that voice anywhere. She opened one eye to see her imaginary tormentor standing in front of her.

"Long time no see," Mailman sneered.

"Go away." Claire turned her face into the armrest on the couch. This time, the voice changed tones. "I can't. Just like you."

Claire snapped her head up, ignoring the pangs in her stomach. Lily now stood before her, out of the mirror, and in Mailman's place.

"Lily? How'd you—"

"You can't escape. You can't get out. He'll never let you leave."

"Where'd Mailman go?"

"I'm him. And so are you. Now listen, no matter what you do, Ben will stop you. He's not going to let you go that easily."

Claire shook her head. "No. I can escape. I can."

Lily's eyes were swimming in sympathy, then, suddenly, they were flaming with anger. Lily morphed into Mailman, his dark figure looming over Claire, contrasting with Lily's feeble form.

"Don't you see?" Mailman spit out. "Ben doesn't care about you anymore. He's gone. He's already sick of your existence, so he just picked up and left. Even if he does come back down, you won't be able to get out, you're too stupid—"

"Shut up."

Mailman stopped dead in the middle of his sentence. Claire could feel his hatred towards her radiating off of him like a heater.

"You ignorant little—"

"I said shut up. Stop talking."

Claire couldn't see the features on his face, but if she could, she knew he'd be gaping at her right now.

"Now listen," she mocked. "I want you to disappear back to wherever you go. Okay? I *will* get out. I don't care what you think. I'm done listening to you."

And just like that, Mailman was gone, without a trace. Claire was sad Lily left too; despite her harsh words, Claire considered the two of them to be friends, they were so similar.

Claire allowed herself to wallow in self-pity for only a short time longer, then forced herself to stand and get ready for bed. She went to the bathroom, but as soon as she stepped foot inside, a sharp pain stabbed her side, and she had to bend over to console it before it consumed her whole body. The pain ebbed and her stomach growled.

She straightened up, her hand resting just above her hip—in case her stomach decided to defy her again. Claire looked in the mirror for Lily, but no one was there. The only person standing in the mirror was Claire.

Her brow scrunched in confusion.

"Lily?" she asked. But no one responded.

Claire touched the reflective surface. The other Claire did the same. Both of the Claires stuck their tongue out. Both Claires wiggled their eyebrows and pulled their lips out to make a funny face. Both Claires watched each other's faces fall and back away from the mirror. Both Claires said goodbye to Lily, but neither knew if she could hear them.

Claire didn't bother brushing her teeth. She shuffled into her bedroom and laid down on top of the covers. She was already wearing sweatpants, so she didn't change her clothes.

She laid in that position for a long time. She didn't know if she fell asleep or if she just imagined that she did, but either way, when she looked at the clock, it said eleven fifty. She sighed and flung her head back into the pillow.

"Claire? Are you awake?"

She lifted her head and squinted in the dark to see Ben standing in the doorway of her room. So that's what had woken her up.

"I, uh, I need to talk to you, sweetie."

Claire mumbled something incoherent into her pillow.

Ben whispered even quieter, "Please."

The raw emotion in his voice made Claire raise her eyes to see if he was serious, and he was, so she sat up in her bed.

Ben didn't turn the light on, but he came to sit on the side of her bed anyways. From the moment he sat down, Claire could smell the alcohol on his breath. She knew that scent far too well.

Ben laughed, but nothing was funny. "This is so stupid. But I think I need to explain myself to you, why I've been such an asshole recently." He sighed and rubbed the sides of his head. "Let me start at the beginning?"

Claire nodded, but she didn't think he could see her in the dark.

"Okay, actually, about ten days ago, I lost my job. I stole from the register and couldn't afford any food for you, because I had to stay alive first, otherwise I couldn't take care of you. Heh." Ben rubbed the back of his neck. "Anyways, my wife, Amy, and my daughter—" Ben gulped. "My daughter, Claire, they disappeared. I don't know why they left. One day, I came home from work, and they were...they were gone." He was choked up, and Claire wanted to pat his hand or his shoulder, to show him that she was sympathetic, but if he wouldn't care for her, she wouldn't care for him.

"They left some of the bigger furniture at our house, but they took most of their stuff with them. Amy and I, we had our troubles, but I always loved her enough to push through, to make it work— for Claire. And I thought that she would do the same, but I guess...I was wrong."

Ben balled his hands into fists, and his voice increased in volume. Claire knew where this was going.

Sure enough, Ben punched her mattress.

There it is, she thought.

"She's a cruel woman. She just picks up and leaves with no warning or anything, not even a note. She's just—and then she has the *audacity* to come back and take all her stuff."

Claire didn't say a word, just let him rant, because if she said something, he might come after her instead of the bed.

"After she took everything, she had another person leave a message on my phone saying that I wasn't allowed to follow her. But I still looked for her. I asked her old friends, our neighbors. I talked to the people at the stores she shopped at, I figured out who Claire's old friends were and asked them.

"No one knew where they had gone. I had to sell our beautiful two story home because I couldn't keep up on the payments. Amy's job was the one that brought in all the cash." Ben scowled. "So I had to buy this dump, but I managed to salvage most of the furniture from the old house—I mean, I went back and got it before the realtor kicked me out. I had to drag it here—strapped it to the roof of my car or took it apart and threw it in the trunk—in like, four trips back and forth. I was surprised to get this house— with a finished basement—at such a cheap price, but then I discovered that it had a rat infestation." Ben shuddered, but Claire thought of Tommy. "I got an exterminator to come in here and get rid of them all, and I haven't seen one since, so I guess it worked."

Is that why you're so lonely, Tommy? Claire thought. *Did Ben kill your whole family? Did he ruin your life too?*

Ben sighed again and rubbed his hand down his neck. "That's when I found you. You were huddled in a corner in some backyard, but I knew you were mine. I knew you were the one who was going to fill the gaping hole in my heart. I kept you fed and warm. And then, when the right opportunity came around, I took you. I never thought you'd be as close as you were, though. Just a quick jog through the woods.

"You and I, we've had a happy life together, I'd say. I tried to get Amy to come back and be your mom, so all of us could start over and we could be a family again. But she wasn't interested. And I couldn't let you outside because there would always be someone waiting to take you away. I wasn't about to have another daughter be taken away from me. You're *mine.*" Ben had reached behind Claire and was smoothing her hair, and it was all she could do not to puke. He was so repulsive. His greasy hair, the alcohol on his breath, and his justification for taking away what little childhood she could have had, everything was gross. But she was also disgusted with herself for allowing him to take her, and not arguing when he locked her down here.

Ben dropped his hand. "Then Amy filed for divorce. Two years of no contact whatsoever, and she wants a divorce. At that point, you'd been with me for a year, and you were making such good progress, I didn't want to give you up. But I went to court anyways, we got a formal divorce, and that *monster* managed to convince the judge to give her sole custody of Claire. *My* daughter. But what they didn't know was that I had you. They could take away one daughter, but I still had you here with me." Ben laughed. "And that idiot smirked at me. She walked away, her shoulders back, standing tall, and I wanted so badly to laugh in her face. Amy thought she had won, but really, I did. Because I had you. "

Claire shuddered. Ben was creepy. She didn't want to be near him anymore. She wanted to leave.

"Amy said I was a terrible father. She said I wasn't good with kids, and that she would never understand why she chose me to have a baby with. She said that my father must've had a horrible influence on me if I treated my own child like that. At the time, I could kind of see where she was coming from. But that's why I wanted her here with us now, to show her that I am capable of being a good dad. I've treated you so well.

"Amy walked out of the courtroom and out of my life. I thought she would come with social services, or the police, or the judge himself, and knock down my door to take you too, because she never wanted me to be happy. I was all prepared for that, but they never came. She never came."

Ben began to tear up, and a small place in Claire's heart opened up for him. As tough as she was trying to be, her kindness was fighting its way through.

He tried to speak in between sniffles and sobs that choked his words. "My own daughter was ripped out of my life, and I had no way to stop it. I don't know what I would've done if I never found you. But you're mine now, Claire. So amazing and smart. And I helped you become this way."

Ben turned to her again, and even in the dark, Claire could see his eyes glistening with tears. She kicked herself internally for doing so, but she put her hand on top of his. He smiled. Claire frowned. His hand was rough and scaly and not at all like the soft, warm, loving Ben that she trusted not so long ago.

Ben spoke, but Claire could barely hear. "I'm so lucky to have you." He leaned forward to kiss her forehead and despite any sympathy she felt, the place his lips touched left a searing burn on her skin. One of his tears dropped onto her cheek, and Claire had to physically restrain herself so she wouldn't wipe it away.

Claire thought Ben would leave, but he stayed, patting her hand that was resting on top of his. She regretted ever trying to comfort him at all.

"Well, goodnight, Claire," Ben said. He crumbled down onto the floor and fell asleep.

Claire stared at him for a while, juggling his story back and forth. Did she stay with him because he had no one left, or did she go through with her original plan and give herself the life she deserved?

There seemed to be an obvious answer, but Claire's conscience was telling her otherwise.

She sighed and settled down into bed.

"What do I do?" she asked the air.

The next morning, Ben was no longer on her floor. She didn't know when he dragged himself upstairs, but she was glad he left.

Claire's stomach growled. She put her hand over her bellybutton and pressed in to shush it.

"Claire, wake up. Come get breakfast," Ben shouted from the kitchen, presumably.

"Not today, I guess," Claire sighed. She needed to be awake before Ben gave her breakfast, because she needed to find Tommy and put him in the tub. She groaned as she sat up and forced herself out from under the warm covers. She yawned and scratched her head as she went out into the chilly air of the basement. As much as she wanted to stay away from Ben, he had food now, and the starving animal in her stomach was propelling her forward.

"Rise and shine," Ben exclaimed, suspiciously happy considering his mood the night before.

Claire grunted.

Ben laughed heartily. "There's that grumpy teenager we all know is waiting inside you."

Claire sat at the table and let Ben serve her. He slid a bowl of cereal towards her, with the dust from the end of the bag resting on top. "Eat up."

When the first bite touched her lips, it tasted like heaven. Even though the cereal was obviously stale and old, it was the only food she had eaten in days. She finished and slurped the rest of the milk up.

"Is there more?"

"A little bit, yeah." Ben laughed again.

Claire squinted at his back. *Why are you so happy?*

Ben poured another bowl of cereal—again the end of an old box he's probably had in his cupboard forever—and hovered it over her. Claire reached for it, but Ben said, "Ah, ah, ah, what do you say?"

"Thanks," she mumbled, and snatched the food out of his hands. She devoured that as well, but Ben didn't have anything else for her.

At one point during her breakfast feast, Ben made a comment that really got under Claire's skin: "Did you know you were completely out of food?"

Yeah, I noticed, thanks for the concern.

When Claire was semi-full, a feeling she didn't know if she'd experience again, Ben washed the dishes for her, "For being such a bad person recently." He put a couple granola bars, a bag of chips, and a candy bar on the counter so she would have something else to eat later.

As usual, Ben didn't stick around too long. He went upstairs— Claire couldn't even imagine where he went now that he lost his job—leaving her alone again.

She refused to play with any of the toys Ben got her, so she was bored all day. She kept checking to see if Lily was back, but she never made an appearance. And, as hard as she tried to resist, her hunger won out. She didn't want to eat the food he gave her, but it was all she would have for a while, she assumed. Soon, the counter was littered with wrappers. She didn't bother throwing them away.

Claire did have some resolve, though. She didn't eat the candy bar. At least, not the whole thing. She allowed herself a few bites, then dropped it on the floor. Being slobby was her way of being defiant.

Late that night, when Claire was in bed, she felt a sense that something was missing.

"Tommy." He didn't make his daily visit.

Claire crawled out from under the covers, hoping that he just decided to wait until later. She checked under all the cabinets in the kitchen, then even looked under the couch and in her room. She'd never seen Tommy leave the tiles, but that doesn't mean he wouldn't start now.

"Tommy," she whispered. "Tommy."

Claire crawled on her hands and knees around the kitchen, searching for her friend, and that's when she saw it.

"No."

She covered her mouth and tears welled in her eyes.

"Tommy," she cried.

Tommy, her only friend now that Lily was gone, was lying motionless on his side next to the chocolate bar.

Claire wrapped her hand around Tommy. She wasn't afraid to pick him up this time; she knew he couldn't bite her. She held her friend close to her chest and let her tears fall freely.

She made herself stop grieving after a couple of minutes. If she had any doubts about escaping, Tommy's death pushed them out of her head.

"I'm not going to die down here," she declared. "I have a life to live, and Ben won't ever let me leave."

Tommy lived a big part of his life with Claire, and he died down in the basement. Claire didn't want the same to happen to herself. His death emphasized her inevitable peril if she stayed. Claire stood up, his body cradled in her arms, and laid him down, gently, into the tub.

"I'm going to escape. I'm going to get out of here."

Chapter Fourteen

Claire woke up at five that morning, and couldn't fall back asleep. As much as she hated to admit it, her nerves were getting to her. She forced herself out of bed, shook out her arms and legs, and got dressed. She put on her most comfortable pair of jeans, a long sleeved shirt, and a coat. If Ben asked why she was wearing a coat inside, she'd simply shrug and say it was cold. Claire also hid by the stairs an unused hat and pair of gloves that she found stashed somewhere in her closet—the closet. No. It wasn't hers anymore.

Claire took a deep breath. "This is it."

She calmly wandered around the basement, her house for the past two years. She really didn't like it here, but she knew the time wasn't completely wasted. She learned how to walk, how to wash herself, and how to use a toilet. She learned how make her own meals, how to be polite and respectful, and how to read. Claire could wash dishes, form sentences, and have her own thoughts and ideas. She had a home.

Each and every piece of furniture downstairs with her received a thoughtful pat and a thank you. She lingered in the bathroom, holding her fingers to the mirror one last time, and said goodbye to Lily once again. As one final preparation, Claire pulled a chair out from under the table and positioned it closer to the bathroom door.

When Claire had made her rounds, she sat in the chair she always chose in the kitchen—hopefully for the last time. A wave of remorse and regret poured over her, and she almost changed her mind about leaving. There was no place for her to go. She had nowhere to sleep, nowhere to live. She wouldn't have any food or water. What was she thinking?

"No," she said. "Someone will find you and take you in."

"Would that be such a good thing? I mean, look at what happened last time," Claire argued with herself.

"Maybe the doctor will help you. Or the nurse, or the lady who gave you the sucker. Any place, any*one*, is better than this."

All of her doubts were followed up by reason, and Claire sunk into her chair. She was slumped in her seat, thinking through the plan over and over again.

Finally, the door opened. Claire had begun to think that Ben wasn't going to come down again, and she couldn't figure out if she was relieved or disappointed.

"This is nice, you're up early today," Ben said. "It's not even seven yet."

Ben sat and ate breakfast with Claire—another bowl of cereal. But this time, at least, it was a brand new box, and she had three full bowls. Ben was chipper, chatting away about anything and everything. But Claire didn't say a word. She could hardly even hear what Ben was saying over the drumbeat of her heart and the thoughts that were rushing through her mind like a roaring river.

"Excuse me," Claire mumbled as soon as she finished eating. She stood up and walked stiffly to the bathroom. She didn't close the door behind her, like she usually did, and she wondered if Ben noticed and was suspicious.

"Bye, Claire, I'm gonna go."

What? No.

Claire turned to see Ben beginning to climb the stairs. Her breathing grew heavy as he neared the top.

Now or never.

Her shrill scream pierced the otherwise quiet basement. "What? Claire?"

She barely heard Ben's concern and his footsteps running towards her over her own voice.

"Hey, stop! What's wrong? Are you hurt?"

Anxiety and fear clogging her throat, Claire stopped screaming and repeatedly pointed to the tub. He was still standing in the doorway. She needed him to be farther in.

Claire positioned herself on the other side of Ben, so he had no choice but to go into the bathroom. Suddenly, her voice was freed. "Get it out Ben it's a rat get it out it's so gross why is it here get it out please!" Everything rushed out at once, but it did the job. Ben calmed her down, or so he thought, by bending down and reassuring her.

"I'll get it out, it'll be okay. I don't know how a rat managed to climb into the tub, though. But, hey, don't worry about it, I'll get it."

A pang of guilt sliced Claire's heart. He really did care about her, it was just for the wrong reasons. She took a step back as Ben turned towards the tub. Another step and she was out of the bathroom. Ben peered over the side of the tub. Claire slowly dragged the chair she got out earlier in front of the door. Blood pounded in her ears and her heart jumped from her chest and into her throat. Ben crouched down to grab Tommy.

Claire threw door shut with all of her might and shoved the chair underneath the handle.

"Hey!" Ben yelled from inside.

Claire fumbled with the lock, her fingers shaking badly, but it clicked into place.

She didn't run away at first. Claire stood where she was, her feet rooted to the ground, and watched in horror as the handle jiggled up and down. She held her breath; what if the chair wouldn't hold? What if the lock breaks? What if Ben comes storming out here and gives her the worst beating of her life? What if he kills her?

But none of that happened.

Ben screamed unintelligibly from the bathroom. The door was shaking and the chair was bobbing at his strength. But the door was solid. It held.

"Now you know how I feel," Claire screamed back at him. She paused, listening to Ben's endless shouts punctuated by her own heaving breaths.

Calm down, she told herself.

"Ben?" she called when she was ready. "I'm sorry. I know you love me. I know you want me to be your daughter, but I can't. Not like this. Not at all. I was happy down here for a while. But now I know things. Things you taught me. You've done so much for me, more than I ever could've hoped for. But I have to leave."

She didn't know if he heard, but she didn't care. Her words unbolted her feet, and she flew.

She took the stairs two at a time, her knees knocking together at the awkward motion.

The door is going to be locked. I won't be able to get out.

The bitter words rolled around on her tongue and made her feel sick.

Claire basically jumped onto the handle, and the door fell through. Claire screamed as she fell to the ground. She caught herself with her hands sticking out in front of her, and fell hard on her wrists. She got her bearings, stood up, and whipped her head around.

"Which way, where do I go?" she whined. She started to run away, but remembered the door. She pushed the basement door closed behind her, for the first time hearing it from this side rather than from all the way below. She searched for the lock that kept her contained all these months, and twisted it. She backed away.

"Claire," Ben moaned. He had protested loudly throughout her whole speech, beating and kicking the door, yelling about how she was going to be in so much trouble when he got out of here, but he had still heard everything she had to say. When her uneven gait flew away, Ben quieted down. He had run out of steam.

"Claire," he shouted. "What did I do wrong?" He sank to his knees and didn't even care when his head cracked on the tile floor. His chest was heaving with sobs and he repeatedly banged his fists onto the floor. "Come back."

Ben's voice was wretched and raggedy, but there was nothing he could do. He was stuck in this bathroom whether he liked it or not.

He sat back on his knees and relished in the physical ache that the bump on his head brought because it distracted him from his heartache. He heaved himself up to a standing position and leaned against the counter to stare at himself in the mirror. He tried to imagine what Claire saw when she looked at him, because all he could see was a man. A defeated man, who, although always putting others ahead of himself, no one appreciated.

"I did everything right," he rasped. "I don't deserve this." He punched the mirror with a shout and his knuckles split open. Small drops of blood were on the mirror and splattered onto the counter. That's when he transformed in front of his own eyes. His hair wild, eyes crazy. "I'm a monster," he said, without remorse.

"Let me out, get me out of here!" But he didn't know if he was talking about the bathroom or his own mind. He tugged at his hair before pummeling the bathroom door again. He screamed until he lost his voice.

"This isn't real, this isn't real," she said, the words spilling out in a breathless whisper. She never thought about what she would do if her plan actually worked.

"Where do I go?" she yelled. Which way did they go when Ben took her to the doctors? She took off running blindly in one direction, since her eyes had yet to adjust to the sun's glare. Claire stumbled around, passing a couch, a TV, and finally. A door.

"Please, please, please," she begged. She ripped it open, but it was just a bedroom.

"Noooo," she moaned. She ran back the way she just came. "There has to be a way out. There *has* to be!"

Claire passed the basement door again. She half expected it to fly off its hinges and for Ben to explode out, but that didn't happen. She could still faintly hear Ben shouting from below.

She sprinted away, through a kitchen with its own table and chairs, not having to run far before another door appeared.

"C'mon, please." She yanked it open, and a blast of natural light smacked her in the face. Blinded and confused, Claire tripped out into the world.

It was like she was being born again. She forgot how to walk, how to speak. She fell to her knees and babbled, tears streaming down her face as though she was a newborn, crying because she was *free*. Trapped, for over two years, and finally, she was *free*. Claire crawled on the cement and it scraped her palms and her knees but she didn't care. She crawled away from the house that kept her captive for so long, only turning back once.

When Claire reached the sidewalk, she pushed herself to her feet. She stared at Ben's house, no longer hers anymore. Her gaze fell over the old car that drove her to the doctors and the door she just came out of. Claire took a deep, shuddering breath, and that was when she knew that she made the right choice.

Claire barely felt her feet hit the ground as she ran away. She heard the slap of her shoes against the pavement, then the *squish* once she reached the grass. Claire looked down and saw that her hands were empty. She had nothing with her.

"The trees," she panted. "I have to get…to the trees."

At any moment, the door to Ben's house could fly open, and a very angry Ben could come after her. Claire staggered to the cover of the trees so she could hide if she needed to. As soon as she stepped foot inside of the woods, everything changed.

The sun disappeared, leaving only elongated shadows in its wake. Thin strips of sunlight were scattered over the ground, intermixed with dark patches left by the branches and leaves who were all desperately trying to impress the sun by being the greenest.

She missed the smell of the outdoors. Inside, her nose was only filled with the cleaner she used to wash dishes and the soap she used to wash her hands. Claire paused, safe under the guard of the trees, and let her senses be overwhelmed with everything.

The scent of grass that hadn't been cut in a while mixed with dirt wafted up to her nose. Crisp, clean winter air flowed through her nostrils and down her throat, and she tracked its movement into her lungs with ease. Claire felt a scratchy wooden tree trunk. She closed her eyes and touched every knot, every turn of the wood, like she was reading Braille. Claire was back in her element; this is where she should be, not holed up inside a maniac's house.

She continued walking, any potential danger she might be in pushed out of her thoughts for the time being. Tall grass that reached past her ankles caressed her as she walked by.

"Don't worry, I'll be back," Claire said, but she didn't know why she didn't just stay at that moment. Maybe it was because she was still too close to Ben, maybe it was because she knew there was something waiting for her up ahead.

Claire made it a point to step over patches of weeds and plants, so she wouldn't disturb their peaceful living. She had to climb over and under some branches and logs, ripping and scratching her clothes and skin in the process, but she didn't mind. She was so blissful having escaped that nothing out here could faze her.

Out of nowhere a swarm of bugs attacked Claire's head. She swatted at them, spitting and closing her eyes to avoid accidentally eating them or having them crawl inside, and in the process, her foot got caught on a root. She stumbled backwards, crying out as she fell, then again as she hit the ground. She spit again for good measure and groaned.

"Stupid bugs. What did I ever do to you?"

The bugs snapped Claire out of her dreamy state. She stood again and brushed her hair out of her face to clear her eyes. She picked off big clumps of dirt and leaves that were stuck on her clothes.

In the midst of the attack, Claire fell over onto a big bush, squashing it, revealing what was on the other side. Standing again, Claire could now clearly see a rusty old chain link fence that was barely standing up anymore, only about a hundred feet away.

Her breath hitched in her throat.

"The light's turned on," she whispered, stunned.

The light pole that stood, unwavering, unilluminated, for all of Claire's years in the yard, was now shining brightly, competing with the sun that was gradually climbing the sky.

Then Claire scanned the house. It looked the same as it did all those years ago: dingy, dirty, and so ready to fall apart that it seemed like it would crumble if the wind blew.

"Maybe I'll be like the boy in that book. Brian and Shannon might be happy to have me back."

From this distance, Claire couldn't tell if anything else had changed, but she was about to find out. Against her will—or maybe fulfilling her deepest wishes—Claire picked up her pace towards her old yard.

Up close, the house looked worse than it did from the edge of the woods. Maybe it always was this way, but Claire had never seen it from this side.

She was standing on the sidewalk—barely two slabs of cement held together by some dirt—in front of Brian and Shannon's house. The white panels looked even drabber from this angle. They were grimy and yellowing, and Claire couldn't believe—after all this time, saving so much money without having to feed her—that Brian and Shannon couldn't have improved their style of living at all.

Claire gulped as her heart beat out of her chest for the second time that day.

"They probably don't even live here anymore. Shannon always said they were going to buy a new house. Maybe that's why it looks so bad," Claire said to the empty front yard. "But they're not gone. The light's on in the back. Maybe there are new people who live here. Maybe..." Claire wrung her hands. "I won't find out unless I go knock though, right?" She looked around for confirmation. "Yeah, I'll go knock. No one's going to answer. Or if they do, it won't be Brian or Shannon, no. They're long gone."

Claire was talking to herself the whole time it took her to ascend the driveway and step onto the front porch.

"Just knock on the door, what's the worst that could happen?"

Before she could comprehend what she was doing, her knuckles were rapping on the faded red door. She put her hands behind her back and stared straight ahead.

"See, no one's home. But at least you tried—"

The door swung open.

Claire gagged. A waterfall of horrid smells rushed at her, making her bend over in shock. The scent of beer—stale, fresh, and regurgitated—hit her like a truck, and she almost emptied her stomach onto the feet of the man standing in the open doorway.

"Well, well, well, what do we have here?" Brian said.

Claire straightened up at the sound of his voice. He looked exactly the same, save for the larger gut, less hair, and the overgrown, scraggly beard.

"No." Claire took a step backwards. But Brian wouldn't let her get away a second time. He grabbed her roughly by the arm and yanked her into the putrid house.

"No!" Claire screamed, but the door had already locked behind them.

"Who is it?" Shannon's voice was raspier and deeper, and it grated in Claire's ears like gravel in a garbage disposal.

"Our stupid, filthy brat came crawling back," Brian jeered. "And she got a makeover."

Brian shoved Claire to the ground and stood over her cowering figure. He bent his face down close to hers, and she could smell the alcohol on his breath. "I knew you couldn't stay away for long."

Claire desperately wanted to shove him backwards and run out the door—according to his breath, he was drunk enough that a fly could knock him over—but old habits die hard, and Claire found herself shrinking into a ball on her side to deflect the worst of his hits.

Shannon came around the corner, her voice a knife stabbing into Claire's brain. "I've missed starving you. Where've you been?" Her voice was dripping with fake sympathy, and Claire just wanted Brian to hit her, because then maybe he would make her furious enough to stand up for herself.

What're you doing? Claire screamed at herself. *Get up and run!*

But her body wouldn't listen to her mind, so she laid, shaking, on the spotted tile floor.

"Get up," Brian ordered, nearly ripping her arm off of her body as he lifted her off the ground. She scrabbled to make her feet useful, but Brian was moving too fast, and ended up just dragging her through the house.

He was panting and huffing by the time they cleared the small space, and he spit, "You got fat."

Claire, up to this point, wasn't completely sure about what Brian's intent was. But as soon as the door to the backyard was opened, she knew. The familiar clanking of the metal fence rang in her ears, and a new rope tied to the brightly lit pole burned her eyes.

"No," Claire screamed. "Ben! Help me!"

Shannon kicked her from behind, and Brian yanked her harder and shouted, "Shut up. You came back here for a reason."

And, for a split second, Claire couldn't remember what that reason was. And her life flashed before her eyes.

"No, let go!" she screamed. She was *not* about to be trapped again. "Get *off*!"

Claire twisted violently away from Brian. He lost his grip.

She scrambled for purchase on the grass, falling forward and jarring her arms on the unforgiving ground. She stood up and made a break for the fence, but before she could make it very far, someone grabbed a handful of Claire's hair.

Her head was jerked backwards, and she was face to face with an upside-down Shannon.

Claire screamed as loud as she possibly could, right into Shannon's sneering face. Her expression changed from sinister to stunned in half a second, and Claire took her moment of weakness to twist around and run away, ripping out a chunk of her hair in the process.

She tripped once on her mad sprint away, but wind-milled her arms and regained her balance. She ran straight into the fence, struggling to open the gate, but she didn't know how the latch was supposed to work. She turned her head to look over her shoulder, and both Brian and Shannon were huge hulking beasts storming towards her.

Another scream sliced the air and Brian winced like it had cut him. Claire gave up on the latch and hoisted herself up on the cold metal fence to jump over.

She got one leg over and was about to make a break for it when Brian's meaty hand grabbed at her ankle. Helpless in the position she was in, Claire just kicked her leg, making it harder for him to get a good hold. But, in effort to separate herself from Brian, Claire wasn't focused on staying on top of the fence. The next thing she knew, she was on the ground with the breath knocked out of her, on the opposite side of the fence. She wasted no time, just coughed a couple times as she stood and staggered away.

She glanced behind her as she ran, and Brian and Shannon had opened the fence and were advancing on her.

"Wait!" a voice yelled right before Claire ran right into another person. A shrill noise was cut off as she hit the person, and Claire realized she had been wailing the whole time.

Without even thinking, Claire tried to run around the man in her path, but he grabbed her shoulders tightly to keep her in place.

Half hoping and half fearing that the man was Ben, she bent her head back to look at his face.

Too tall to be Ben. She breathed a sigh of relief, but that was soon dissipated when Brian snatched her arm again.

"Hey, no," the man said, firmly pulling Claire back, but not hurting her.

"Who do you think you are? This is my daughter, hand her over."

The man took another step backwards with Claire. "Um, I don't think so."

"Who the hell are you?" Shannon barked.

"I just moved here. This is the only place I could afford, but I figured I'd take a walk around and meet my new neighbors. I didn't even know there was a house down this road. I was down that other street and I heard screaming."

Brian lunged for Claire, but the man was too fast. He shoved her behind him and spread his arms to protect her.

Brian got really close to the man's face and demanded, "Give me back my daughter."

"She doesn't look like she wants to be with you."

Claire fell to the cement behind her savior and wrapped her arms around her knees, trying to control her trembling. The voices above her were yelling at each other, but their words were floating through clouds in her mind. It was like she had cotton balls stuck in her ears.

"You have no right—"

"I do if it'll save her life—"

"She's our daughter—"

"She's *terrified* of you, that much is obvious."

Claire glanced up and saw Brian's hands forming into fists. She knew, by the tone of his voice, that he was about to explode. The man better watch out.

Shannon grabbed Brian's arm. "It's not worth it. We never wanted her anyways. Take the stupid brat and leave."

Claire was shocked. And so was Brian, apparently.

"Shan—" he started, but Shannon cut him off with a curt shake of her head. The two threw evil looks at their former daughter, then an even nastier stare at Claire's hero, and retreated back into their home.

When they were gone, the man crouched beside Claire.

"Let's go get you somewhere safe okay?"

Claire nodded. She allowed the man to help her stand up, but then all of her senses were on red alert. This was happened with Ben: he saved her from Brian and Shannon and locked her away.

Not again, she thought.

"I can't—no, I can't," she whined, her arms still wrapped around her body.

"Sweetheart, we need to get you help." The man's eyes showed real concern, but then again, so did Ben's.

Claire got an idea.

"Can you smile?"

"Um…"

"Please, I need to know. Can you?"

The man glanced around and looked unsure, but gave her a huge, genuine smile, showing off his white teeth.

"Good, okay. Let's go," Claire said. The man's eyes had crinkled in the corners, just like the nurse and the doctor. Ben's eyes never smiled with his mouth.

"Um, yeah," the man said. He offered his hand to Claire and he led her down the sidewalk. "My house is over here. We can get in my car and I'll drive you to the police station."

Claire and the man walked a couple minutes in silence. She couldn't help but notice that there was no other movement in this neighborhood. No other people were out walking on the streets, there were no trees swaying in the wind. All of the houses were shabby and dreary like Brian and Shannon's, and a grey and brown film seemed to settle over everything here.

"Here we are." He opened the side of his car, which looked nothing like Ben's, and let her climb inside. The man walked to his side and revved the engine.

"Can you put your seatbelt on?" he asked timidly. "I'd feel a lot better if you were safe."

Claire didn't know how, though, so the man clicked it in place for her. She didn't feel the need to hold it away from her body this time.

The man started driving and Claire was able to look out the window without getting sick or dizzy. The scenery amazed her as if she was seeing it all for the first time. And in a way, she was. This was the first time she was seeing nature when she wasn't tied to someone or something.

"Oh, my name is Sam, by the way. I forgot to mention that earlier," the man said with a little chuckle.

Years earlier, Claire would've been too scared to speak, but now she spoke with conviction. "My name is Claire." But as soon as the words left her mouth, her eyebrows furrowed. The corners of her mouth turned down. She didn't like her name anymore.

Sam was quiet for a little bit after that.

Then he said, "I know this is a dumb question to ask, but are you okay?"

Claire thought about that, then nodded, then shook her head. "I don't know. I think I will be."

"Good, good."

The rest of the ride was quiet, except for Sam saying, "Sorry, I still don't really know my way around yet—I think it's over here. Yeah, there it is."

He shut off the car and grabbed her hand, leading her inside. He took her up to a desk and talked to a person behind it for a minute, both of them glancing at her every once in a while.

"What's your name, sweetie?" the lady behind the desk asked. Claire was trying to take in the scene around her so she didn't hear the lady's question at first. Sam nudged her and the woman smiled kindly, repeating what she had asked.

"Claire."

"Okay, well, how about you two come with me?" the lady said. She led them to a small room with a table and a couple chairs.

Claire imagined the room as though it was the basement, and was about to sit in the chair she normally would've, but changed her mind. Sam sat next to her, releasing her hand. Claire felt completely exposed with the lack of contact.

Two more officers entered the room, one male and one female, and the man had a paper in his hand. The male officer had a big, round stomach like Brian, but had a head full of hair and a mustache that sat on top of his upper lip. The woman was thinner than the man and had short, dark-brown hair that almost blended in with her skin.

"Hi, Claire, I'm Officer Baxter and this is Officer Reed," the man said. "We just want to ask you a few questions, to get a better understanding of what's going on."

Claire nodded.

"Okay. Officer Reed?" Officer Baxter motioned for Officer Reed to begin and he picked up his pen.

"Claire, can you tell me what your home life is like?" she asked, a small smile teasing her lips.

But Claire's face was hard and cold. What did she have to smile about? All hope that she may have had while walking up to Brian and Shannon's door had disappeared. "What home?" she spit out.

Officer Reed's smile faltered. "What do you mean?"

"I don't have a home. I had Brian and Shannon's house…"

"Yes, that. Tell me about—Brian and Shannon you said?"

Claire nodded. She told them everything, and Officer Baxter's pen scribbled across his page. The tears that were cascading down her cheeks barely grazed her skin, and Sam wrapped his arm around her. She looked up at him and tears of his own were making their way down his face.

"Is that all, Claire?" Officer Reed asked, her voice quiet. Claire nodded. Then shook her head.

"Lily. It used to be Lily," she said between sniffles.

"What used to be Lily?" Officer Baxter asked, finally glancing up.

"My name. Ben changed it to Claire when he took me."

Officer Baxter scanned his papers. "Ben? You didn't mention a Ben earlier."

Then out came the story of Ben's superhero rescue.

When she was done, a fresh wave of tears washed both her and Sam's faces, but the officers were both grim.

Officer Reed cleared her throat and asked, "Do you think you could show us where Ben's house is?"

Claire nodded.

"Would it be okay if you showed us now?"

Claire hesitated. Her heartbeat spiked once, then twice.

"Don't worry, you'd be safe. You'll be in the car with another officer the whole time."

Claire picked at her lip. She whispered, "Sure."

"Sam, you can go now. We'll take it from here," Officer Reed said.

Sam had red streaks striping his face. "How can I go home after this? You're going to arrest those people who hurt her, right?"

Officer Baxter glanced at Claire. "We don't know what's going to happen yet."

"You better make them pay for what they did. They deserve it."

"Sam, please, go home, get yourself a hot meal and try and distract yourself," Officer Baxter said, standing up, prompting the rest of them to stand as well. He led Sam outside, and Officer Reed told Claire to come with her.

The officer helped Claire into the police car, and the sky was turning dark already. While Claire sat there, Officer Reed went and asked Sam for directions to his neighborhood, or so Claire assumed.

"Okay," the officer said as she climbed inside. "We're going to go drive by your parents' house and we'll see if you can show me where Ben lives, alright?"

Claire nodded tightly. She wasn't so sure if she wanted to go back there.

As if she could read Claire's thoughts, Officer Reed said, "I know it's hard, but this is really important." Another police car followed Claire's on the drive over.

Claire's mood mimicked the descending darkness of the impending night as they neared Brian and Shannon's home.

"There's a house down here?" Officer Reed asked.

Her headlights illuminated the road in front of them, but before they could land on the dreaded house, the officer stopped the car and the road went dark again.

"It's up there," Claire whispered.

"That's where your parents live?"

"Yeah."

Officer Reed was quiet for a second. "So where does Ben live?"

"Through the trees."

Officer Reed shifted. "So it's down that other street then? The one we just passed?"

"I don't know. I only know how to get there through the trees."

Officer Reed brought her radio close to her mouth. She requested backup, gave whoever was listening the address, and told them to come in quietly.

"They'll be here in a couple of minutes. We'll put you in a different car, and some more officers and myself will go to Ben's house," Officer Reed said.

Claire didn't respond, but just stared out the window and waited for the backup to arrive.

Soon, two more police cars pulled up, and four officers poured out. Two cars stayed behind to get Brian and Shannon, but Claire's car and another went over to Ben's. Officer Reed left, but someone else came to stay with Claire. Officer Reed and another officer were nearing the house.

"Ben's probably still in the basement," Claire told the officer in her car.

"What was that?"

"Ben. I trapped him in the bathroom in the basement. He's probably still there."

The officer used the radio to tell Officer Reed and the other one who were just about to kick open Ben's door.

"If they find Tommy, can they bring him to me? He's the rat in the tub. He was my friend."

"Uh, sure. Yeah, they can do that."

Again, he radioed Officer Reed. Then he said to Claire, "I'm going to have to go outside now. I'll lock the doors. Will you be okay in here?"

Claire almost laughed. *I've handled much worse. I think I can sit in a car and live,* she thought. But she could tell the policeman was trying to be nice, so she nodded.

In the dim lighting, all four police officers held up their guns and crept towards the house. Claire couldn't tell who was who, but two of them kicked down the door and ran inside, while the remaining two knelt down and pointed their weapons at the open door.

Claire held her breath.

Chapter Fifteen

Ben had given up trying to escape by the time he heard thumping coming from outside.

Footsteps? Are those footsteps?

"Claire?" He pushed himself up from his position on the floor and crawled over to look out the crack underneath the door. He gasped and sat up on his knees, palms flat against the door, and put his cheek against it. "Claire, I'm so glad you came back for me—" The door flew open and Ben tumbled forward.

"Freeze!"

"Don't move!"

The officers pointed their guns at him and pushed him onto the floor with their shoes. Ben's face was pressed against the cool tile and the police were talking, but his ears were ringing; he couldn't understand a word they were saying. The world began to blur, but his eyes focused on a brownish-blonde clump of hair under the counter. He reached his hand out to grab it, but was stopped by the crunch of the officer's boot on his fingers.

"I said, don't move."

Ben's hands were ripped behind his back and forcibly connected together by cold metal handcuffs. The fuzziness of the world was back, but Ben could tell he was being pushed through his own house by the police. Claire's small face was peering out of a police car window, unemotional, detached, just like how she was in the beginning. Ben struggled and pulled against the officers, jumping, doing anything he could to get away from them and to his Claire. He was screaming her name but it was like he had the volume down low; his voice didn't sound real to his own ears.

Ben was dragged away to a different vehicle, leaving Claire behind.

Claire couldn't breathe until the car with Ben inside drove away, lights flashing and sirens blaring. Officer Reed joined Claire in her car, and sighed.

"You know, you were very smart for locking him in there," she told Claire, who just nodded. "Now we can go back to the station. You did amazing."

She turned the key in the ignition. "Oh, I almost forgot." She dug into her pocket and pulled out a rumpled plastic baggie. "Do you still want this?"

Claire grabbed the bag from her, holding it to her chest. "Hi, Tommy," she whispered into the plastic.

She knew that Officer Reed was staring at her, but Claire didn't look up.

Claire looked at Tommy's still form through the clear plastic. Her voice barely audible, she said, "You're all I have left."

Back at the police station, Claire was sat in a room and given so many different tests, and asked so many more questions. Someone told her that she was going to go to a doctor's office soon, and she hoped she would get to see the nice bearded doctor again.

Different people, either in uniforms or in regular clothes, kept coming into the room and telling her how smart and brave she was. Claire was tired of people congratulating her for something that wasn't even good, so she put her head down on the table.

She heard someone walk up to the door, but she didn't raise her head.

"Claire?"

She focused her eyes on the doorway again, where a woman was standing, wearing a brightly colored dress with pink and yellow stripes covering it.

"I'm Michelle. I'm your social worker." Michelle came and sat across from Claire.

Claire swiped at her face, not wanting her to know that she was crying.

The social worker smiled broadly, the corners of her eyes crinkling. Her teeth were bright against her dark skin. "You're free. Do you know that? You're finally free. Your parents and Ben, they'll never hurt you again."

"That rhymed," Claire said, mostly to herself.

"What was that?"

Claire just shook her head, but a small bubble of laughter rose in her throat. A giggle escaped her, and she covered her mouth, but was a little too forceful and hit herself in the face instead, which made her laugh harder.

She was engulfed in giggles, bent at the waist, grasping her stomach. Honest, pure laughter exploded from her and tasted light and sweet on her tongue.

Michelle was laughing to now, not as manically as Claire, but happy all the same.

It was only when tears threatened to roll down her face from sheer happiness did Claire calm down enough to speak. "I'm free," Claire said, feeling the way the words rolled off her tongue. "Free." One last giggle burst out.

"Claire, I understand that this is great news, and I am so happy for you. But now we need to talk about something a little more serious okay?" Michelle said.

Claire nodded and bit her lip to hold back her excitement.

"We're going to have to find a foster home for you, do you know what that means?"

Claire shook her head absently. She wasn't really listening to what Michelle was saying. The word "free" kept bouncing around inside her head. But now, every time it came back around, it made her increasingly resentful. Her delight was gradually replaced by a bitter mixture of a need for vengeance and extreme loss.

"They stole my life."

Michelle looked stunned. "I'm sorry?"

Claire hadn't even realized that she interrupted Michelle's speech about the foster home process. "They wanted me dead. They didn't love me. They never did. Mailman was right."

Claire tried hard to sever the bond between her words and the emotional section of her brain, but it didn't work. Her bottom lip began to quiver and her eyes refilled with salty tears, this time for the opposite reason from about five minutes before.

Her words were enunciated strangely. It was hard for her to speak. "They were selfish. I trusted him. He trapped me. He wouldn't let me go."

Michelle opened her mouth to speak, but decided against it. She just listened to what she had to say.

Claire felt the all too familiar heat growing behind her eyes and her head begin to ache as she desperately tried not to cry. She sobbed once and covered her mouth to hold the rest in.

"I want them to feel what I felt. Put them in prison forever. See how they handle being trapped." She burst into tears. She bent in half and cried into her hands.

Michelle was dumbfounded. "The police are doing everything they can…"

"They locked me up. They ruined my life." She sobbed one last time. "Now I want you to ruin theirs."

It was three years later. Ms. Nicole was watching her from the front seat. Mr. Jason kept looking at her in the rearview mirror.

"Are you sure you want to do this? Nobody's making you," Ms. Nicole said.

"Is she ready? I don't know if we should let her go in," Mr. Jason said softly to Ms. Nicole.

"I need to." Bri looked both of her foster parents in the eyes.

Ms. Nicole nodded. "Is it still okay if I come in with you? Mr. Jason would be happy to if you'd rather go with him."

"No, that's okay."

"Alright, well, if you're ready," Ms. Nicole said. She had a soft smile and an even sweeter personality. She was the one who took Claire to get her name changed to Brianna; she helped her choose it because it meant "strong."

Bri's lips were pursed together and she pushed open the door to the jail with Ms. Nicole not far behind. She let her foster mother tell the guard what they were there for and fill out all the necessary paperwork. Within minutes, Bri was sitting behind a thin sheet of dirty glass—or plastic, she couldn't tell—waiting to pick up the phone that was hanging on the wall. Ms. Nicole was waiting outside the room, right near the door. After learning about their situation, the guard said that Ben could become unstable and dangerous if Ms. Nicole was in there too. Apparently they knew each other way in the past; Ben had done something horrible to her and Mr. Jason's son—but they wouldn't tell Bri what.

The door opened on the other side of the glass and two people walked in. The guard on the other side held Ben's hands behind his back and sat him down in the chair across from Bri. They picked up the phone at the same time but Bri held the receiver half an inch away from her cheek; everything in here seemed dirty and she didn't want it touching her face.

Neither of them spoke for the first few seconds, but then Bri said, "I'm sorry."

Ben glared at her, but behind the menace, Bri could see a glimmer of something. Was it hope? Love? Regret?

"Stop."

Bri blinked. That wasn't the reaction she'd been expecting. She quoted Ben's words from so long ago. "If you do something wrong, you say sorry."

"I don't want your pity."

Bri thought about that. "Sometimes that's the only thing people have to give."

Ben sneered at her, but Bri still thought he was just putting on a façade to seem tough—or maybe it was just to keep himself from breaking down. "What is that even supposed to mean?"

"It means that I don't have anything else to give you. I don't love you—not anymore. I'm relieved that you're behind bars, where you can't get me or anyone else ever again. But I do feel bad for you. Not just because I was the one who put you in here, but because it's almost not your fault. You're just messed up. Something's wrong inside of you."

This seemed to strike a nerve in Ben. "Claire—"

"I'm not Claire. I don't know who that girl was, but she's not me anymore. I'm Bri. I think I've always been Bri, but it took what you did to make her show herself."

"What I did? What I *did* was give you the best life possible. I thought, after the life you lived with your parents, you'd love to have your own space. You had the whole basement to yourself. I thought that'd be enough."

Bri scoffed. "You were wrong. What kind of kid would be happy never seeing the sun? Who would ever want to go through their entire life in one tiny area, when there's an entire city, country, *world,* to visit and see and explore?"

"I loved teaching you things. I loved seeing you learn and grow and be happy. I knew, coming from that yard, you were better off with me. They didn't love you there. *I* loved you, Claire. Not Brian, not Shannon, not Amy."

Bri rolled her eyes. "I'm not Claire. Yes, you named me that, but I was never your daughter. I thought I was. You thought I was. But the real Claire is probably somewhere far away from here so your wife doesn't have to deal with you anymore. I was never who you thought I was. And now I'm someone completely different. I'm Bri, I'm strong, and I'm capable. You needed me more than I needed you."

Ben's face turned menacing. "Bri," he said mockingly. "You would've died if I didn't save you from that yard."

Bri sat back in the chair. "You know, I don't know what I thought I'd get out of this. I don't know why I thought you'd change. But honestly, I'm not really sure why you would, or what I'd want you to change into. But this was stupid. I shouldn't have come."

Ben wasn't listening to her. "I taught you how to walk, and to read. You became confident enough to start talking because of me. And look where you are now. Forming coherent and profound thoughts."

"I don't think you understand," Bri said, her resolve melting away. "I wish you hadn't stuck me down in that basement. I wish you would've given me a normal life. But I mean, looking back, you did more than you had to. You helped me learn that it was okay to smile. That I can talk when I want to. You gave me some freedom, but not enough. I love space now. The solar system, the universe. It's open and endless and full of possibilities."

Ben at least had enough sense to look ashamed, dropping his eyes from hers to the table in front of him. "Oh, that's—that's awesome. But where'd you learn about all this stuff? How did you get to be so smart?"

"I go to school now. And my foster mother signed me up for a speech and language tutor because I love words so much. She also put me in a writing camp at a library, so I can be around books all the time."

When Ben looked up at her again, his eyes were watering. His voice was small and Claire had to press the phone close to her ear to hear what he said. "I gave you books."

Bri sighed. "Goodbye, Ben. I'm sorry."

"No, please don't—" was all Bri heard before she hung up, but Ben's mouth form the word *go*.

"I'm sorry," she said again, but Ben was already being led out of the room. Their eyes locked, and he was gone.

Ms. Nicole had her hand on Bri's shoulder the whole way back to the car. She was trying to be comforting, but Bri was too dazed to be thankful. She had said sorry three times. But what did she have to be sorry for? She didn't do anything wrong. Then she realized, Ben hadn't said he was sorry at all. He said it plenty while they were down in the basement, constantly apologizing for not having things ready or for leaving her alone, but he never said it when it really counted. He honestly believed that he was doing the right thing, and he just wanted his daughter back. As much as Bri wanted to hate him, as much as she wanted to hold a grudge as long as she lived, she couldn't. She walked out of the jail and into the sunshine with a new aura about her.

The wind that lifted her hair off her neck and kissed her cheek also blew away the weight she was carrying in both her mind and on her shoulders. She could fully become Bri, and eradicate Claire and Lily forever. The spirits of the other two girls finally released their holds on her, and lifted away into the sky.

Bri gasped, softly enough that Mrs. Nicole didn't hear. Something clicked inside of her chest: her heart, sliding back into place. She paused and put her hand over the spot that had been empty for the past five years. That first day in the basement was when it fell from where it should've been, but it was back. Where it was supposed to be.

"You ready?" Mr. Jason asked after Bri stepped into the car.

"I've been ready," Bri said. Mr. Jason must've thought she was talking about going home, but Bri knew what it really meant. She was ready to start her new life.

ACKNOWLEDGEMENTS

To my mom, for listening to my ramblings for hours on end.

To John Rhuby and Jaime Buike, for providing honest, in-depth feedback and advice during the early drafts.

To Robin Holden, Lori Roesler, Jim Gill, Kim Leushel, Melissa Meszaros, Munira Odetallah, Tim Gose, and Dylan Hamilton, for reading and critiquing at different stages.

To Bailey Klingbeil and Sky Gill, for enduring my endless updates on word count, plot changes, and draft number.

To family, friends, teachers, and teammates, for supporting me along the way.

Thank you.

Made in the USA
Lexington, KY
22 May 2019